BERG FARM

Pastor:
Thank you for officiating at the funeral of my mother in law,
Janet Erickson.
I was reminded that I visualized you when I wrote in the pastor (cap-
ter 12) in this book I wrote a few years ago.

Jim

A NOVEL
BERG FARM

JIM HODGE

Published by
Deep River Books
Sisters, Oregon
http://www.deepriverbooks.com

ISBN-10: 193526589X
ISBN-13: 9781935265894

Library of Congress: 2012930163

Printed in the USA

Cover design by Becky Barbier

To Sue, Kirstin, Doug, Kelli, Addie and Devin Lynn

PROLOGUE

"My friends, you have just entered an amazing new country. There is nothing standing in your way to accomplish whatever it is you want to accomplish here. It is all up to you. I myself, and the Immigration Department, wish you the best. Seven years ago America came out of a bitter and deadly civil war. Many people died to preserve the right for each man and each woman, no matter who they are or where they come from, to enjoy freedom. As I am sure you know, we have no king in this country. We have no nobility. When our founding fathers wrote our Constitution they broke the chains of European royalty. Where you go and what you accomplish is all up to you. Make the most of it and God bless you all."

Elmer felt a surge of excitement. The immigration officer's words were just what he wanted to hear. Even though he had put his faith in his Lord regarding the success of this enterprise, his human frailties gave him cause for concern. Now, hearing this man's words, his heart and soul were as full as a fjord at high tide!

The belief that people will seek familiar surroundings, even after crossing an ocean, seemed to be true. Cold winters followed by damp springs and green, growing summers brought the hardy Scandinavians into much of America's heartland. During the last half of the 19th century America's Great Lakes and upper Midwest region drew these robust people by the thousands. Typically the Swedes, Norwegians and Danes arrived in Chicago. Those who did not stay in the city spread themselves up both the Michigan and Wisconsin shorelines of Lake Michigan and into the hinterland of Illinois, Wisconsin, Minnesota, Iowa and the Dakotas. The Finns flocked to Michigan's Upper Peninsula.

For Elmer Berg, two issues led to his decision to come to America; economic opportunity and religious freedom.

As tenant farmers, the Bergs labored on thirty-two acres outside the hamlet of Storen, where the icy waters of the narrow and swift flowing Gaula River made its decent to the huge Trondiem fjord. It was a treadmill life of heavy labor with no foreseeable opportunity to purchase their own land in the tightly controlled countryside.

The Bergs worshiped as part of the Lutheran Bible Church, a more gospel oriented denomination than the dominant Lutheran State Church. The Bible Lutherans were very much discriminated against.

It was for these reasons that Muriel Berg and three small children made the wagon trip to the harbor at Trondiem in the cold April chill of 1872, dropping off the family's husband and father. As was the case with some who left the homeland, Elmer would arrive in America alone, leaving his wife and children to come later. Limited finances and a fear of the unknown made this a common practice.

The family had carefully planned so that they could survive the coming growing season and the following winter without their breadwinner. Their wellbeing in Norway was now far from certain and there was no assurance that Muriel would ever see her husband again. As she embraced him one last time on the waterfront's ancient wooden docks, she felt, at one and the same time, anxiety and confidence. The night before the couple had prayed together at their bedside. They prayed that God's will be done in their lives. They prayed that they would watch and listen for His leading.

As they finished praying Elmer opened his Bible to Proverbs.

"Trust in the Lord with all thine heart; and lean not unto thine own understanding. In all thy ways acknowledge him, and he shall direct thy paths." He looked determinedly into his wife's eyes. "These will be our verses. These verses must sustain our hearts when all else around us sends doubt to our minds."

≠ ≠ ≠

When Elmer arrived in America he carried with him the homestead document assuring him that he would be awarded 160 acres of land. In return the document stated that he would "build a dwelling and cultivate the soil." If, after five years, Berg had established himself on the acreage to the satisfaction of the government, he could apply for title to the land at a nominal fee.

For immigrants of meager financial means and only basic education the move to America was a move into the unknown. Elmer Berg knew only that Chicago was a large city far from the Atlantic shore. It was from this city that he hoped to have the promise of homestead land awarded to him. It was not confidence and a sense of adventure that sparked Elmer Berg's journey to America, but desperation for a new and better life.

ONE

From a distance the tractor appeared and disappeared in the contours of the gentle hills. The black earth, turned over by the field cultivator, stood in sharp contrast to the brown corn stubble that had endured the bitterness of the previous Wisconsin winter.

Thirty-six-year-old John Berg sat high and gratefully proud in the 1953 Persian orange Allis-Chalmers WD45, carefully turning the rich, pungent soil so as not to miss even an inch of the precious ground. The drone of the tractor engine and the thump of the tires as they angled across the previous year's furrows did not deter him from humming one tune after another. His large hands, weathered and calloused from years of outdoor work, slapped against the steering wheel in an amateurish attempt at keeping time with his humming. The unmarked blue baseball cap—faded, sweat stained and somewhat rumpled—that crowned his tousled brown hair was as self-effacing as the man himself.

This was his land. This had been his father's, his grandfather's and his great grandfather's land and he had long ago acknowledged that he was a steward of all that his Lord had entrusted to him. He well appreciated the courageous homesteading legacy of a man he never knew—his great grandfather. On this spring morning in 1957 John Berg felt, as he almost always did, like the luckiest man in the world.

Indeed, life had been good to Berg, but no more so than it had been to most people. It is just that he seemed to know it and appreciate it. He had grown up during the years of the Great Depression and had served his country as a soldier in World War II. He now basked in the relative tranquility of the late 1950s. Though he was not an expressive man—often his quietness left a doleful impression—he was a contented man. As a husband, the father of three and the business partner of his father,

Berg was a man fulfilled. Yes, there was concern over the ways of his second born, but he was realistic enough to know that his family was not exempt from worries. The weight of responsibility for a family and a two hundred-eighty acre dairy farm did not seem to daunt him.

Back at the two-storied, white farm house, John Berg's wife was rolling out the dough for the bread she would bake that afternoon. No one ever called her Gertrude. Scandinavians very often gave their children cumbersome given names that were not at all trendy. Gertie, however, was a most acceptable shortening of Gertrude.

At age thirty-three she was in the prime of her womanhood. Her sandy blond hair was always pulled back in a short, no nonsense ponytail. Her eyes were an open, friendly blue. When she smiled she showed just the beginning of crow's feet wrinkles. Her strong, supple and striking figure, which she in no way tried to advertise, was very much up to the demands of home and family.

The rigors of farm life were nothing new to Gertie. She was a Mehlborg, born and raised with three brothers and three sisters only six miles away on the farm of Steven and Karen Mehlborg. Like most of the members of her large family her conversations were always to the point, unadorned with either unwarranted praise or the scorn of superiority. These things endeared her to all who knew her.

"Boys? Johnny! Clark!" Gertie's voice could be heard upstairs. "You need to get on that job that your father gave you. You'll not dawdle away this whole Saturday. You get down here." Her voice was bright and friendly but each of Gertie Berg's three children knew that she always meant what she said. The thumpety-thump of feet coming down the stairs could be heard by Gertie back in the kitchen. A quick smile crossed her face as she thought of the eleven- and twelve-year-old sons with whom God had graced her and John's life.

It was their oldest, Johnny, who bounced into the kitchen. A mop of straight, but still unruly, blonde hair crowned his youthful frame. The junior size bib overalls that he was wearing were a testament to the great pride he took at being part of Berg Farm. He was fully aware of his obligation in the tractor barn but, nonetheless, he was prepared to raise an objection.

"Mom, can't I chore this afternoon? I have all day to do that job." His eyebrows rose above his wondering blue eyes in hopes of a softened response from his mother.

Gertie did not look up from the bread dough she was working.

"John Berg Jr., your father said he wanted that seeder cleaned up and lubricated this morning, not some time this afternoon. Your father also said the job shouldn't take more than a couple of hours. A strapping twelve-year-old youngster like yourself should have a lot more responsibility on a Saturday than one job out in the barn. And where is your brother?"

"He's upstairs still." Johnny's response was without concern for his brother's usual apathy.

Now Gertie looked up. She wiped her flour-covered hands on the apron she wore over her checkered house dress.

"Now, out you go. I don't want to see you back in here until dinner at noon time."

The youngster gave a shoulder shrug, a resigned, yet cheerful, "Okay," and headed out the back door.

Gertie wasted no time in summoning her other son. "Clark! Get a move on!"

It was another two minutes before she heard the slow footsteps of her eleven-year-old coming down the stairs. With hands in pockets he sauntered unenthusiastically into the kitchen.

His hapless attitude was as large a contrast to Johnny as his brown eyes and dark, curly hair.

Gertie had little patience for Clark's lack of interest, but as she looked right at him she was calmly deliberate.

"You need to get out there and help your brother with that seeder."

Expressionless, and without a word, the boy shuffled out the kitchen door.

As she returned to her bread dough Gertie could but shake her head.

≠ ≠ ≠

First Lutheran Church stood at the corner of Washington and 4th Street, just a block off State Highway 51, the road that served as Stoughton, Wisconsin's main street. As on all Sunday mornings, the church parking lot had as many pickups in it as it had sedans, for the farmer was a major presence in this community.

In the same pew as always, John and Gertie Berg, their three children and John's parents sat together as a family. Their presence each Sunday was a reflection of the anchor of support the family had been to the congregation for many years. In 1909, John's grandfather Gus had been instrumental in building an addition on the original church, located across the street.

In 1942, the church suffered a fire. For the next four years the congregation met in the Dunkirk Town Elementary School at the other end of town. World War II had left few resources and even fewer men to rebuild the church. When restoration took place in 1946, John Berg and his father Mack helped rebuild the church on property across the street from the original building.

The church was certainly much grander than the humble Evangelical Lutheran Church that Elmer and Muriel Berg had been a part of for so many years when they homesteaded the Berg property. When the survey officer showed Elmer his land that day in 1872, he was delighted to find the church perched on a prominent hill just off the wagon trail that served as a Dane County road, within sight of his land. He had come so far and hoped to find a fundamental Bible-based church like their own in Norway and here it was! The church was often called the Bovre Congregation because it was built on property donated by Lars Bovre. For the next fifteen years the Bergs did their best to be good stewards of their church until that day in 1887 when the tiny congregation felt it could no longer support itself. The Bergs then began to attend First Lutheran and were delighted to find that it too was very much a Bible believing, Bible preaching church.

Johnny and Clark Berg silently rejoiced when Pastor Kiel announced the closing hymn. An hour for Sunday School and another hour for church were a test of the boys' energy restraint.

Back at the Berg house after church, the two chickens that Gertie had slow roasting during church service were almost done.

"Woman, I thought I saw you putting an apple pie together yesterday afternoon." Mack Berg peeked under the clean dish towel that covered the two pies that Gertie had baked on Saturday.

The senior Berg, at age sixty, was still a full time dairy farmer. His once blond hair had turned a gleaming silver in just the last couple of years. His blue eyes showed a man of earnest, hard working character and jovial spirit. He retained a rugged, heavily muscled frame. He had the full face and strong jaw typical of men of Scandinavian decent.

In 1917, Mack, at age twenty, had been thrust into the family leadership when his father Gus died from a wicked strain of influenza which had ravaged much of the upper Midwest in that year. The next year Mack married. He and his wife, Ann, had spent a lifetime building the farm, strengthening the vision that had led his grandfather, Elmer Berg, to this place.

"You just stay away from those pies, Mack Berg," Gertie ordered. "I might just have some for you after your dinner."

Mack rumbled his subdued, throaty laugh as he backed away from Gertie's kitchen domain.

"I guess it's just something I'll have to live with; getting bossed around by my wife and my daughter-in-law! But, what's a man going to do."

Gertie gave a mock scolding as she mashed potatoes on the stove top. "Mack Berg, as far as I know you've never missed a meal around here, whether it's my cooking or Ann's. Unless you want that to change you would do well to leave the kitchen to us."

The Berg home was a great source of pride for the family. During the winter of 1922 Mack and his neighbors, most notably his childhood friend Harold (Skorpie) Johnson, did the back-breaking work of cutting virgin white pine from the twelve acres of high, heavily wooded ground on the southeast corner of the property.

Cut and milled into lumber to satisfy the needs of the Sears and Roebuck "Gabled Farmhouse No.6" plans he had bought three years prior, Mack and his friends got the basement dug and the home roughed in before the next winter. Before the snow flew, Mack and Ann painted the place white with green trim.

When he came home from World War II, John and Gertie built a modest home on the northwest corner of the farm. In 1952, with a young, growing family, they sold it and bought the family homestead from Mack and Ann. Three generations now shared the home. Where the long driveway leading to the house met Spring Road, Mack had, many years before, hung a small wooden sign. It was painted white with dark blue lettering spelling out BERG FARM. The modest sign was a visible indication of the great pride this family took in their home, their family, and the five generations that had worked this land.

John said grace for the Sunday dinner.

"Our Lord, we give thanks to you for the great gifts you have given us and for the everyday gifts that you have given us. Though we try to be honest and dependable in our work we need to understand that all we have we owe to your grace to us. We thank you for providing this family with the necessities of life. Thank you for the greatest gift of all, the gift of eternal life through the sacrifice of your son, Jesus. Amen."

Being typically Norwegian, the conversation at meal time was subdued, even at its crescendo.

"Ike said that if the Russians want to keep threatening with the nuclear stuff we are going to match them." Mack would sometimes throw out a broad statement in order to create some conversation.

"I don't know about that but I do know that since the Russians launched that Sputnik up around the world the amount of homework the kids are getting has greatly increased," Gertie said.

"I have lots of homework now, mama. Our principle said that it is a shameful thing that we should fall behind the Soviets. I think she said that the Soviets are the same as the Russians."

Elsie was eight years old, John and Gertie's youngest. She had freckles, straight blond hair, was wiry and quite tall for her age. She had the same blue eyes and the same no nonsense way about her as her mother.

"I expect you can handle any work they send your way, Elsie." Ann

Berg was certainly not a big talker but when she spoke it was usually something sincere and supportive. She was grandmother to ten children. Besides John and Gertie's three, she and Mack's two daughters, one living in Madison and the other in Milwaukee, gave her the other seven.

"Did you get the seeder cleaned up and lubed for me yesterday?" John looked straight at Johnny.

"Yep. We got all the grease fittings. Had to use a hammer and a piece of pipe to knock out a lot of the dirt that was jammed up in there." Johnny met his father's gaze, eye to eye.

John had not questioned his sons about the chore until now, even though he could have mentioned it anytime from Saturday afternoon on. He felt that questioning the boys too soon would be hovering over them, showing a lack of confidence in them. With a degree of uncertainty he accepted Johnny's use of "we" to mean that his brother had helped with the work.

"Good. I'll spring-tooth the two west sections starting tomorrow and we should be ready to plant later in the week. That's if it doesn't rain."

A look of uneasiness crossed John's face.

"It's not right. The government pays cash crop farmers to leave some acreage fallow. It doesn't affect us because we use our crop for feed, but it just always seems strange to me."

It was Elsie who spoke up. "Dad, Mr. Long says that the American farmer should accept subsidy payments proudly because he succeeds so well in producing. The American farmer feeds the world!"

John Berg mulled over his daughter's words for a few seconds. "Who's Mr. Long?"

"He's my social studies teacher."

The farmer's uneasiness about the government's involvement in the affairs of agriculture had him staring blankly at his daughter while he let her statement sink in.

TWO

"So do not fear, for I am with you; do not be dismayed...."

ISAIAH 41:10 NIV

As she did every morning, rain or shine, in the heat of July or the frigid temperatures of January, Gertie walked the 200 yards to the mailbox that stood where the Berg driveway met Spring Road. It was now 1965, and on this day, a damp, blustery morning in early May, the mailbox contained a letter addressed to Johnny, now a strapping twenty year old, almost two years a graduate from Stoughton Area High School. The letter's return address said The Pentagon, Wash. D.C.

Gertie caught her breath. She thought of how she and John had talked, just a month ago, about the possibility of their two sons being drafted someday.

"If they get drafted, then so be it," John had said. "This life is full of things we would rather not do. We are not going to allow ourselves to be vessels of sympathy. That won't do either of the boys a bit of good."

She had affirmed her husband's thoughts at the time, but now she felt a queasiness that was foreign to her. Her heart sank for the briefest of moments as she thought of the families around Stoughton, and around the country, that lived day to day on the edge; fearing for their young men.

She righted herself with a brief prayer.

"Lord, I know that this family is no more immune to the tide of world events than anyone else. I don't know what the future holds, but I do know that it is You who holds it. It appears the time has come for our son to leave us. To maybe even go to war. Give me, I ask you now, the courage and the serenity to support him in any way that I can. In your Word it says that You will not give us anything more than we can bear if we will just put our faith in You. I don't know what You have in store for us but I pray You will give me the strength and the wisdom to hold on to that truth."

That afternoon, as she and her mother-in-law prepared the evening meal, Gertie allowed a stray thought to come forward.

"Ann, wouldn't this be an ideal life if we could just avoid the snares of this world."

Ann gave Gertie a puzzled look, for she had never heard that kind of statement from her daughter-in-law. Gertie had not yet revealed the letter from the Pentagon.

The men were working the fields relentlessly now, for once the soil was firm enough it had to be prepped for planting. The chisel plow, the spring-tooth, the cultivator-seeder; these things were their allies. Any delay meant planting was moved back. John, Johnny and Mack each had their roles in this process. They were in the fields at dawn, toiled with dedicated perseverance the entire day, and then worked with headlights burning until well after sunset. Clark was just finishing high school but he was expected to work a few hours immediately upon getting home.

Despite this schedule, the men did not lack for nutrition for Gertie and Ann brought both breakfast and dinner out to their men, meeting them individually or as a group on whatever ridge line the women were able to maneuver the family's trusty Ford pickup.

But supper was different and on this evening Gertie was particularly grateful that it was. Years before, she and Ann had insisted, spring planting or not, that the family sit down together and have a full meal. For the men to stuff down a breakfast and dinner at their tractors was enough. The women would not let the demands of work overshadow the stability a family supper offered.

That evening, right before supper, Johnny sprawled out on the davenport in the family parlor. After a hard day in the fields he loved to wash up and then, even if only for a few minutes, lean back into the deep cushions of this piece of furniture, his lanky 6-foot2-inch frame recovering from the vibration inflicted by the tractor work.

Gertie called from the kitchen. "Johnny, can you come here?"

Though he heard his mother's call the young man did not immediately respond. In a few moments, and only half awake, he staggered down the hallway into the big kitchen. With his eyes half shut, a contented smile crossed his face as the scent of his mother's cooking filled his senses.

"Oh yes. Meat loaf. And is that homemade bread I see?"

"It is," Gertie responded weakly. She picked up the letter off the counter. Looking directly into the eyes of her son she handed it to him.

When he saw the return address Johnny's reaction was typically low key. He gave a grunt of recognition. "Ugh. Well… I think I know what this is all about." He gave his mother a quick snippet of a smile and returned to the parlor.

Ten minutes later John and Gertie, their three children and Mack and Ann were at the supper table. Gertie wondered if and when Johnny would mention his letter. He didn't wait long.

"I'm being drafted. Got the letter in the mail today. Have to report to Camp McCoy for a physical and induction on May 16th." He spoke matter-of-factly, as was the usual Berg way.

Not a word was said for a number of seconds when Elsie, now sixteen years old, spoke up quizzically. "You have to work the farm. Aren't you excluded because you have to take care of the farm?"

"Nice try Els, but this is grandpa's and dad's farm, not mine." After a pause he continued. "Besides…I wouldn't try to get out of this. I've been having a funny feeling seeing other guys go. I'm sort of glad I got drafted. I want to get on with it. It's only two years."

John Sr. did not immediately respond to son's announcement but the joy that he always experienced at eating the meals prepared by both his wife and his mother seemed to leave him.

After a good thirty seconds it was the grandparents who spoke up— in the usual reflective and affirmative way.

"Uncle Sam will be getting the best." Mack spoke with confidence.

He looked around the table at everyone when he said this. "I know you will make us all proud."

Ann had something to say.

"Your grandma has but one thing to ask of you, Johnny. Please hear me and take heed. Do not go out of your way to seek danger. Ask the Lord to use you as he will and ask Him to give you the courage to handle that task, but I urge you, don't go out of your way to seek danger."

John Sr. rapped his fist around his fork, the prongs sticking up in the air. He stared at his oldest son.

"Your grandmother is right. I saw it for myself. Men who volunteered to come to our unit in North Africa. Just so that they could see action. They were the first to crack. Probably because they realized that they had brought on the whole thing themselves."

"I think our son is level headed enough to know all this and, besides, you've all got him in Vietnam already." Gertie spoke with annoyance in her voice. She put an end to the subject. "Goodness sakes. There is many a place the Army could send him."

But it was eighteen-year-old Clark who broke the sullen atmosphere. "Besides, he probably won't even make it through basic training. Pass the c-rations buster!"

The mood around the table lightened except for John Sr. After everyone else had left the table he continued to sit, seemingly deep in thought. Gertie stopped her cleanup work and came up beside her husband.

"I'll just bet your mind is back in North Africa."

John snapped back to the present moment. He gave his wife an affirmative nod.

The next morning the mailbox again brought a significant bit of news to the Bergs. The letter was addressed to Mr. Mack Berg. When Gertie retrieved the letter she would have thought little of it except that the return address was from the Pleasant Springs Town Property and Zoning Board. Pleasant Springs Town was the rural township just north of Stoughton where Berg Farm lay.

That morning Mack came in from the fields to make a minor repair on his tractor. He spent time in the barn closest to the house, where the Bergs had their workshop, replacing a leaking hydraulic hose. The repair finished by 11 o'clock, he decided to eat his dinner in the kitchen, before the women took food out to the fields. Like many farm folk, the Bergs referred to the noontime meal as dinner, not lunch. The evening meal was always supper.

"Grilled cheese, tomato soup and coffee. That should keep you going till supper."

It was Gertie's habit to announce what was to eat for dinner, whether it was around the kitchen table or out in the fields. She would, however, never let on what she was going to be cooking for supper. It was just a little game she played. Her way of saying, "'This is my kitchen, you just bring your appetite and I'll make sure you get plenty to eat."

Mack kicked off his muddy boots at the back door. "That sounds good to me, I'm hungry. I'll bet you made that grill cheese on homemade bread. Where's that wife of mine?"

"Mack Berg, I've never known you when you weren't hungry and, yes, your grilled cheese is on homemade bread. Ann wanted to lay down awhile. She was feeling a little tired."

The farmer had washed his oily hands at the repair barn's wash basin so he sat right down. Gertie handed her father-in-law the letter.

"Here. I know you're in the habit of opening your mail just before suppertime but this letter is from the property board. Thought you might want to see what it's about. Have you been up to some no good that we don't know about?"

"Haven't done anything wrong lately." He fumbled to open the letter. "That husband of yours keeps me too busy to have time to get into trouble and, besides, I'm too scared of that wife of mine to be out gambling, drinking or chasing wild women."

After a slurp of coffee and a bite from his grill cheese Mack began to read. By this time Gertie was at work over the kitchen sink, her back to her father-in-law, when she responded.

"Goodness knows, you and John have never given Ann or I concern over such things. We've enough frustration just picking up after you."

When she received no response she looked over her shoulder to see the strangest look on Mack's weathered face. It was a look of puzzlement, astonishment and annoyance, all at the same time. She turned, leaning where the small of her back met the sink counter, as she folded her arms. "What in the world has got you looking like that? You look like you were the one who just got the draft notice."

"It wouldn't surprise me anymore than this. Have a seat."

Mack's strange look was replaced by his soft, throaty laugh and a shake of his head. He handed the letter to Gertie. She started to read aloud. The farther she got the softer her voice became until she was reading silently.

From: Pleasant Springs Town Property and Zoning Board.
May 3, 1965

Dear Mr. Berg:
This letter is to inform you that a "Right to Purchase Land Claim" has been filed in the office of Pleasant Springs Town. The land in question belongs to you.

By law the claimant has the right to a hearing before the town supervisor to present the claimant's case. Since the land in question belongs to you be advised that you are requested to attend this hearing. The purpose of the hearing is to expedite the resolution of said claim, thus preventing the need for a legal confrontation in the courts. Barring an amicable settlement upon the conclusion of this hearing the claimant has the option of filing a law suit against you. Be advised that you may wish to have legal counsel present at the time of the hearing. Filing information for the above stated claim follows:
Claim No.: 24-5; Right to Purchase Land Claim
Wisconsin State Real Estate Code reference: section 12, paragraph 7

Date of claim declaration: April 30, 1965
Claimant: Mr. Gerald Hicks
Brief description of claim at issue:
Concerning deed of property sale and pursuant addendum between Oscar Knudson (seller) and Mack Berg (purchaser) dated December 5, 1936.

Property in question is two sections (eighty acres) from coordinate plat line longitude 34 to coordinate plat line latitude U, Town of Pleasant Springs, County of Dane, State of Wisconsin. Common language border recognition is at north acreage of Berg property along the north side of Koshkonong Rd. to intersection at Kinney Rd. to where it meets Knudson Lane.
Time of claim hearing: Tuesday, May 24, 1965; 9:00 a.m.
Location: Pleasant Springs Town Hall, room three.
1325 County Highway B, Pleasant Springs Town, Wisconsin.
Any request on your part to change the time of this hearing may be addressed by calling the following number: Su 8-4407.
Thomas Evans
Pleasant Springs Town Supervisor

As she finished reading, Gertie's face was flushed with irritation. She slapped the letter down on the table.

"Why, this is just about the most outlandish barrel of hogwash I've ever had the opportunity to know of. Who in this wide world of ours is Gerald Hicks?"

Mack had no answer for her for the name meant nothing to him. But before he could say anything Gertie was on her feet and back at her sink counter, handling her kitchen wares with an angry authority. Though he always admired his daughter-in-law's spunk he felt it best to offer a moderating tone.

"Gertie, let's keep this our little secret until supper. We'll let everyone know about this at the same time."

≠ ≠ ≠

"Mother, I have no doubt that you make the best pineapple upside down cake in the entire state of Wisconsin." This was Clark's favorite dessert and in one way or another he always let his mother, and his grand-mother, know that he appreciated their efforts. Despite his sometimes irreverent behavior he could be a real charmer.

Upon the conclusion of dessert it was normal for Clark and Johnny, and sometimes Elsie, to leave the table to their mother, father and grand-parents, who would relax over their coffee for another ten minutes. On this evening, Gertie asked her kids to stay put, grandpa had something to say. Clark's expression showed his impatience with staying at the table, but then he received that glare from his mother that told him it would be wise to stay put.

Mack put on his reading glasses. "Got a letter today. Want to read it to you."

When he finished there were a few seconds of stunned silence.

"Who in the world is Gerald Hicks?" John Berg leaned back in his chair. "Is this really addressed to us? There has to be some kind of mis-take. My great grandparents settled here in 1872. I haven't got time to go to court on May whatever it is for a hearing about being forced to sell the land we've been farming for the last ninety-three years."

He took the letter from his father and read it himself. He looked up quizzically, at no one in particular. "Gerald Hicks? A Right to Buy Prop-erty Claim?"

He shifted his gaze to his father with an expression of both amaze-ment and concern.

"You or I need to call Tom Evans tomorrow and see what this is all about. In the meantime, Dad, you've got the homestead land grant deed somewhere, don't you? In your safety deposit box at the bank?"

"Yep. Got it somewhere," replied Mack. "I don't know where, but we've got it somewhere. I think it's in our dresser, in the bottom drawer with a lot of other papers. I don't believe I ever got around to putting that stuff in the safety deposit box."

"And the receipts or the deeds from when you bought the acreage from the Knudson place?"

"Oh yea, got those also. And I know I've got the deed from when Dad bought the north forty acres from the state shortly before he died." He rubbed the back of his neck.

"You know, the two sections this letter is talking about. That's the land Oscar Knudson sold me when he retired."

Mack stared into his coffee cup for a second or two and then repeated the thoughts that his son had just expressed. "What kind of a crackpot is going to come along and claim the right to buy a person's land away from him?"

Clark was now glad he stayed at the table. "Grandpa, maybe this is a practical joke? Maybe this is another one of Skorpie's practical jokes? I wouldn't put it past him."

"Ah! That old bird isn't smart enough to come up with something this good. Harold Johnson has been sticking it to me since I was five years old but that dumb Swede isn't smart enough to come up with something like this. Besides, look at the letterhead. This looks pretty official."

John raised his hands to his chest with his palms out, a gesture suggesting an end to this subject, at least for the time being.

"I'd be happy to know that this was some of Skorpie Johnson's mischief…but I don't think so. I'll call Tom Evans tomorrow and see what this is all about."

He sat at the table, motionless for a few moments, before thinking out loud. "Who in the world is Gerald Hicks?"

THREE

"Not that I speak in respect of want: for I have learned, in
whatever state I am, therewith to be content."

Phillipians 4:11 kjv

That Saturday Johnny Berg came in from the fields at two o'clock. This was his regular practice. He spent the rest of the day with the girl who had been his sweetheart since his sophomore year in high school.

Jenny Watson had moved to Stoughton with her family when she was eleven years old. Her father had bought the hardware store in town in 1956 when his career as an engineer at the American Motors plant in Kenosha seemed to have no real future.

Jenny was the oldest of three girls and one boy. She was bright, sincere and had a mind of her own. If the latter quality indicated stubbornness, it was of a positive nature. She was a person, even at the young age of twenty, who thought independently. She could not be easily swayed from what she believed to be right and she was more than willing to speak up for those beliefs. Young John Berg was not the same. Though just as principled as Jenny, he was so laid back and, to an extent, unsure of himself, that he often let the comments of others go unchallenged.

Johnny received his draft notice on Thursday and had only talked to Jenny on the phone Friday night for the briefest of moments. The intense field work left little time for talk and besides, the singular telephone at the Berg home was considered a tool to be used as needed, not as an instrument for extended conversation. He did not mention the induction notice at that time, preferring to wait until he saw Jenny in person.

As they often did, the couple drove the Bergs' Ford pickup twenty-five miles into Madison to eat. They liked a place on Highway 12 called Tom's Grill. The place offered a great club sandwich that Johnny could not stay away from.

While waiting for their food Jenny challenged him. "I know you are one of the most soft spoken people on this earth, Johnny Berg, but you hardly said two words on the way over here. Sometimes I wonder how you ever put the words together to say that you want to marry me."

Jenny tilted her head as she met John's gaze. "In case you forgot, you did say that you want to marry me. You do remember saying that to me, don't you Mr. Berg?" She gave her boyfriend that smile that always brought him around to her way of thinking.

John cracked a smile. "Of course I want to marry you." He gave a long hesitation that made Jenny take pause for concern. Her tone was upbeat, but demanding.

"What is the matter, John? It's like you are about to tell me something that I don't want to hear. What is it?"

He leaned back in his chair and rubbed his left hand on the back of his neck. It was a mannerism, not uncommon to his grandfather, that he unconsciously used when concerned about something. He took a deep breath and looked directly into Jenny's eyes.

"I've received my draft notice. I have to report to Camp McCoy for a physical and induction in twelve days."

Jenny was caught totally by surprise. For a brief moment they just stared at each other.

"Camp McCoy. It's over near LaCrosse. Dad says it's an old army camp they closed a few years ago and they probably reopened some of it to process new guys since Vietnam started."

Johnny knew that his girlfriend was not really interested in the history of Camp McCoy, but it was an awkward moment and he did not know what else to say.

Jenny's eyes went down to her coke. She took a sip, gathered her thoughts, squared her shoulders and returned her gaze to the young man she loved.

"I don't know if this war is right or wrong or what. The one time we talked about it you said that if they called you then you would do your best."

Though she was not finished with her thought she stopped for a second. Tears welled in her eyes. She was fighting her disappointment while trying to face this news head on.

"Well, now the draft board has called you, Johnny Berg. I won't be the first girl to have her fiancé, well, almost fiancé, called into the Army. Is that what it is; the Army? Or is it the Navy or the Air Force or the Marines or the paratroopers? I would prefer that you not be jumping out of airplanes."

At this moment Johnny felt a wave of love for this girl that went beyond anything he had yet known. Here she was getting the news that her future with the guy she wanted to marry was going to be put on hold for the next two years and yet she took the news bravely. He reached across the table and squeezed her hands.

"I want to go and get this over with, Jen. Then I want to come back and marry you and share your bed and make babies with you and all that goes with it."

Jenny was speechless for a moment. She had never heard him speak with such authority about anything, including their future together. She was wide eyed and her mouth was agape.

John realized he had somehow said something, or spoken in some manner, that had struck her.

"Anyway, I don't know much about the military Jen, but I do know that they don't draft guys into the paratroopers. They are a part of the Army. I think paratroopers is something you volunteer for."

It took her a few seconds to regain her composure. Jenny loosened her hands from his and squeezed one of his forearms. "Well, I hope you have the good sense not to be volunteering to jump out of airplanes."

John laughed softly. "Jen, I don't know what I'll be doing. I could spend two years cleaning out toilets."

"Besides," he spoke with light hearted conviction, "I've already been told by grandma not to volunteer for anything dangerous."

Jenny took a long drag on her coke and controlled a smile that was trying to break out. "Does that include cleaning out toilets?"

Johnny broke into a big grin. "It certainly does!"

It was well past dark when the couple returned to the Watson house. Jenny opened the door and turned and looked up to the young man she cared for.

"I just…" Her eyes welled up instantly. Tears rolled down her cheeks. She took a deep breath and exhaled. "Whew! I'm sorry! I just hadn't expected something like this."

She reached up and wrapped her arms around her boyfriend's neck. She gave him a more passionate kiss than she had ever previously offered. She immediately turned and went into the house.

Johnny stood there, alone on the porch, for a good five minutes. He realized, perhaps for the first time, how much more fragile a woman's emotions were than a man's.

As he drove home a number of things raced through his mind. One second it was Jenny and how special it would be when he returned from the Army so they could begin their lives together. He knew before he pulled into the farm that he needed for them to become engaged before he went away. He wanted to buy her a ring immediately. If it weren't so late he would charge back to the Watson house and take her to the Christenson jewelry store in town. Before the next week was out he would do that very thing.

Then he realized how much he was going to miss his family and how amazing his life, this simple, unglamorous, but amazing life, had been. And then he thought of the uncertainty of these next two years. Would he be up to whatever experiences were ahead of him? Would he be the kind of soldier, the kind of man, that he should be? Would he be the kind of person that, as his grandfather said, "would make them all proud?"

As these things cartwheeled through his mind, he felt an insecurity in himself that had always been his Achilles heel. He realized how steeped in his own comfort zone he was. Was that why the farm meant so much to him? Did he really love farming that much, or was it because the farm was a safe haven? A place he had always known and understood. A place that allowed him to avoid stepping out into the unknown.

"Well Berg," he told himself, "you are about to step into that unknown."

Johnny quietly entered the back door of the house. It was 10 o'clock and everyone was asleep. He knew that at 10 o'clock on a Saturday night much of the world was out trying to make life fun and exciting. He stood there in the dark kitchen. He shoved the feeling of insecurity and doubt to the back of his mind. A feeling of gratitude came over him as he realized that all the fun and excitement and all the contentment and peace that he needed had already been his for the twenty years of his life.

FOUR

lark Berg knew that he was different. Different than his brother; different than the whole family. He knew he was from a family of soft spoken, sincere and hard working folks but he was determined that he would not be one to hide his light under a barrel.

He was a handsome young man. He was of solid build, almost six feet tall; dark, curly hair and brown eyes. Some said he reminded them of a popular actor of the day, Montgomery Clift.

His choice of friends had never pleased his parents, even in elementary school. There was the time, when as a fifth-grader, he was caught along with two others looking at pictures in a girly magazine. Gertie was summoned to the school for what the principal called misguided grade school curiosity. She considered it to be a symptom of a more serious trend in her son's disingenuous character.

When John and Gertie confronted the youngster about the incident they were certain to make sure that Clark understood that they were not people to be trifled with.

"Your mother and I have not just fallen off the turnip truck," John told him. "We see your adventure with the magazine as a sign of some overall disregard for what is right and what is wrong. You've just inherited some additional chores around here, young man, and your mother has asked your homeroom teacher to notify her for the rest of the school year anytime you begin to falter in your school work."

For the remaining ten weeks of the school year the most excitement Clark was to know was completing his school work and doing more than his normal share of chores.

Now, a senior in high school, John and Gertie were disappointed to know that his behavior had little improved. He was part of a crowd that could charitably be called fast. Clark never drank or smoked anywhere near the farm but, again, John and Gertie were not unaware of the world around them. Elsie and Johnny had never been any trouble but Clark was another matter. He could be very much a rebel. He was the one that nobody could figure out where he came from. He possessed a charm that could endear him to people one minute and an insincerity that left people feeling betrayed the next.

Where Johnny always knew his vocation would be to carry on the farm, Clark seemed less interested in his future and more interested in the delights of the next weekend. He had always managed to pass from grade to grade in elementary school, not because of any work ethic, but rather because he possessed a natural aptitude for memorization and deduction. Then, in the ninth grade, part way through the fall term, his behavior got him expelled for the reminder of the term when he and three others were caught by the truant officer launching a rowboat out onto Lake Kegonsa during school hours. When he reentered school his attitude was so poor that he flunked that same first half of the ninth grade. He had lost an entire year.

Clark graduated from Stoughton Area High School on May 18, two days after Johnny left for the Army. He faced graduation with no plans other than to spend that summer working on the farm; something he did not want to do. But then a stroke of good fortune gave young Berg the direction he needed. Occupational direction, anyway.

Clark's Uncle Frank, husband to John Berg's sister Catherine, was sales manager for WWMR, a 50,000 watt, major radio station in Milwaukee. It competed staunchly with the likes of WGN and WLS out of Chicago for a share of the Wisconsin audience. Like many stations of the day the morning and afternoon drive time programs featured music with an adult appeal. Conversation was light hearted, covering subjects from human interest stories to occasional interviews with local athletes and politicians. Though the station did not cover the Green Bay Packers' games play by play, it thoroughly followed every aspect of the beloved team. They did cover the play by play of the Milwaukee Braves and had done so since the team came from Boston in 1953. Mid-morning programming included a popular and well done documentary program covering something from Wisconsin or Midwest history. The farm report came on after the noon news and Arthur Godfrey's syndicated radio show followed. The station was a CBS affiliate.

Frank Smith had been sales manager at the station for eleven years. Selling radio advertising was a difficult, high pressure business that required perseverance, discipline and a desire to compete. Smith was aware that Clark had little of these qualities. But over the years he had come to see a likeability in his nephew that could often go a long way in sales. Could Clark learn the discipline he needed? Frank Smith felt it was worth a try. After all, Clark was family. The son of his wife's brother. Smith felt that somewhere inside the young man must reside the character so abundant in the rest of the Berg family.

And so on the Tuesday after the Memorial Day weekend, just five days after his high school graduation, Clark borrowed the family station wagon to keep an appointment with his Uncle Frank at his office, one floor above the WWMR studios in the Kramer Building in downtown Milwaukee.

Frank Smith was an imposing figure from behind his desk. With the sleeves of his white dress shirt rolled up, the shirt unbuttoned at the top and a conservative blue tie dangling loosely, he appeared all business. He was a rangy, athletic looking six foot three inches tall. His black hair, graying at the temples and receding just a bit, was conservatively cut. He was already well tanned despite the cool spring weather.

Smith came around the desk, welcomed his nephew with a handshake, and asked him to take a seat. Smith sat on the edge of his desk. He skipped over the family small talk and got right to the point.

"Clark, I told you over the phone that I had a job offer for you. I didn't tell you anything about it over the phone and I did that purposefully. I believe the most important thing I do as advertising sales manager here is to hire the right people to sell time on this radio station."

Smith had succeeded in getting and holding his nephew's attention. This, Clark could tell, would be no family favor hiring. The thought made him anxious for a moment, for in his immature mind he had hoped for some sort of cushy, "let's help Clark out" offer.

"What I want to do is show you what goes on here, what is expected of you should you be interested in this work and make sure you understand that you sink or swim here based on your own performance, just like everyone else."

A formal, "Yes sir," was all Clark could manage.

"If you're interested, you are going to have to look at the big picture. Our advertising account execs all have university degrees. What I see in you is some raw talent. Over time, with some long-range planning and commitment on your part, I believe you have the opportunity for a lucrative career in radio ad sales. Before I go any further, do you think that this holds any interest for you?"

For one of the few times in his young life someone had Clark's complete attention. His mind buzzed quickly with thoughts of adjustments. All of a sudden the responsible attitudes that he had so easily cast aside throughout his boyhood were being put up to him by an uncle that he had really only known peripherally.

"Yes sir, I'm interested. I'm very interested."

Smith moved right along. "What I am proposing is this. I know you are a senior. Have you finished school yet?"

"We graduated last week." Clark was on the edge of his seat, keenly anticipating Frank Smith's projected plans for him, while at the same time trying hard to convince himself he could meet the coming responsibilities.

"Fine then. If your answer is yes to this opportunity, be ready to start here next Monday morning. Your position will be assistant ad exec. What that means is you'll be doing everything from assisting the ad execs with their paper work, taking phone calls when the execs aren't available, going out on presentations when the exec needs a hand, organizing files and whatever else is required. We have six ad execs here and we have one assistant. It's too much. We need a second assistant. Your starting pay will be $150 a week. If all goes well, there will be incremental increases as soon as I deem appropriate."

Before Clark could give any response Smith continued, all the while keeping piercing eye contact with his nephew.

"Now, before you give me a final answer as to whether or not you want this, I need to know something. I want to see you make every effort to get yourself enrolled in college for the fall semester. I know that it's a little late to get started in this effort and maybe your grades are not the most impressive, but I am of the belief that a person can accomplish most anything if he puts his mind to it. We will deal later about how you go to school and work here at the same time. Are you still interested?"

Clark swallowed hard and took a deep breath. He knew full well that this was an opportunity that he must take. Here he was, one minute drifting along with no plans after high school, and the next minute having a chance to get started in a business with a legitimate future. A chance to break away from the farm and have something he could identify as his own.

"Yes sir. I'm very interested. I do want this opportunity."

Frank Smith stood. He continued to stare directly into his nephew's eyes. "And the discipline? Are you going to be disciplined enough to work and go to school? I don't need you to be an assistant sales exec forever. You'll have to be energetic enough and disciplined enough to work toward a future."

Clark stood to meet his uncle. He exhaled the air of tension that had accumulated in his lungs. His uncle had been upfront with him and he owed the same to him.

"I want this opportunity very much. I, uh. Well, I may be telling you something that you already know when I tell you that I don't have the best work reputation. I've sometimes been one to ...."

Smith held up his hand for Clark to stop. "I know something of your work ethic. And I know something of your good time Charlie reputation. What I am interested in is what lies ahead of you. There's no reason why you can't be an achiever. You work hard, be willing to learn and to be sincere with your employer and with our customers, and I believe you can make it."

Smith offered his hand and Clark met it with a firm shake.

"So I'll expect you Monday morning at 8:30." He spoke matter-of-factly to his nephew.

Clark responded with a, "Yes sir. Thank you." It came upon him that this was no moment for a "thanks Uncle Frank" good-bye.

FIVE

John brought the Ford F-150 to a stop when it reached the crest of the rise. He occasionally took this bumpy, two-track trail along the edge of the Bergs' land, the very high ground from which Mack had harvested the pine to build the family's home in the 1920s, to take in all around him.

He spoke audibly to himself, thinking of his great grandfather's move to America.

"Yes sir, Elmer. You did good. You did real good."

Having been born and raised in the dairy business, John accepted without need for acknowledgement the demands on the American farmer. It is unlikely that in any other work are the qualities of self-discipline, physical endurance, optimism, patience, pragmatism, business savvy, and the acceptance of disappointment so well required. And then, beyond all else, the need for humility is essential. A humility that says a higher power than man has control of the weather that is needed for success.

It was not uncommon for John to come to this spot on occasion. From here he could take in the farm's 280 acres. Looking beyond his land to the southwest, with the morning sun at his back, he caught the glimmer of its reflection off of Lake Kegonsa. Farther south he could make out the top of the Romanesque-style bell tower of Stoughton's town hall.

He smiled as he thought of the annual Syttende Mai festival and parade that had taken place the previous month. He thought of how his dad proudly flew the family's Norwegian flag during that week which celebrated the town's ancestral heritage. Mack always broke out his elaborately embroidered Norse sweater, sent to him years before by relatives near Trondiem, for the Sunday parade. It had been an especially warm

May afternoon this year, but Mack proudly perspired through the festivities.

On this morning, John had called for a nine o'clock meeting with Mack and his two hired hands at this location. He thought that from here the young man that he had hired through the University of Wisconsin's placement service could get a view of the entire farm on this, his first day of employment. As he heard the station wagon strain as it reached the top of the hill, John's gaze settled on the eighty acres that was now, thanks to a man named Gerald Hicks, in doubt. The contented feeling that he was experiencing began to slip. He was of a belief that the Lord was in charge, but he was also mindful of the expression that God helps those who help themselves.

"Georgie, welcome to Berg farm, home of the Vikings. If Mack here or John get on your case just remember that Gertie and Ann's cooking will make it all worthwhile."

It was Rollie Leach, the farm's regular summer help, who offered an official welcome to young George Wistoff once all four men were gathered around John's pickup. Though Rollie and George had first met while taking care of the milk hookups earlier in the morning, Rollie now had an audience.

"Where's home, Georgie?"

The soft spoken nineteen-year-old was put at ease by Rollie's outgoing style.

"Minot, North Dakota. It's about nine hundred miles west and a little north of here. My folks have a farm there."

"North Dakota? North Dakota, eh! Do they have electricity out there yet? Berg farm must seem like the Las Vegas strip to you!"

They all chuckled, then Mack put his two cents worth in. "Don't mind Rollie here, George. I thought that Canadians were a soft spoken, well mannered bunch but I think Rollie here's been hit too many times in the head by the puck."

Rollie gave a quick retort. "Oh mighty Thor, like I've said before, it's the stick that does the damage. A hockey player will get hit twenty times in the head by a stick for every time he gets clobbered by a puck."

Leach had come to the University of Wisconsin on a hockey scholarship in 1958. In his sophomore year he suffered a severe knee injury that ended his playing days. Being unable to play, and with his scholarship money partially revoked, the starch had been taken out of him regarding school. When the opportunity to take work as the team's equipment manager presented itself, he quit school and took the job. During the off season he had taken work with the Bergs.

There is no doubt that Rollie had taken on the appearance of many an ex-hockey player. He had the thick calf and thigh muscles and high, rumpy gluts of a man who had been skating hard almost from the time he could walk. He had a barrel chest and the beginnings of a pot belly. The barrel chest was the result of the aerobics of his sport. The pot belly was from the favorite form of hydration of many an ex-player—full-bodied Canadian beer. He always wore one of two baseball caps over his reddish brown brush cut. One was red and white with the word Badgers spelled out. The other was blue and white displaying the word Hespeler. With unabashed pride Rollie Leach loved to tell anyone he could about his beloved hometown of Hespeler, Ontario.

John brought everyone's attention to the work at hand.

"I brought you all up here so George could get the lay of the land. Dad is going to continue with his tractor work for the rest of the week. Rollie, I want you and George to spend your time cleaning out a number of culverts along Koshgonong Road. We've neglected them for a number of years and they can't take much more rain before they start backing up. I'll be in the repair barn for the rest of the week with three jobs. Kaiser's called yesterday and said the yoke was in for the little Massey."

Rollie couldn't help but make young George feel more at home.

"John, I think old Georgie here might be cleaning out culverts for the first time. Up in Minot it stays so cold the damn, I mean the darn, drains never get a chance to thaw out, eh!"

By this time George Wistoff could sense an unfamiliar lilt to Rollie Leach's speech pattern.

"Where are you from, Rollie?"

George could sense both Mack and John stiffen, as though he shouldn't have asked the question.

"Georgie, I'm from the greatest little town in North America; Hespeler, Ontario. It's a great main street community. Not so many Vikings to put up with. Mostly Scotch and English up our way. Hespeler is the hockey stick capital of the world. Most all your major brands are cut and milled there. Bauer, Sherwood, our own Hespeler brand. A lot of the Northland Pro brand is done in Hespeler for teams in the National Hockey League. And some of the minor league teams."

"You can't beat it. Right John?"

Berg shook his head in resignation to Rollie's enthusiasm. "Right Rollie. Scotch, English and hockey sticks."

He redirected the conversation toward his new help. "George's family has a big grain operation out there in Minot, but he shouldn't have any trouble adjusting to the dairy business. You're replacing a good man, George. We're glad to have you."

George was already aware that Johnny was away in the Army. "I've got two older brothers. Twins. They got drafted about a year ago. One's in Vietnam."

It was quiet for a few moments as the uncertainty of America's commitment to this war in Southeast Asia gripped these men.

Mack broke the silence, speaking with Berg pragmatism.

"We just gonna have to see how it all works out."

Before the summer was gone both John and Mack were to find out that Johnny's Army time and the land dispute with Gerald Hicks would become secondary to a more immediate concern.

SIX

Are you up to no good with me again, Johnson?" Mack had the words out of his mouth before he plopped into his chair.

"I'm up to no good every chance I get when it comes to you, Mr. Berg," replied Mack's lifelong friend. "Trouble is you're just too easy a mark. What did I do this time?"

It was the usual Saturday morning coffee bull session for Mack and three of his buddies, all farmers. None were yet retired, but they were to the point in their lives where, once a week, they could find time for a couple hours of down time at Rasmussen's, an unpretentious breakfast and lunch diner on Stoughton's main street. The place was well suited to these men who lived close to the land, unimpressed by the fads and fancies of some establishments. The place was clean and the service was fast. Bud Rasmussen made no attempt at creating atmosphere for his place, save for one enlarged, framed photograph that hung above the doorway leading back into the kitchen. The picture was a black and white print of Bud and three other locals showing off an impressive stringer of walleyes. In the bottom right corner of the picture was scribbled "Lake Kegonsa, May 23, 1948."

Mack shook his head and grunted. "I wish it were one of your shenanigans."

He rubbed the back of his neck. "Got a letter yesterday from the town office. Some guy has claimed that he has the right to buy some of our land. Those eighty acres that Oscar Knudson sold me in the thirties. I've got to go for a meeting to see if it can be resolved to avoid a legal action. Can you believe it!"

Skorpie Johnson stared over his reading glasses at his friend for a good five seconds. Over the years he had kept himself almost in as good a physical condition as Mack, although he now carried a few extra pounds on his six-foot-two inch frame. His blue eyes looked gleeful as he saw the humor of it. "Ah! That's a classic. I'd a loved to have thought of that one."

"Thought of what?" Tom Edgerton and Edgar Friske found their seats as Edgerton asked the question.

Mack again rubbed the back of his neck and explained what he knew.

"What's the guy's name?" It was Eddie Friske who asked, hoping the name would ring a bell with one of them.

"Uh? I don't know. I forget. I've got it here." Mack fumbled for the letter and put on his reading glasses. "Uh. Name's Gerald Hicks."

They all reflected for a moment. "My family's been here almost as long as yours, Mack. I don't recall anybody named Hicks from around here," said Friske.

"Yeah. Well, whoever he is he's got a lot of explaining to do come the twenty-fourth," grumbled Mack.

The mood at the table was always jovial with a great deal of kidding and exaggeration. But now the mood was somber. A man's land was being questioned. In this part of the country, where the business of farming was passed on from one generation to the next, where pride and tradition were as important as making a dollar, a man's land ranked only behind his God and his family.

Betty Smith, Rasmussen's longtime waitress, filled the foursome's coffee cups and put down a plate with a generous number of slices of Swedish coffee bread from Kronberg's, the renown Danish bakery directly across the street.

"Eat up boys, it's not getting any fresher." It's the same line she gave this group every time.

Skorpie looked up. "Betty, you get better looking every day. If I wasn't so afraid of that wife of mine I'd be sweet talking you on a regular basis."

Indeed, Betty Smith was a good looking woman. Now 45 years old, she had been widowed seven years previous when her husband, Tom

Smith, the town's postmaster, passed away after a long struggle with colon cancer. Betty had a million dollar smile, had been able to keep an attractive figure and, possibly with a little help from the right hair color, had been able to retain her shiny, naturally curly chestnut brown hair. Better than all that, Betty Smith had a great sense of humor and a no nonsense way of keeping her acquaintances, including customers, in line.

"Harold Johnson, you mind yourself. If I were to tell Esther how you carry on here I believe they'd have to cancel your life insurance."

The men chuckled and Eddie Friske asked Betty if she knew anyone named Hicks from around Stoughton.

"Beats me," she replied, as she took off for another table.

Five minutes later she was back. "You know, I think I do know that name Hicks. When I was a young girl my mother's best friend was Maggie Knudson. Well, you guys knew the Knudsons, Oscar and Margaret.'"

"Yeah, sure," replied Mack. "They had the farm right next to us. Oscar Kundson sold out to Bobby Pierson and myself during the Depression."

Betty continued. "Anyway, they had two daughters. Maggie was the oldest and she had a younger sister. Name was Gretchen. No. No, it was Greta."

"It was Greta." Eddie Friske seemed to have the sharpest recall of the four men. "As I recall, a good looking girl."

"Oh, yeah. I remember now," chimed in Edgerton. "A very attractive young woman."

Skorpie grunted, "It's good to know that a couple of geezers like you can still remember such things."

"Do you guys want to hear what I have to say, or not?" With hands on hips and a look of mock impatience on her face Betty continued. "She married somebody from Chicago named Hicks. I remember they lived in Chicago and I don't believe they ever came back here much. Come on! I'll bet you guys were at the wedding."

After a second of reflection none of them could remember being at such a wedding.

"Had to have been near thirty years ago," said Mack. "That wedding isn't ringing a bell to me, Betty."

"Ah!" Betty shook her head. "That's because you're men. It's beyond your powers to remember anything as significant as a wedding. For goodness sake. I remember and I was just a kid."

She folded her arms and softened her voice. "Anyway, there it is. I'm pretty sure you all remember hearing about the car accident. Fifteen years ago, or so. Maggie was killed. Down south somewhere; where she lived. She never had married."

Betty left for another table.

Eddie Friske spoke to no one in particular. "Yes, I think we all remember hearing about that one. When you think about it, the Knudson name is gone. That is, if Margaret is gone, which is likely. She'd have to be somewhere in her nineties."

"She's gone alright," said Mack. "I remember reading it in the obituaries a number of years ago. Knuddy died first. Funny, they brought him back up here, had a memorial service and all, but they must have buried Margaret down there somewhere."

"Gone but not forgotten," said Edgerton. "Old Knuddy was a hard, hard worker." He looked to Mack. "You think this might be the Hicks guy that married Greta?"

"Must be. Still doesn't make any sense to me." Mack reached for another slab of coffee bread. "How in the world could this Hicks character have any claim on our land? I'm going to forget about it for now and just be at that meeting."

SEVEN

"God is our refuge and strength, a very present help in trouble."

PSALMS 45:1 KJV

On June 24 Mack and John appeared at the Pleasant Springs Town Hall. They arrived with a great deal of curiosity and a keen desire to confront Mr. Gerald Hicks. Mack, in particular, arrived with a chip on his shoulder. John could sense that he would need to keep a lid on his father's emotions.

The Pleasant Springs Town Hall was a modest, one-story office building. It had a reception area and three rooms. It was in the conference room where the meeting was to take place. When Mack and John walked in the town supervisor, Tom Evans, was already seated at the head of the conference table. Along one side were three men, all dressed in three-piece suits and each sporting a leather valise filled, no doubt, with pertinent papers. The Bergs never had need for a lawyer, save the time papers were drawn up to create a partnership of the farm, bringing John into ownership with Mack. They brought no lawyer with them on this day. They were, however, armed with the property deeds and bills of sale for the transactions that had occurred at the farm going back to the homestead award to Elmer.

If some people felt intimidated by such a legal looking battery it was not the Bergs. Besides, Mack had known Tom Evans for almost forty years. He was a man of unquestioned integrity. He wasn't going to let any intimidation take place.

The job of Pleasant Springs Town supervisor was a part-time position. Evans was a lifelong resident of the area. Now retired from running his own insurance business in Stoughton, he did light farming on his forty-acre Pleasant Springs property. He had accepted the supervisor's position when asked to take it thirty-one years before. The compensation he received was nominal. It was out of a sense of duty to the community that he had kept the position all these years.

Evans made the introductions. "Mack and John Berg, this is Gerald Hicks, the petitioner, and his two lawyers, John Patterson and Charles Diehl."

Hicks sat between his two lawyers, as though insulating himself from the very process that he had set in motion. At the introduction he said nothing, giving only an expressionless nod of recognition. He was a man of rather athletic build, appearing to be in his late fifties, possibly early sixties. His well greased hair was combed straight back, without a part. If he had any gray it was hidden by jet black hair coloring. The wire rim glasses that he wore did little to soften the hawkish look of his eyes.

The Bergs were not judgmental people but they later agreed that the man left an untrustworthy impression. They could not help but sense that he must make his living manipulating other people.

Evans continued. "Mr. Hicks, would you get this started with your statement."

One of Hick's lawyers read the contention. As far as the core content was concerned, the message was the same as the letter received at Berg Farm. However the legal wording, party of the first part, party of the second part, etc., drew a look of uneasiness from both Mack and John. They glanced at Tom Evans for reassurance.

"A very legal way of saying the same thing your letter says. Gerald Hicks is claiming the right to purchase those two sections of your farm."

Mack turned his gaze toward Hicks. The twinkle that normally was present in his eyes had turned steely.

"We are aware of what you are claiming. I want to know how in the blazes you think you can make such a claim?" Mack displayed an air of calmness but John knew his father was working up a head of steam inside.

Evans interjected. "That comes in a second statement. Shall we hear it, gentlemen?"

Before reading, the lawyer, Charles Diehl, held up a copy of a hand-written note for all to see. He then read.

If one of our daughters or a member of her immediate family should want to reestablish themselves on the 80 acres of property sold by Oscar Knudson to Mack Berg on December 5, 1936 Mack Berg is obligated to sell the property to that person. The price of the sale would be based on market conditions at that time.

Oscar Knudson	*December 19, 1936*
Margaret Knudson	Notarized on this day,
	December 19, 1936
Mack Berg	Thomas L. Evans
	Supervisor, Pleasant Springs Town
	County of Dane
	State of Wisconsin
	Thomas L. Evans

Diehl continued.

"On February 18, 1940 Greta Knudson, daughter of Oscar and Margaret Knudson, married Gerald Hicks. We have here in our possession a copy of that marriage certificate. Last year, on October 13, 1964 Greta Hicks past away. We have in our possession a copy of that death certificate."

Diehl held up both certificates for everyone to see. He then offered them to Mack and John for viewing.

"Gentlemen, based on this documentation just presented and on the Wisconsin State Real Estate Code, section 12, paragraph 7, Mr. Hicks has a perfect legal right to purchase the property in question."

In an attorney's voice, trained to be separated from the emotion that he knew resided in the Bergs, he continued.

"Gentlemen, this note is straight forward. We do not know if you have in your possession a similar hand written note, Mr. Berg, but the significant thing is that you put your signature to this one. State law indicates that this note stands as a legal document when placed as an addendum to the notarized deed as registered in the Pleasant Springs Registrar of Deeds. We have researched the deed relating to this sale and found, in fact, that this information is legally attached to the deed in question. Oscar Knudson, Margaret Knudson and Mack Berg signed that deed and this addendum. This handwritten note is legal and binding."

There was silence for a few moments, then Tom Evans spoke.

"Mack, do you agree that this is your signature?"

By this time Mack had a hollow look on his face. The kind of look a man gets when he is forced to face an unpleasant and certain fact. He took a deep breath and reluctantly looked at the note. "Yeah, that's my signature all right."

Before he could say anymore, John grabbed his father's forearm. He knew that an emotional response to this claim would be of no value. He also knew that an emotional response would be just what a man like Gerald Hicks would like to see. Here was a man, John realized, sitting between two lawyers, saying not a word himself, but apparently knowing how to let the law work for him.

Staying as composed as he could, John spoke. "I don't know what kind of game you are trying to play here, Mr. Hicks, but our family has been on this land for ninety-three years. My father bought those two sections from the Knudson's twenty-nine years ago. That eighty acres has been good to us, and as a boy I remember the sale of that land during the Depression was a lifesaver for your wife's mom and dad. Go ahead and have your lawyer here say whatever else he needs to say. We want you to know that we have no intention of selling any of our land to anyone."

Mack could be contained no longer. His normally husky voice took on an even more raspy quality. "Who the hell do you think you are? Are you a dairy farmer, Hicks? I don't think so. More like an opportunist. More like somebody who's trying to pad his own pockets at the expense of others. My grandfather came here with nothing and built a shack...."

John again grabbed his dad's arm. "These people aren't interested in what we have to say, Pop." He looked at Tom Evans. "What else do we need to hear?"

Evans gestured toward the lawyers and Diehl continued. "We just need you to know that this will be turned over to Mr. Hicks' real estate representatives and they will be contacting you about the purchase of the two sections in question. I believe that is all we have, gentlemen. Thank you."

The threesome stood in unison and began to exit the conference room.

Mack repeated himself. "What would you do with this land if you had it, Hicks? You don't look like much of a farmer to me."

In the doorway Gerald Hicks came to a stop and spoke without expression.

"Good day, gentlemen."

It was the only words he said during the meeting.

John said nothing for a few moments, trying to digest what had just taken place. He knew he had to approach this situation logically and pragmatically. "Tom, where do we go from here? This guy is not going to go away."

"You're right. He, and his lawyers, are not going to go away. I think you both know that as supervisor I have to be a neutral facilitator. But let me advise you here. You need to get a lawyer and you need to get the right kind of lawyer. You need to get the services of a lawyer who knows something about farm real estate. That note you signed, Mack, will carry a large amount of weight. It was a long time ago and I certainly had forgotten about it, even though I notarized it. But what matters is that it stands as a legal document."

Staring blankly down the length of the table Mack now spoke like a man whose spirit and zest for life had just been shaken. "I had forgotten about that note. I had completely forgotten about it."

In an apologetic voice, a tone of voice that John had rarely heard from his father, Mack continued. "Oscar and I agreed on the sale as a way to help his family. It was during the Depression. After he had no takers on the sale after about, I don't know, maybe a year, he came to me. I had all I could handle at the time but he was not well. And he had no sons. Knuddy was a happy Norseman when I agreed to buy those sections. I agreed to the price he wanted. Never tried to offer a lower price.

Figured I had nothing to lose. And then, a little later, he wrote that note. I didn't mind. If one of the girls wanted it back Ann and I would probably make a little profit. Knuddy sold his equipment off at auction but before he did he sold me his tractor as part of our deal. A good machine. A 1925 Case A 25-45. Still got it. Stashed back in the corner of our repair barn. Gave me a real good price. It helped me a lot to offset equipment expenses."

He looked over at his son. "I'm sorry John. Now we've got a mess on our hands."

"You did nothing wrong, Dad. Everything you did was honorable. We for sure have a mess on our hands, but it was a mess created by this Hicks guy, not you."

John looked to Evans. "I want to get that right lawyer you mentioned. Who do I go see?"

"I know some people at the Law School at Madison," replied Evans. "I'll make some phone calls and get back to you."

As the Bergs began to leave, Mack turned to the supervisor.

"Tom, what about the other property; the two sections that Bobby Pierson bought? I don't know if Bobby signed that same kind of note or not."

"He probably did. In fact, I remember now. I remember notarizing that one, too. But that doesn't apply here. Such a note applies only to the original purchaser. When Pierson sold the farm to his nephew, what, about fifteen years ago, that paper became null and void. That's state law."

"Ugh. State law." Mack spoke distantly, to neither Evans or his son. "Seems to me like this Hicks guy is breaking a greater law. He wants what is not his."

EIGHT

"God is our refuge and strength, a very present help in trouble."

PSALMS 46:1 KJV

There is an old, but untrue, saying that if you ignore bad news it will go away.

Gertie went to the mail box one morning in the second week of July to find two letters. One was from Johnny, now in his sixth week of basic training at Fort Knox, Kentucky. The other was from DeVries Real Estate Brokerage in Milwaukee.

Johnny had been writing to Jenny Watson almost every day and to his family once a week since he had left home in the middle of May. In his letters to the family he always spoke of how he missed everyone and how he missed working the land. When he mentioned how much he missed his mother's and his grandmother's cooking he always referred to particular items; things like homemade bread, cakes and pies; meatloaf and Swiss steak suppers, and grandma's homemade grape juice.

He wrote of how there were so many guys from so many places in his platoon. "Even though we are all so different we seem to get along and I think that is for one reason; we all want to get through basic training."

He always liked to sign off his letters with a light hearted P. S. after his signature.

P. S. "How's Rollie? I sure miss hearing about Hespeler!"

The other letter was the bad news that wasn't going to go away. The real estate firm said it specialized in the buying and selling of farm land. It had been hired by the law firm representing Gerald Hicks to make an offer on the acreage in question. Mr. DeVries would soon call, requesting permission to look at the acreage. "A fair and equitable offer would then be forthcoming."

That evening John, Gertie and Mack sat on the porch of their beloved farmhouse as the last glow of the summer sun melted into the western horizon. Anne had been tired and had already gone to bed.

Mack and Skorpie Johnson had added the porch, as well as a hard-wood floor in the parlor, in 1924. The porch was as much a gathering spot for the family during the summer and fall as their kitchen table was at any time of year. It extended the breadth of the house. Hanging cedar flower baskets, made years ago by Mack, adorned the length of the entire porch. Ann took great delight in growing a variety of flowers in them.

Ann and Gertie were diligent in keeping the area tidy, but in the summer months this spot was so central to the Bergs' family life that it always had a very lived in feeling. Two swings were hung from the porch ceiling, one on each side of the front door. Six rocking chairs held their places there, in no particular arrangement other than to allow family and friends to visit easily. A table that could accommodate eight people was at the west end of the porch. Over the years it had been the site of many a summer evening meal.

"It's not like Ann not to be out here, especially on a Saturday night," said Gertie.

Mack was in his familiar pose: his hands behind his head, fingers interlocked, as he gently rocked in his chair.

"Oh, I think she knew we would wind up talking about the Hicks thing and she's had enough of it. But there's nothing more to talk about right now."

He rocked in silence for a few more seconds and then spoke with a tone of disgust in his voice; something uncommon to him. "A fair and equitable offer. Ha."

John leaned forward in his rocker. "Dad, you've made me partner in the farm and you've given me free range to make decisions. I don't ever want to take that flexibility for granted but I'll say this. Tom Evans sent us that list of lawyers to choose from and I don't want to let any more time go by before we speak to one. You're going to be sent an offer on those sections and we need to know what to do to fight it."

For a few moments Mack stared straight ahead with a sour look on his face. "Yeah. The time has come. I never thought a simple dairy farmer would have to seek out a lawyer. But then, some people would say I'm behind the times."

"You have worked hard your entire life to build this place!" Gertie was on her feet now. Though a bit irritated, the tone of her voice also expressed an optimism that the right thing would prevail. "You men have to make the decisions here but I will tell you this. You can be sure that Oscar Knudson would not have wanted you to lose that land to someone like Gerald Hicks. You need to settle on a lawyer. He'll know where to go from here."

Mack gently smacked the arms of his chair with his weathered hands. "What a time of year to have to take time out to go explain what this is all about to some lawyer and then hope that he's the right one to help us."

"No." John spoke with resolution. "No, we are not going to go chasing after a lawyer. I'm going to make a phone call or two on Monday. If one of these outfits is interested they can come out and talk to us."

Monday morning at about ten o'clock John roared up to the back of the house on his tractor. Gertie was hanging out laundry to dry when she saw her husband walk very purposely toward the back door. With a clothes pin clamped between her teeth she mumbled audibly to herself. "Lord, help us out here."

It wasn't but ten minutes later when John came out the back door and walked over to his wife. She could tell immediately that the call went well. Without much expression but still with a tone of relief in his voice he told her that the lawyer he contacted would be out to see them on Wednesday at 7:00 P.M.

Gertie gave her husband a long hug then looked him in the eye. "Did he give you any idea of what he thought? Did he think he could help us?"

"He said from what I told him the law looked to be on Hicks' side but there are always a few skeletons in the closet. I asked him what he meant and he said he'll be able to have a better idea once he sees the letter from Hicks and the note that Oscar Knudson wrote."

Gertie's voice was uplifting, as usual. "I'm glad your father found his copy of that note. You've done the right thing, John Berg. We'll look forward to Wednesday evening then."

They gave each other another quick hug and John turned to go back to the Massey. He stopped, turned back and looked at Gertie. With his spirits buoyed by the phone call he made a suggestion. "I think you and I should take a break. Right now, I mean."

Gertie didn't say anything for about ten seconds as she returned to hanging her laundry.

"John Berg, along with you I have three other men looking forward to dinner in the field in another hour and fifteen minutes. I haven't got time for the kind of break that you've got in mind."

John showed a "can't blame a guy for trying smile" and returned to the tractor. As he was climbing into the cab Gertie shouted over the noise of the idling diesel engine. "We'll take that break tonight."

Wednesday evening at five minutes to seven the lawyer that John spoke to was at the Bergs' door. His name was Charlie Stroud. He appeared to be in his mid-fifties. He sported a brush cut of once black hair that had gone mostly gray. He was not a distinguished looking man, as some folks would expect a lawyer might be. He had a modest middle-aged spread. He appeared work worn, with pronounced bags under his tired, but earnest looking eyes. The suit he wore hung on him in a bit of a haphazard fashion. No three piece suit here. No doubt he had already put in a full day.

As was customary for the Bergs when anything of family concern was discussed, everyone sat around the kitchen table. During coffee and some of Ann's wonderful Danish sweet rolls, Charlie Stroud explained himself.

"I have my own firm in Wes Allis. I am not part of a partnership. I just feel that I can do a better job representing people when I can work with them one on one. It's a matter of wanting to know each client directly. You could call me a no frills country lawyer, I suppose. Anyway John, you told me Tom Evans said you needed a lawyer with some farm real estate experience and that he recommended me."

Stroud continued. "After you called me I spoke with Tom. He told me your story, but I'd like to hear it directly from you folks."

It was John who explained. The lawyer gave a half smile and gently shook his head affirmatively. "Could I be forward enough to ask you ladies for another cup of that great coffee?"

"Oh! Where's my manners?" Gertie bounced to her feet, came back with the coffee pot and filled everyone's cup. "Mr. Stroud, you have another Danish."

"They are most delicious." Stroud reached for another of the sweet, buttery, tender and flaky raspberry Danish. "My dad used to call this his boarding house reach." His attempt at a little down home humor drew courtesy smiles. The lawyer straightened up in his chair and tapped a knuckle on the table.

He looked around, making eye contact with each of the four Bergs, and spoke plainly. "I want to tell you that I do believe I can help you.

"After I spoke with Tom I did a little research on Gerald Hicks. I knew I had heard the name before. He's in the real estate business. In fact, he's president and owner of Midwest Properties, a large commercial out-fit in Chicago."

"Real estate!" Mack set his jaw hard as he looked at John. "We knew he didn't know a disc plow from a York rake. But real estate! He's got to be up to no good."

As was his habit while he was thinking John had his chair tipped back on its two back legs, allowing a gentle rocking motion back and forth. "It makes sense, I guess, but the outfit that contacted us was DeVries Real Estate in Milwaukee."

"Sure. A guy like Hicks wants to keep a low profile. He wouldn't want to advertise that he was in real estate. He just wants to be the inno-cent beneficiary of his father-in-law's note. Anyway, I stopped over at your town hall this afternoon and took a look at the plot of the area around you. I see that Midwest Agra Group owns and operates two hundred and forty acres that butts up to the north side of your property. If I'm not mistaken that north side of yours is the acreage that Hicks is after?"

"Yes, that's the acreage, all right. Midwest butts up against us there. They bought the Buhl farm a few years ago. That's it then," said John. "He'll just turn around and sell to Midwest and make a little profit."

Stroud was emphatic. "Maybe make a big profit, if he could get a so called 'fair price' from you folks. Has Midwest Agra talked to you about buying some of your land before?"

"Bout a half dozen times," Mack said with equal emphasis. "And not just some of our land. They offered to buy it all."

"Sure," the lawyer said. "The two hundred and forty acres Midwest has is not near enough for a commercial enterprise like they run. It has just allowed them to get their foot in the door."

Stroud continued. "I talked to a friend of mine in real estate. Residential, actually. I asked him if he knew anything about Gerald Hicks. He knew about him, all right. He said Hicks was very successful and he also said he had a reputation of being ruthless. He was aware of two deals where attempts to sue him had been made. Anyway, that note you signed, Mr. Berg, is, under Wisconsin law, a legal document. It is binding."

There was silence. The lawyer could sense an air of inevitability at the table.

He clasped his hands together and continued. "That is the bad news. However, state law most certainly has some qualifiers that could make Hicks' claim invalid. Those skeletons in the closet that I mentioned to you on the phone, John, could trip up Mr. Hicks."

John righted his chair on all four legs, put his elbow on the table and cupped his chin in his hand. "What kind of skeletons are you talking about and how could that help us anyway?"

"May I see the note?" Stroud grabbed his reading glasses, then carefully handled the twenty-nine year old piece of handwritten paper. He read to himself and then aloud.

If one of our daughters or a member of her immediate family should want to reestablish themselves on the 80 acres of property sold by Oscar Knudson to Mack Berg on December 5, 1936 Mack Berg is obligated sell that property to that person. The price of the sale would be based on market conditions at that time.

Duly signed on this day of December 19, 1936

Oscar Knudson	*December 19, 1936*
Margaret Knudson	Notarized on this day,
	December 19, 1936
Mack Berg	Thomas L. Evans
	Supervisor, Pleasant Springs Town
	County of Dane
	State of Wisconsin
	Thomas L. Evans

The lawyer stated the obvious. "Of course the biggest obstacle in Mr. Hicks' plan has been removed with the death of his wife. It's very likely she objected to buying back the eighty acres or else he would have pulled this stunt years ago."

Stroud moved right along. "Now that phrase, 'reestablish themselves on the Knudson farm.' That, I know will be interpreted as requiring that the purchaser reside on the property."

Mack's eyes darted hopefully from the lawyer to John and back to the lawyer.

"If that's the case we should be able to beat this. I can't picture this guy leaving his business in Chicago to move out here. Believe me, he's no farmer."

Stroud held up his hand to slow Mack down. "Unfortunately state law interprets the concept of residence very liberally. There are some legal alternatives here. Hicks can beat this rather simply by taking up legal residence on the farm. That doesn't mean he has to actually live there. Then again, he may need to live on the property for a certain period of time, or even be required to farm the land for a certain period of time. Any of those alternatives are possible. I can't give you a definite answer on which would apply, the reason being that this is such an unusual situation. I've yet to deal with a note of this type where the seller requests an agreement like this from the purchaser. Whatever the stipulation might be, Hicks would just wait for a prescribed period of time before selling to Midwest."

As Stroud said this it reminded him of another question.

"Oh, yes. Who lives in the Knudsons' old house? Is the house still there?"

Once again Mack stretched his mind back almost thirty years. "Knuddy sold the house with about five acres when they moved south. Been a few folks in there."

As Mack said this he could see a puzzled look on the lawyer's face.

"Knuddy, that's how we all knew Oscar back then. It was the Depression, Mr. Stroud. I wasn't looking to buy any land."

Mack told his story about the purchase.

"Anyway, I never put a plow to it till five years time. Now we've got an operation big enough that without those eighty acres we couldn't support our herd."

Stroud kept the conversation moving right along. "I think I know the answer to this but I'll ask anyway. Is there any chance Mrs. Knudson is still alive?"

Mack was gulping down a mouthful of coffee so he shook his head before speaking.

"Nope. They both passed away down south. Knuddy first, then later Margaret. She had to be well into her seventies somewhere. They brought Oscar back up here. Had a memorial service before they put him in the ground. I remember seeing in our newspaper's obituary about Margaret's passing. I was a little surprised that they didn't bring her back up here for burial. It said she would be buried down there somewhere."

Ann spoke up. "Why did you say you think you know the answer to your question, Mr. Stroud?"

"Because Gerald Hicks is much too knowledgeable to make a move for this land before both his father-in-law and his mother-in-law had passed away. If the Knudsons were to object to him buying the land it would probably not be worth a family battle, or even a court battle, for Hicks to pursue the whole thing. But now, with no one to stand in his way, and Midwest Agra Group an eager buyer, well, he decided to make his move."

One more gulp of coffee and Stroud continued. "Now, this is just an option, and I am sure a weak option, but one possibility for you, Mr. Berg, is to sell the farm to John. New owner, the note becomes worthless."

Mack straightened in his chair as, again, he thought he had just heard the solution to the problem. But before he could say anything Charlie Stroud again held up his hand.

"I said a weak option because there is room for interpretation here. John is your son, not a person outside the immediate family. And, anyway, the court would likely rule this as manipulation because you sold to him after Hicks made the offer."

"Dad and I are partners in the farm. We formed the partnership about twelve years ago." John wondered what effect the partnership might have.

"Does the partnership stipulate you as senior partner? If so, then you may be on solid legal ground." Stroud was quite sure he knew the answer before he continued.

"But, if your dad is senior partner…then nothing changes."

Mack let out a deep breath of frustration. "Yeah, I'm senior partner. But why would it matter who is senior partner and who is junior partner?"

"State won't allow it. Too great an opportunity for people to hide themselves from responsibility. A person takes on a junior partner; maybe just a small percentage partner to deflect all kinds of litigation against himself. The state still considers the senior partner the one subject to all kinds of litigation. In this situation I'm sure, Mr. Berg, that your partnership with your son would not void your written agreement with Knudson." Stroud spread his hands in a gesture of sympathetic frustration.

In her quiet and dignified way, Ann Berg spoke. "It appears that there are some variables here that cannot be answered around this kitchen table." She looked at both her husband and her son. "We are going to need help."

When neither John nor Mack responded the lawyer spoke. "You're correct, Mrs. Berg." He clenched his fist and tapped the table resolutely. "This is an unusual case, but not a complex one. Whether you choose me to represent you or not you are going to need council on this. As I said I am not in a partnership with anyone so I do not have the resources that some firms do. But I do have a small staff that will work hard for you. And I have two private investigators that do work for me."

John was quite sure that Stroud was right, but he wanted his father to say something first. After a few moments Mack questioned the lawyer. "Mr. Stroud, how much would all this cost us?"

"It works like this. I have a retainer fee of three hundred dollars. Beyond that you pay me by the hour. My fee is twenty five dollars per hour. This can add up to a lot of money, I know. But I don't foresee a lot of hours in a case like this. And you should know that a larger firm would charge as much as forty dollars per hour."

Stroud knew well enough to let the Bergs digest this news before continuing, even if it meant getting no answer until later.

John questioned. "By the hour? How does that work?"

"If this were a situation where you were seeking punitive damages, I would be paid by receiving a percentage of your award, if you won. In this situation, the time spent by myself and my staff is compiled."

Silence.

Finally Mack spoke. "I want to wring his neck. I just want to wring his neck!"

Stroud looked a little startled. "Not me, I hope?"

"Uh? Oh, no. Hicks." Mack cracked a smile. "Hicks, not you."

The lawyer offered a ray of sunshine. "That was the bad news, but here's the good news. If Hicks brings this to court, and is deemed to have brought you into court under a fraudulent claim, he can be held liable for your legal expenses. For example, let's say I were to find that Greta and he had divorced before her death. The judge could determine that Hicks is responsible for dragging you into court fraudulently, since he no longer is a family member. Now, Hicks and his lawyers know this and if they know you can, in some way, present him as making a fraudulent claim, they most certainly will back down."

Gertie shook her head. "He would have some nerve trying to pass himself off as a rightful family member if he and Greta had divorced."

"Yes," said Stroud. "I'm sure he's much too smart to try something like that, but you would be amazed at what some people will try and do. His deviousness is probably of a much more subtle nature. The one thing we do know for sure is that you can expect that offer from DeVries Real Estate sometime soon."

Mack quickly brought the discussion to a head, for in Charlie Stroud he believed he saw an honest man.

"I've known and trusted Tom Evans for almost forty years. There's no one finer. He recommended you. You seem like the kind of man who will help us out here. And I want to tell you this. We try to be a God fearing bunch here. It's my feeling that the Lord's sent you to us."

Mack looked over to his son. "I think we should have Mr. Stroud help us."

John nodded at Stroud. "Your integrity and your honesty with us is what matters more than anything. We'd like to pay you that retainer, Mr. Stroud, and you can get started."

Stroud gave a gentle smile. Not a smile like a man who had just closed the deal on selling a commodity to a buyer, but a smile that said, "I'm glad you are putting your trust in me."

As they all stood the lawyer put his hands to his stomach. "In closing I have but two things to say. If a man is going to go off his diet he might as well do it in style. Ladies, those Danish of yours were just wonderful. And, secondly, I hope you'll all call me Charlie from here on."

Mack reached out to shake Stroud's hand. "Only if you call me Mack. I'm getting old enough without this Mr. Berg stuff!"

NINE

Over and over again, in his mind, it kept repeating to Clark Berg. Frank Smith's words. "What I see in you is some raw talent that could, over time, with some long-range planning and commitment on your part, make available the opportunity for a lucrative career in radio ad sales."

What I see in you is some raw talent? What raw talent?

Wasn't he the one that no one could really count on? The one shirking responsibility in a family of responsible people? He thought back to the first job his father had assigned him and Johnny as youngsters: keeping the repair barn squared away. Keeping the tools clean and organized. Twice a year scrubbing down the cement pad. Johnny took the work as an acceptable prelude to field work. But Clark? If he could only be out in the fields with his father and grandfather. Yes, then he could take some pride in the farm. But then, of course, as the years passed the field work became as unsatisfying to him as anything else.

He not only did not like the farm, but even showed disdain for it. Wasn't he the jerk that just a few months ago, when confronted by his mother for letting his father down on some work, blurted out "Dairy farming! Milk! Who needs milk when there's beer to drink!"

He apologized to her later, but it was probably because he wanted something. That is how he had always been. Manipulative. That's the word that one of the girls at school used. She said he was a manipulative person. He shrugged off the comment, just as he always shrugged off the comments of anyone he let down. After all, he was the Berg who didn't have his head buried in the manure pile. He was the one who could deal with more sophisticated people. He was the good looking one. He was the one that always had two or three girls interested in him at the same time. Not like Johnny; quiet and shy. Sure, he was going to marry Jenny Watson, but that's the point. He'd been so slow socially, such a hayseed, that Jenny was the only girl he ever dated. Not him. He'd had experience that his brother did not have. A couple of sexual experiences; two different girls, during his senior year. This despite all of the solid background he had received. This despite all he had been taught and all he had seen in his own family.

Now his uncle was saying that he had some raw talent. Clark didn't even know what that meant. He was going to start work at the most conservative, most profitable radio station in Milwaukee. He didn't know a thing about the radio business, but even that wasn't the point. He was beginning to realize that he really didn't know anything about anything. Not just about radio advertising, but about how to really treat people. How to be, as he had heard it said, a genuine person.

Now, all at once, he realized he needed to grow up. His brother might be quiet and unassertive but he was fair, sincere, honest, reliable. These were the qualities that mattered to people. So it took a job offer from his uncle for him to realize these things?

On the Friday of his first week of work, Clark went out on his first sales presentation with one of the execs, Andy Quince. The potential client was available late in the day so it was six o'clock that evening before a very successful meeting ended.

"Clark, I'm in a bit of a jam. My wife and I have to be somewhere tonight. Could you get this paperwork filed back at the office?"

"Sure," said Clark, though to himself he instinctively reacted, "What about me? I've got places to go, too."

After they parted company Clark decided he would arrive early Monday morning to file the papers.

Monday morning Andy Quince asked Clark to stop by his desk. He spoke in subdued tones.

"What gives, my friend. I came in on Saturday to, among other things, get a head start on this new account. I find no papers, yet this morning I get here and wa-la, here it all is. What in the hell is going on? If you say your going to do something, my man, then do it."

"Andy, I'm sorry. I…" Quince held up his hand, indicating that he had said his piece and wasn't really interested in Clark's response. His face red with embarrassment, Clark realized he had slipped into some old "me first" behavior.

The rest of the day he told himself, "You've got to be a whole new person or you're not going to make it. I don't know if I can do it."

He thought of how this job offer had jolted him to the realization that he had been living in this shallow, selfish way, since when? Maybe age ten. At least. Maybe longer, if he could really see himself as his family had since he was young. He thought how, year after year, the example of those who loved him had been so completely and flippantly ignored. It made him feel weak in the stomach. Now, how was he going to change completely, like a car going from high gear to reverse without first coming to a stop?

"One day at a time," he told himself. "One day at a time." He felt like the lumberjack balancing on the floating log during Stoughton's Syttende Mai Festival. One slip and the real Clark Berg would come crashing down.

TEN

"Put on the whole armour of God, that ye may
be able to stand against the wiles of the devil."

EPHESIANS 6:11, KJV

Though the course of the nation's events had taken young Johnny
Berg away from his home and had potentially placed him in harm's
way, he held none of his brother's apprehensions. He was a soldier
now. That is, he was being made into a soldier.

Fort Knox, Kentucky. A world, and a way of life, quite different than
any other he had known. He boarded the Greyhound bus, a military
charter full of recruits that had all been given a physical and been sworn
in at Camp McCoy. It dawned on him as they crossed the state line into
Illinois that he had only been in one other state besides his own Wisconsin. That state being Illinois; twice to see Chicago with his family.
Indeed, those two trips had been in winter; the Christmas to New Year's
school break. Harold Johnson had done the milking for them. To leave
Berg Farm in the spring, summer or fall was not even a consideration.
Too much work to be done. Nature's time clock demanding that it be
done on schedule. The influence of the sun on the ever rotating earth was
the clock by which the Bergs lived.

Now he would be living by another clock, one set by the military
machine known as the American Army. Generations of young men before
him had done the same, and now it was his turn.

It all seemed so strange, so completely different than the life he knew.
Basic training. Every minute accounted for. Everything being done by
the numbers. Strict adherence to military rules and regulations. Com-
mands to be followed, one's own opinion meaningless. Don't think; react.

The objective of basic training as old as the military itself: Break the individual down and make him responsive to a higher authority. None of it made any sense to him at first, until he realized that they were not all like him. Whether it was his lack of self-confidence or just his easy going nature, he found it not difficult to fall in line with the seemingly pointless details and intimidating harassment. Soon, when he saw the defiant spirits and surly, independent attitudes of some of his fellow trainees, he understood. The exaggerated discipline was the only way to take a mass of individuals from different backgrounds, most whom did not want to be there, and turn them into an effective unit. The alternative would be chaos and disaster. His father's words when he left home were ringing true. John Sr. had told his son, "You'll be giving up your own freedom to help secure the freedom of our country."

Johnny was never one to try and be anyone but himself. This unassuming quality brought him a challenge early in the first week of training. It was just before lights out when one surly young man, a six-foot-three-inch Philadelphian named Cassel, who seemed to be establishing himself as an intimidating leader in the barracks, saw Johnny as an easy mark.

"Hey, you, Berg. Big mouth."

Some of the others stiffened as they could see a confrontation coming with the likeable Berg.

"What the hell is with you, my man. Don't they teach you people out in farm country how to talk?" By this time Cassel had approached Berg, thoroughly expecting to intimidate Johnny and add to his own reputation.

Johnny, dressed only in his underwear, came to his feet.

"Come on man," said Cassel in a mocking voice. "Time might come when you have to be a leader over there in Vietnam. What kind of leader are you going to be if you can't even talk?"

With that Cassel gave a toothy, mock grin and tapped Johnny on the chest with the back of his hand. Johnny grabbed his hand and squeezed. Cassel felt the strength of the strong right hand of a dairy farmer who had done his share of manual milking. For fifteen seconds Johnny squeezed.

"Hey man, that's cool. That's cool man." Cassel's words were desperate.

When Johnny let go Cassel tried to control his breathing but they all heard an exhale of a man totally surprised and relieved. As Cassel returned to his bunk he tried to regain his swagger with a face saving comment.

"Strong, silent type. That's cool. That's cool my man."

Berg thought it strange, but his immediate thought was of the man named Gerald Hicks, the man who was invading the peaceful lives of his family back home. Each in his own way, Gerald Hicks and Cassel were bullies.

Many a young man of Johnny Berg's character had entered the military service, only to be swept up in the cynicism, bravado and worldliness of the barracks atmosphere. It was an atmosphere where young men bragged about their sexual conquests, even if the stories were only half true. Where they told of their beer drinking prowess—failing to mention about the throwing up afterwards. The cussing. The oaths. Taking the Father's or the Son's name in vain. Sometimes just a fountain of four letter profanities. That transformation of the human psyche was as old as any army. All an attempt to hold one's ground in the masculine environment these young men now found themselves in.

But Johnny Berg would stay the soft spoken person he had always been. When he said something it was said without embellishment. He never tried to build himself up at someone else's expense. When others talked amongst themselves and belittled the platoon's drill instructor, Staff Sgt. Hence, as a loser, a guy who had flunked out at life and was reduced to barking at forty army recruits, the forty-some year old who was rubbing their faces in the dirt for eight weeks, the loser who was living in a room at one end of their barracks on the second floor, Berg would never join in. He would continue to be the decent person he had always been. Did his lack of self-confidence indicate a certain vulnerability? Yes. But a superficial vulnerability only. Beneath what appeared to be a worldly innocence John Berg Jr. was rock solid, dependable, loyal and true to his word. He possessed a quality that left him unshaken and unchanged by circumstances beyond his control. Though he was not one to express his faith to others, his Christian upbringing had influenced him with a spirit of peace that allowed him to face uncertainties with a calm nature.

His physical strength was deceptive. His six-foot-two-inch frame was what some might call thin, but a better description would be rangy. He didn't possess a showy muscularity, but rather the deceptive physique of long muscles with great elasticity. It was muscle that had spent its young life working the rigors of a Wisconsin dairy farm. Tossing hay bales, shoveling manure, cutting and clearing land with a chain saw and even a manual crosscut saw. Countless different chores from the time he was first able to help his father and grandfather.

The first morning they marched, drill instructor Hence screamed at their sloppy incompetence. They joined the rest of the training company in the esplanade under a barrage of insults.

Physical training. P.T. The daily dozen. The time tested twelve exercises designed to begin toughening these young men from all walks of life. The strong, the weak, the athletic, the softies, the lean, the fat. The brash who needed to be cut down, the timid who needed their confidence built up. The four count pushup. The eight count pushup. The turn and bounce. The airborne squat. All twelve exercises. Every day.

It was here that Berg first felt a confidence that he was as capable as the next man to survive, even excel, in his Army experience.

Sgt. Christian was the fittest of the company's drill instructors. Five-feet-eight-inches tall, one hundred and sixty pounds of rock solid muscle. He stood on the wooden platform demonstrating each exercise to the new recruits—teaching them to perform each movement to his cadence count. After each exercise, when he began to demonstrate the next one, he kept them at attention. Arms to their sides, fists closed with the thumb over the top of the index finger, knees locked, chin up, eyes straight ahead. Later, in coming days, he would say, "At ease, shake it out," and they were given a few seconds to relax between exercises. But not in these first few days. They were going to be taught who was boss. They were going to have to earn those few moments when they could "shake it out."

Berg survived the first day of P.T. quite well. Oh, he was sore the next morning, but not like some of them. Hardly able to get out of their bunks. Some of them had been unable to complete even a third of the repetitions demanded by Sgt. Christian. Some recruits "fell out" after four, three or even two repetitions. The other drill instructors patrolled the rows of groaning bodies. They screamed in the faces of those who "fell out" early. They belittled, humiliated and threatened them. John made it as far into the counts as anyone. He completed at least nine repetitions of all twelve exercises, ten or eleven of some and he was one of only six recruits to complete all twelve repetitions of the eight count pushup. The quiet one who didn't have any exploits to brag about. The one who didn't pepper every sentence with a barrage of four-letter expletives. Yes, they came to call him hayseed or pork belly or John Deere, but they did it with respect.

Basic training was just the beginning. Eight weeks of learning how to think like and perform like a soldier. Then it would be AIT; advanced individual training. The word individual was a misnomer. Nothing in this man's army was tailored for the individual. But it was training in one of a number of specific areas. There were areas like communications, radar specialists, hospital technicians of one sort or another. These were the types of career opportunities that the Army publicized. But it was infantry, armor or artillery that most of them would train in. And maybe then to a combat unit. Who knew. None of them did. When the training was done, then they would each receive orders telling them where they would go. Career officers in the Pentagon, officers who had the grand scheme of personnel movement in front of them, would make that decision. And wherever any of them should be sent they should all be so fortunate to have a young man like Johnny Berg at their side.

ELEVEN

"Casting all your cares upon him; for he careth for you."

I PETER 5:7 KJV

The raspy irritation in her throat began to bother her part way through that August, but Ann Berg refused to allow herself to think anything was wrong. This life she loved was too full for her to be slowed down.

She was 67 years old when her two grandsons went out on their own. One in the Army and one now working in Milwaukee. She was proud of them both. Sure, Clark was a handful, but it was her job, her privilege, to love them both, unconditionally, just as she loved Elsie and her other grandchildren. It had been a long and bumpy road for Ann to become the person she was. She knew more than any of them about the value of a strong family. She was the product of a broken home.

Her father had been a professor at the University of Illinois. George Hopkins also was a closet alcoholic; carrying himself well enough in academia, but hurting the ones closest to him increasingly as the years went along.

As a very young girl Ann Hopkins had a sweet nature. However, by the time she was ten years old, when her father's vice began to manifest itself in his relationship with his wife and two children, Ann began the long slide to insecurity, self doubt, cynicism and bitterness. She finished high school with only an arm's length friendship with a couple of girls and a total rejection of boys. How could she trust any boy when her own father had let them down so wretchedly? The stream of broken promises made to her and her younger brother Cal. The evening meals when Ruth Hopkins would try to explain her husband's absence to the children with pathetically weak excuses about where he was; after school faculty meetings, helping his mother out, doing after school research for his chosen field of political science. And worst of all for Ann, the fights. Her mother and father yelling at each other as once again he failed to admit his shortcomings, instead accusing his wife of being the source of their problems. Why could he not see what he was doing to them? How could someone so smart, a PhD, a professor of political science at one of the best university's in the country, not realize how selfish his behavior was? How could all he care about be in a bottle of crystal clear liquid? Gin. Distilled grain spirits flavored with juniper berries. Nothing else seemed as important as his gin.

At times he could be contrite with his children. He would sit on the edge of one of their beds, bring them to his sides, put his arms around them and come to tears asking for their forgiveness. But Ann knew that he never asked Mother for her forgiveness. And what did it matter anyway? He would come home, sometimes as soon as the next day, and be in a gin foul mood. His act of asking for forgiveness making the hurt of disappointment even worse.

When Ann was a senior in high school her mother and father separated. George Hopkins took accommodation in faculty housing at the university. Ruth and her two children stayed at the modest house in Champaign. She had seen the inevitable handwriting on the wall. Although it was a time when women rarely strayed from the job of homemaker, she had gotten a decent job two years previous as a receptionist in the City of Champaign offices. The couple never divorced. This was 1918. The stigma of divorce was unacceptable. They never reunited. To his credit, George, in those years, sent money every month to help support his family; no doubt an act to sooth his guilt as much as anything else.

Ann was an intelligent girl, but she graduated from high school confused and drained of the energy she would have needed to continue her education. Besides, in those years, going on to college was a rare step for any woman. Most often the mindset for young women graduating from high school was to find a husband and start a family.

She took work with the Stratton Leather Works Co. This was a small organization that bought cured cowhide from two different tanneries in Chicago. Stratton's dyed the material and fashioned a number of small leather goods. They sold wholesale, mostly to the two mail order giants, Sears-Roebuck and Montgomery Ward. Ann would come home, hands swollen and sore from hours of cutting and stitching leather for gloves, belts, men's wallets and women's purses. But it was her spirit that was beaten more than her hands. She continued to be timid in her relationships, rarely venturing beyond the certainty of home with Mother and Cal.

In that summer of 1918 Ruth Hopkins managed to secure two weeks off. This was not a paid vacation; such was almost unheard of. But the City of Champaign was a progressive bureaucracy and granted her the time off. A drop in orders for leather goods made it convenient for Stratton's to grant Ann the time off. So Ruth took Ann and Cal, now finished with his junior year of high school, to the village of Stoughton, Wisconsin; her hometown.

It turned out to be wonderful medicine for all three of them. It had been six years since they had been to Stoughton. On that trip, with her husband with them, it had been a trip with its share of anxiety for Ruth. And for Ann and Cal, insecure and confused by their parents crumbling marriage, it was a guarded time with their grandparents, aunts, uncles and cousins. But now, for all three of them, Stoughton was a revelation of family ties. A confirmation that family laughter and support were still tangible things.

Ruth Hopkins was a Steingird. Her father, Hans, owned the feed store down near the railroad tracks on the east end of Main Street, Steingird Feed and Supply.

There wasn't a farmer within a radius of twenty miles that Hans Steingird did not know. Some of the time the talk between farmer and store owner was in Norwegian, or a more than adequate combination of

Norwegian and Swedish. And he wasn't bad at getting along with the Germans and the Danes, although he diplomatically made the effort to get those that wanted to speak in their native tongue to speak English. Hans was an anomaly for a Norseman. He was talkative and outgoing with his customers. He was, however, very aware of the limits of the Scandinavian or German farmer's psyche toward backslapping. He never allowed himself to be anything but sincere with customers and friends that walked in.

Hans and Margaret welcomed Ruth, Ann and Cal with open arms. Three of Ruth's four siblings lived in Stoughton or surroundings so the Steingird home buzzed with family laughter. Even at age twenty, Ann, and certainly Cal, reveled in the companionship of their cousins.

On Sunday the family was off to church — First Lutheran.

Ann remembered when they were a church going family; before dad began drinking. At least before the drinking became apparent. And then, gradually, the strain of it all. Dad showing up home so late from a Saturday night drunk that he couldn't get out of bed in time to hitch up the buggy for the trip to church. Missing sporadically at first, then never to Sunday School and finally, they just stopped going totally. It became easier, less painful, for Ruth Hopkins to just avoid the strain she felt when she was there at church. She just didn't have the emotional energy to praise the Lord one moment and deal with her husband the next. Although the problems were rooted in his drinking she began to feel too inadequate to be in church.

Somehow that service with her grandparents, the first time Ann had been in church in such a long time, was an experience she would not forget for the rest of her life. The hymns, the fellowship, the wonderful feel of it all. Even though she would soon forget the pastor's message, the joy and overwhelming peace that she felt kept her fighting tears throughout the service.

She was reminded of what she knew as a young girl, that God loved her enough to sacrifice His Son to wipe away her sin and that, as a believer, she would know eternity in heaven.

In the same service that morning was Mack Berg. He was only

twenty-one years old but owner of a then 200-acre dairy farm six miles north of the village. When his father died from the flu strain the previous year, Mack was yoked with a great deal of responsibility. But he was up to the challenge. He always knew it would be his duty, his desire, to carry on Berg Farm. He had learned everything he could since, at age seven, he first tried squeezing milk from a cow's teats. He never expected that time to come so soon.

From the benediction Mack, Inga, Steven and their mother exited church where they were greeted by the Steingirds. Mack's mother needed no introduction to Ruth Hopkins for the two had been only one year apart at Stoughton High School.

Mack and Ann had, no doubt, been aware of each other when the Hopkinses last visited, but they were much younger then. Now, as the families paused outside church, they each felt an attraction toward the other. This was a feeling new not only to Ann, but to Mack also. He, so dedicated to carrying on the farm that he never took pause to consider women. So concerned for his mother's, sister's and brother's welfare that he hadn't thought about the need to share his life with someone. Inga had taken to calling her brother the "bachelor farmer." It wasn't that he was not yet married. It was just that he was so focused on the farm that he never gave himself a chance with any of the girls around Stoughton.

He was rather handsome, in a rugged sort of way. His unruly curly hair, pure blond as a youngster, was only a shade or two darkened now. He was powerfully built on a six-foot frame. He did not possess the classic facial features some would consider necessary to be called handsome, but his rugged masculinity more than compensated.

Ann, if she could only learn to smile again, was an attractive young woman. Her English rose complexion, inherited from her father's family, was a joy to behold when she did smile. She stood there on the church steps, one moment feeling so good about what she felt from the service and the next realizing that she felt an attraction to this young farmer. It was a new feeling for her not to instinctively put up her defenses. Somehow she felt that this young man was not in any way like her father.

≠ ≠ ≠

All through the first part of the next week Mack could not get his mind off the Hopkins girl. His concentration on his work was nothing less than a shambles. It was a good thing that it was the end of July, not the end of May. It was still ten to twelve hours a day of work but late spring, the most critical time of year, was past.

He experienced something new; a queasiness in the pit of his stomach. His hardy appetite took a turn downward. He always devoured everything his mother put in front of him. His normal breakfast of three eggs, four sausage links, four pieces of toast and two cups of coffee was cut in half. Ruth Berg was puzzled by her son's diminished appetite.

By Wednesday morning Mack made up his mind that if he were any kind of a man he would call on Ann Hopkins. He felt the need to speak to Ann's grandfather, face to face, about such a visit. He made the trip into Steingirds Feed and Supply. He bought something he didn't really need and asked Hans for a moment of his time.

He gathered his nerve and spoke.

"I'd like to see your granddaughter, Hans. I'd like to see Ann. I guess I'm asking your permission. I'd like to pay her a visit, Friday evening, if that's possible?"

Hans Steingird handled young Mack's request with the same ease he dealt with his customers. "You'll not come over Friday unless you come over for supper. Do you think you can pull yourself off of that farm of yours early enough to get over to our place at 6:30?"

"Sure Hans. Thanks. I'll be there. Thank you."

Mack exited the store quickly. He climbed back on his wagon, flicked the reins on his two horses, and sped away. As soon as he made the turn to go north on county road N he stopped. He took a couple of deep breaths to settle himself down. All of a sudden he felt like a new man. It was as though a twenty-pound weight had been lifted from around his neck. He had summoned the nerve to do what his heart was telling him to do. Ann Hopkins may reject him, but Mack knew that he could deal with that easier than if he made no overture at all to get to know her. All of a sudden he felt powerfully hungry.

When Mack had pulled away from the store, Hans, who had made his invitation to Mack in matter of fact fashion, gave himself a little smile, knowing he may have helped get something good started.

Friday evening Margaret Steingird served a wonderful chicken pie dinner and a fine pie from their own black raspberry patch for dessert. She took the awkwardness out of the after dinner proceedings when she ordered Mack and Ann to visit alone. "We'll clean up the kitchen, you two young ones go get acquainted out on the porch."

Mack and Ann did just that. They sat and talked for some time before Mack invited her to walk with him in the remaining minutes of the setting July sun.

The Steingird house was just off Stoughton's unpaved Main Street. They walked on the narrow concrete sidewalk that fronted the businesses along the street before returning to the house. Their conversation was quite guarded, as one might expect. She, with her uncertainty about men; he, with his awkward inexperience with girls. But it was the beginning of a familiarity that would grow in the next few days.

Mack joined the Steingirds and the Hopkinses every evening except one for the remaining days of the Hopkinses' visit. Sometimes it would be for dinner, other times later in the evening. On the coming Sunday afternoon Mack took Ann on a picnic. Just the two of them. By this time they were talking much more openly. Mack and his dreams for the farm. His need to gather the confidence to carry on his father's and his grandfather's work. Even stating his desire to share those dreams with someone. Ann, for the first time having a feeling of security about talking to a man. She spoke of her family's difficulties. She told Mack how difficult she thought it would be to ever go out on her own. How she thought there might never be a man she could trust. How all three of them were so enjoying this time in Stoughton.

"I know I should not think this way, but I just can't tolerate the thought of how my mother agonized so with my father's drinking. She kept it so much to herself, but I know she suffered dearly—for years."

Mack allowed his sense of humor to do the responding.

"All those Germans making all that beer over there in Milwaukee; and I don't even like the stuff!"

As the time drew close for the Hopkinses to return to Champaign, Mack knew he must ask Ann to marry him. They had known each other only nine days. Such a short time. A nine-day courtship, if you could call it that. But they would soon be separated by 240 miles. Mack knew he would never be the kind of man to court a number of women and choose among them to marry. Besides, it wasn't as though there were girls lining up all over Dane County just to know Mack Berg. And above and beyond it all Mack had been raised to be a sincere person, limited in his number of relationships with people, but always committed to honesty and forthrightness in those relationships. He knew what he felt and he had to know if Ann felt the same. Could she commit to a Wisconsin dairy farmer after less than a two week acquaintance? It had been a wonderful time for Mack and he told her so. She had said the same. Now he was going to ask her to marry him.

He did that very thing just the day before the Hopkinses left for Champaign. They walked that evening and Ann remarked with a puzzled look that something seemed wrong with him. Mack had them sit down on a bench along Main Street, close by the bridge that allowed the Catfish River to cross under the road. It was almost ten o'clock. The street was almost deserted and the sun was gone, leaving only an orange glow on the western horizon. Mack spoke slowly and earnestly, as was his nature.

"Ann, I don't know how to say this except to come right out and say it." He looked down, inhaled deeply, then looked up to her. It was difficult for him to continue, not because he was unsure of what he wanted to say, but because he was afraid her answer would be no.

"I want to marry you." He now increased the cadence of his speech, concerned that any hesitation on his part would allow her time to decline before he said his piece.

"I know I'm asking you this and we've only known each other for a few days, but I know this; that we were all made to share our lives with someone. It's in our nature. It's in my nature. I know that I love you and I want to marry you. I know it's asking a lot to expect you to come up here and be part of this life with me. But I'm asking. Will you marry me?"

She stared at him, motionless for a good ten seconds. She then shut her eyes as tears ran down her cheeks. "Yes Mack Berg. I will marry you. I will marry you and come to Stoughton and help you with your farm."

Twelve weeks later Mack Berg and Ann Hopkins were married in Stoughton at First Lutheran Church.

And now it was forty-seven years later. She was wife, mother, grandmother. None who did not know could suspect the heartache of her childhood. She was beloved by all that knew her.

The raspy sensation in her throat carried no pain with it—initially. Gertie was the first to notice the raspy sound to her words and say something about it. It was in the morning when the two of them were making sandwiches for the men's dinner in the field.

"Ann, you're starting to sound like one of those Hollywood bombshells. You know, with the deep, affected voice that gets the men all tingly."

Ann told her it had started off and on about three days earlier. "I don't know what could be causing it. Here it is summer and I have acquired some kind of cold."

They had arranged for one of the men to come in from the fields to pick up their dinners at eleven o'clock. It was Rollie who showed up. He bounded up the steps of the back porch and spoke through the screen door.

"We've got some hungry farm boys out there, eh. Some of that good Berg chow should set us straight. Old Thor himself says he could stand a gallon of whatever we're drinking today."

Gertie had gone upstairs. Ann had just finished putting all the items in two boxes. "Come in Rollie, come in. How is my favorite hockey player this morning?"

Rollie walked in, the gentle clank of the wooden screen door closing behind him. His face was covered with a combination of sweat and the dust of the fields. His red Badger cap was heavily sweat stained.

"Ex-hockey player, Mrs. B, and I couldn't be finer. But you said morning? You know how to deflate a chap. We've been going at it for seven hours and it's still morning?"

Ann gave her gentle laugh. "Well, it is only eleven fifteen, but I do suppose it seems later to all of you. There is plenty of ice tea in there to keep my husband and the rest of you happy."

Rollie grabbed the first box, took it out to the tractor and was back for the second box.

"I'm hearing a little burr in your voice, Mrs. B. Had a hockey coach in bantams with a rough sounding voice. Could hear him all over the rink. I think it was all of the cigars. He used to smoke 'em right down to the end. Burned his nose a few times. A hell of a, excuse me, a heck of a coach."

Ann stood listening to Rollie with her hands clasped gently together. She looked in his eyes with a smile, as though she were delighted at every word he spoke. Rollie quickly realized he had started carrying on about his life in Hespeler. He was happy to burden the men about such things but he became faintly apologetic to Ann.

"Enough of my talk, Mrs. B. We'll enjoy all this food, for sure. Hotter than a pistol out there, otherwise it's a lovely day."

Ann laughed gently and shook her head.

Rollie was puzzled. "What is it, Mrs. B?"

"Oh, it's the way you use the word lovely so often. We say things like wonderful, great or outstanding. But you say lovely. I think it's very nice."

"I'm glad you like it. Your husband and your son and your grandsons too, if they were here, give me a rough time about it. They say, 'I thought you were a rough and tumble hockey player. How come you say everything is lovely?' Your husband is the worst. Says it sounds girly.

It's just the way we say things in Canada. At least my part of Canada—Ontario."

"Yes, of course," smiled Ann. "Hespeler."

The raspy irritation in her throat persisted. By Labor Day weekend it had become painful.

One afternoon in the kitchen Mack continued to press her about it.

"I'm sure it is nothing," she replied. "I can't be running to the doctor over a sore throat."

In his own light hearted way Mack put his foot down. "You haven't been to the doctor since you gave birth to Catherine; and that was more than thirty-four years ago. You can betcha that the world will not stop spinning cause Ann Berg makes an appearance at the doctor's office."

He kidded with her. "Got a young, good looking doc in there now. I'm sure you'll enjoy the visit!"

Ann responded with thanksgiving. "I've been a blest woman beyond all that's owed to me, and that's surely the truth. One case of the flu in all our years. I'll give the Lord credit for it all."

Deep down she did feel that something could be wrong, but she humored her husband.

"I worked in those fields with you for our first twenty-five years, Mack Berg. I cooked and cleaned and raised three children. I don't recall you giving me up to the doctor in all those years. Now that you think you can spare me for a few hours, you just want to see if I'm ready to be put out to pasture."

He patted her on the butt on his way out the kitchen door.

"That's right deary. I might be need'en to trade you in for a newer model!"

Ann eventually relented and agreed to be looked at. The doctor in Stoughton ordered tests for her at the hospital in Madison. This included a throat biopsy. When the results were in Mack and Ann went together and received the bad news. A malignant tumor had been found in the larynx.

They arrived home from Madison around dinner time. John, Gertie and Elsie anxiously met them out at the car.

"Well?" was John's one word question.

"We've hit a bump in the road," responded Mack. He rarely displayed affection toward Ann in the presence of other people, but with his arm around his wife he briefly explained the doctor's report.

Elsie instinctively hugged her grandmother.

On the drive back home Ann had tried to put this development in the context of her faith.

As she continued to share her granddaughter's embrace, she gave her thoughts.

"We all need to know that this is not something we are going to get all flustered about. I want all of us to remember our future is in the Lord's hands. It is my responsibility to do my best to fight this illness, and with all your help I am going to do just that. But let's remember the old saying, 'We don't know what the future holds, but we know who holds the future.' None of us know from day to day what could happen next in what I believe to be this wonderful life that we share, but every Christian knows what a glorious future He has for us when our time does come.

"I know that I am grateful for the prayers you will make on my behalf, just as I know Johnny can be grateful for the prayers we offer for his safe return from the Army. I know that we can place these things in God's hands. The Bible tells us that because right there in the book of Peter it says, 'Cast all your cares upon him; for he careth for you.'"

Ann shared these thoughts with an amazingly positive and glowing authority.

Though it was not the Berg way to display any sort of dramatic emotion, they all trembled inside at both the news of this cancer and the Christian strength of this woman they loved.

TWELVE

"Take my yoke upon you, and learn of me; for
I am meek and lowly in heart: and ye shall find rest unto your souls.
For my yoke is easy, and my burden is light."

MATTHEW 11:29, 30 KJV.

By the last week of September the sights and smells and feel of autumn were beginning to show themselves everywhere. The first frost was still a few days away, but the cool night air hung persistently through the morning hours.

"Dad, I think Johnny might be right. He's always said that autumn is the best time of year. The trees are starting to turn now. Won't be long and we'll be surrounded by all kinds of color. Even the smell this time of year. Things starting to die off. It has that mellow smell to it."

John and Mack had walked over to one of the two sections they had planted in corn to see how dry the product was. Harvest time was fast approaching.

Mack rarely expressed sentiment with his son, but his concern over Ann's illness and the realization that the years were moving along may have prompted his comment.

"When you were born and when you were a little kid, it was always my concern whether you were going become a man that could love this land, this farm. It was always my greatest hope that you would have a passion for this place. Ha! It's been a prideful thing for me to know that you, and Johnny too, love this land."

Mack paused. "Funny how it goes. One day I'm ready to drag this son of a…this snake Hicks across a barbed wire fence. Next thing you know your mother is sick and, well, the land thing just doesn't seem so important anymore.

Ann began a series of chemotherapy treatments that did little to slow down the rapid progression of cancer in her voice box. The growth soon invaded her esophagus. It became even more difficult for her to swallow.

For Mack, John and Gertie taking care of Ann at home became increasingly difficult. To keep her suffering to a minimum she needed full time nursing care. But such a move, taking her from her home, to have her be cared for by strangers, no matter how qualified and compassionate they might be, was a heartbreaking decision for Ann's loved ones. The Bergs had never given up one of their own to be cared for full time. Some had died during hospital care, but never before had any family member been taken to a care facility to live out their last days. If such a decision was to be made by the Bergs it might be accompanied by the unwarranted feelings of guilt and failure.

It was, of course, toughest on Mack. One afternoon, after coming in from the fields to check on Ann he found the opportunity to be alone with Gertie.

"Is it me, or is it this way for everyone?"

Gertie did not attempt to ask for an explanation for she knew Mack was about to say more.

"I mean, I've always been able to accept when loved ones get sick and their time has come. But now, I just can't see the timing of it. I just can't get over that it seems like we just got started and now… and now it might come to an end. I mean, my folks, and all the others. Sure it was tough to lose them, but I could accept the order of it. They were supposed to go ahead of us. But Ann? No. It seems as though we have just gotten started. Why, Gertie? Why does it seem to me that it was just yesterday that Ann and I had just gotten started?"

Gertie stared directly into Mack's eyes while he spoke. She could think of but one answer for him.

"It's because of love, Mack. It's because of a certain kind of love between a husband a wife. Ann will always be young to you."

She crossed her arms and felt that now was as good a time as any to say something that was on her mind.

"I'm praying every day that the Lord will restore her to good health, but I'm also thinking of what it would be like if I were to lose John someday. And I'm aware that there's many a person out there who has never had a husband and a family the way I have. We've got a lot more to lose than a lot of people, Mack. We've got a lot farther to fall. But I say praise God for it. I'd rather have the heartache of loss than have nothing to lose."

Ann's cancer rapidly took hold. Difficult though it was Gertie was the first to be pragmatic about it. She gently but firmly confronted her husband. When Ann's condition put her in a state of not being able to feed herself and she became incontinent, Gertie told John he must speak to Mack. He must be made to see that keeping Ann at home had become more of a consoling thing for him than it was a comfort for her.

But Mack resisted. The three of them talked but Mack would not consent to such a move. He took alliance with Elsie, whose tender young emotions resisted any thought of her grandma being cared for somewhere other than at home. And so the days moved along. The strain began to show on Mack. His hearty appetite waned, as it had when he first knew his Ann; when he first knew he had love for this woman.

At John and Gertie's insistence Mack agreed to a home visit by their pastor. In all their years as members of First Lutheran, stretching back to Elmer and Muriel, the family had never requested pastoral counseling. They were indeed a low maintenance family. But now, as he thought about it, even Mack agreed for the need to speak to someone outside the family.

Pastor Fred Mantlund was fifty-four years old; a tall, rangy figure with earnest looking eyes and a personality to match. He had been First

Lutheran's pastor for six years, succeeding Edwin Kiel. Kiel had been much loved by the congregation when he retired in 1959 after thirty years at the church. It was no easy task to follow a man of such revered stature, but Mantlund had been well received.

He was born and raised in Minneapolis, the third child of Swedish immigrants. Though the heavily Norwegian congregation had great affection for their new pastor he was made to suffer the good natured Norse superiority. Mack would often chide him for not being fortunate enough to be Norwegian. "A thousand Swedes ran through the weeds, chased by one Norwegian." Mack had repeated the old Norwegian folk rhyme a number of times when Mantlund first came. He now saved the verse for once a year, having realized that too much of a good thing does lose its punch. He delighted in hitting Pastor with one of his Swedish jokes from time to time. But this meeting with Pastor at the Berg kitchen table was one without levity.

One of the things that the Bergs liked about Fred Mantlund was that he was to the point. Whether it was from the pulpit, or now home visitation, he engaged little in small talk. He possessed a sincere Christian spirit but he never exhibited a forced upbeat personality. He was just himself.

As soon as they sat down and Gertie poured the coffee the pastor asked the penetrating question. "At this point in Ann's illness I suspect there are decisions, tough decisions, that you are facing."

John and Gertie glanced at each other for a split second. It was like he had read their minds. Really though, it was just experience.

Mack showed no visible response to the comment. He stared at his coffee cup.

John was prepared to be the one to have to open up to Mantlund.

"That is true, Pastor. Mom is suffering dearly now. She has trouble talking to us much of the time. We are concerned that soon she may not be able to swallow soft food or even soup. There are times, I think because of the pain, when she doesn't understand us."

"She hears me. She knows what I am saying." Still staring at his coffee cup Mack spoke in an irritated and defensive tone.

John waited a few seconds before responding. "Yes, she does, some of the time, dad. But a lot of the time I think she is in too much dis-comfort to understand." He shifted his eyes from his father to the pas-tor. "Especially when the pain medicine wears thin."

Mantlund said nothing. He waited for John to continue.

"We're having a tough time deciding on what to do." John's voice suggested just the hint of the loss of composure. The pastor leaned for-ward in his chair.

"Decisions like this were a lot easier in years gone by when there were no such things as convalescent homes and rehabilitation centers." He paused as the thought took hold, even in Mack. "As wrenching as the decision is, having the option of full time care is a blessing."

Mantlund could have spent the next moments consoling with the anguish of the decision facing this family, but he moved forward.

"I want to read you something."

Like any good minister he had his Bible with him. It was a small Bible that he had tucked in his jacket pocket. Now Gertie knew why he had insisted on just hanging his jacket on the back of the kitchen chair.

"There's two different things. They seem to be opposite each other in one respect. In another respect they seem to work together. The first is stewardship. In Proverbs it says this. 'Be thou diligent to know the state of thy flocks, and look well to thy herds.'"

He closed his Bible and spoke resolutely.

"I see that verse and I think of stewardship. Of taking care of what we have been blest with."

"Well, I don't need to tell the Bergs about that. About the wonder-ful farm you have here and the great discipline it takes to make it a suc-cess."

Again he hesitated.

"Even more importantly is the stewardship of family. I don't believe there is a family anywhere that shows better stewardship of family than you folks. The pride and the love you all take in this family. What is it now, four or five generations right here together? Supporting each other. That doesn't happen without the discipline of good stewardship. A per-sonal responsibility as individuals and as a family.

"I know, Mack, that you, that all three of you, have done your utmost for Ann. There's no greater example of stewardship than taking care of your family. So that's one thing; the stewardship."

Mantlund turned the pages of his Bible. "Then, the second thing. It's in Matthew. I know you've heard it before, but let's look at it. Jesus said it. 'Take my yoke upon you, and learn of me, for I am meek and lowly in heart: and ye shall find rest unto your souls.'"

The pastor again said nothing for a few seconds. It was just not in his nature to rush his speech.

"I know you folks have taken this principle to heart as well. Different concerns and problems. I know. I've seen it in you. Being able to lean on the Lord. And now you've got a really tough one. The thing is, for a person who does not have Christ in his life, and even for those of us who are Christians, we don't always see the help that He affords us."

Mantlund quietly closed his Bible. "I think the thing is…you've got to decide if having a place for Ann to go to is a gift from the Lord. We usually think of that yoke from the Lord as a source of strength offering us a spirit to see us through difficult situations. And it is. But I also think that yoke can be a very practical form of help. Is a facility a yoke that He is providing that will ease the burden on Ann; and on yourselves?"

The pastor said no more. If any of them wanted to discuss how these words applied to them, he was leaving the door open for their thoughts. But he was not going to preach at them. The Bible's words were clear.

A good minute went by when Mack audibly exhaled to try and release the emotion that was crowding his insides. "What you're saying…" He stopped to try and control the shaking voice that was upon him. "What you're saying. It's just like Ann told us all after we got the news. It tears at my insides to think of giving her up, but she would be saying just what you said."

He paused and fairly trembled as he again exhaled. "I don't know. I just don't know."

Neither John nor Gertie had ever seen him this emotionally wracked, but they could both see that Pastor's words had made an impact.

Mantlund brought things to a close. "I'm going to take us to prayer."

"Our Father, you have promised to never give us a burden that is more than we can bear if we will seek you for our wisdom and our strength. Help these good people in the days ahead. Make it clear to them the decisions that must be made. May they know, more than ever now, that their hope and assurance is centered in You. Amen."

THIRTEEN

t was just a few days later when Johnny completed his eight weeks of advanced individual training in infantry at Fort Leonard Wood, Missouri. John and Gertie prepared themselves for the strong possibility of their son being sent to Vietnam. John Sr. knew that it would be the foot soldier that would bear the biggest burden in Vietnam. It was a war without front lines.

Young John had been gone twenty weeks with almost no personal freedom. Rigid training, rigid discipline. First basic training and then AIT. Now he was going home.

As he rode the Greyhound bus from Fort Leonard Wood to Chicago his mind was spinning with a number of thoughts. It excited him to think that he was a young man engaged to Jenny Watson. She had been in thoughts every day since he left home but the actual thought they were engaged to be married now made him realize that much of his future had already been set in motion.

He thought about his grandmother, mentally preparing himself for the fact that she was not going to physically be the woman he knew when he left home.

From Chicago he took the Greyhound transfer to Milwaukee. From there he took a Trailways bus to Stoughton. The deeper he got into dairy farm country the more his mind tossed between the excitement of being back in the world he loved and the thought that eighty acres of the farm was in jeopardy. When the bus arrived in Stoughton it was late afternoon. He knew Jenny was still at work so he sought out one of his friends to take him to the farm.

Upon his arrival all work stopped. John and Mack came in from the fields. Gertie had spent the afternoon making Johnny's favorite dinner—rolled pork roast and gravy, with potatoes peeled and halved and roasted with the pork, plenty of homemade apple sauce, homemade bread and the very last of the green beans from the garden. Rhubarb pie for dessert. They weren't sure if he would arrive Monday or Tuesday, but Gertie wanted to be ready with his favorites.

Johnny soaked it all up. Being home with those he loved, at the place he loved. They all seemed to be the same, mostly. Mom, in her bright, industrious, in charge way. He could see how excited she was to have him home. His father, giving him a hug along with the handshake. He was not a hugger, except to his wife and mother. He looked into his son's eyes with a look that said "I'm proud of you. I know you've done well."

Grandpa Mack was the last one to get back to the house. They shook hands as Mack looked at his grandson. "This is a good day. This is a good day, John."

For a long moment Johnny did not say a word. Both grandson and grandfather choked back emotion as the unspoken thought of Ann filled their minds. It was a moment when not a word need be spoken.

Finally Mack said, "She's upstairs. I know she'll be glad to see you."

And then there was Rollie. His cheery thoughts helped everyone through the moment.

"Bergie, what'ya think your doing eh, running off to the Army, leaving me with all the work this summer?"

He slapped Johnny on the shoulder with his beefy right hand. It was good old Rollie all right, but not quite the same. He was, as always, lively, exuberant, full of life; but at the same time showing just a touch of reserve. Was it that he felt a little out of place, being there with the family at such a special time, greeting their son after twenty-one weeks away? It's possible, but Rollie Leach always felt completely at home with the Bergs. Was it because of the seriousness of Ann's illness? He did care deeply for Mrs. B. Or was there a little respect for the soldier?

Despite her weakened state Ann lit up when Johnny came to her bedside. They visited for more than an hour.

That evening, after dinner, Johnny excused himself in order to go see Jenny.

The Watson home was just off Main Street on Harrison Avenue, one of the beautifully shaded streets lined with early twentieth century homes where oak, hickory and maple trees predominated. In just a few more days the October temperatures would bring out the reds, golds and oranges of the turning leaves in all their nuances. It would make for an awesome display against the backdrop of the brilliant blue October sky.

Some of these homes, including the Watsons', were a modest two story frame. A front porch for sitting was a prominent feature of this style home. Intricate woodworking details, often called gingerbread, abounded where upright posts met the header boards of the porch overhang. It was small town Midwest Americana. Just three houses away from the Watsons was the home that once belonged to Hans and Margaret Steingird, both deceased many years now.

Jenny met Johnny on the porch with an embrace that seemed to go on forever. He was hesitant of letting go because he was raging so for this girl. He was afraid he could not control his feelings once he looked into her eyes. They pawed at each other as they made their way to the swing that hung suspended from the porch ceiling. Howard Watson was working late, taking inventory at his hardware store. Jenny's mother and sister were in the back sitting room watching television.

Jenny, too, felt a surging emotion as a woman's tears flooded her eyes, but she forced herself to quickly gain control of the situation. She pulled back slightly.

"Oh John. Are you all right? You're out of breath and all the color is drained from your face."

Again they kissed and held each other tightly for the next few moments. Jenny knew she needed to steady this young man of hers. She pulled back again, looking at him with a mixture of amazement, delight and caution. "You're a freight train of passion, Johnny Berg. I think you missed me."

John's heart was still racing as he began to laugh softly. His muffled laughter went on at length. Jenny watched in amazement as he finally got control of himself enough to put some words together. "A freight train of passion. I guess so."

She put her head on his chest and joined him in a soft, affectionate giggle. She herself had just experienced a physical passion as never before, but she had the wherewithal to defuse her fiancé's urges with the skill of a bomb squad expert removing the firing pin from a bomb.

Howard Watson arrived home presently. He greeted Johnny warmly, then left them to their time on the porch, though the cold night air soon drove them indoors. They talked until well past midnight. As he had told his family at dinner, he now told Jenny where he was being sent after his furlough. Beyond that he kept the talk about the two of them, with Jenny, as usual carrying most of the conversation.

"My orders are to the First Cavalry Division. They're in Korea. That's where I'll be going. Somewhere in South Korea."

Jenny gave a puzzled smile as she kidded him. "That sounds like horses. That is what the cavalry means. Wouldn't they rather have cowboys from Oklahoma or Texas than a dairy farmer from Wisconsin?"

Johnny shook his head. "You do know how to keep a guy loose."

"Well, that is a bit strange. I may not know too much about, what are they calling it, the military-industrial complex, but I do think they gave up on horses some time ago."

"Yes," replied John. He went on to explain. "The First Cav stopped using horses some time ago. I don't know, some time after the start of World War II, I believe. From what little I know they travel by APC's now, and by helicopter."

Jenny drew back with an exasperated look. "And I'm supposed to know what an APC is?"

For the first time since he arrived at Jenny's house John was relaxed enough to let his lanky frame sit back. He was chuckling again.

Jenny made a fist and knocked on her fiancé's head.

"So what is an APC? It sounds like an all purpose capsule to me." She smiled at her own humor.

"It's an armored personnel carrier. I rode in one just one time back at Leonard Wood. It's a track vehicle, like a tank, but it's not a tank. It's used to carry guys from one place to another. It's a way of moving foot soldiers quickly."

He shrugged his shoulders, as though to say, "that's about all I know, let's talk about something else."

But it was Jenny who had to have the last word on the subject.

"I'll bet it is terribly noisy. I think you had better take some of those all purpose capsules with you."

Johnny smiled, but Jenny gave herself but an instant to enjoy her own wit. She almost immediately broke down. She covered her face as her body shook with quiet sobbing.

Johnny was startled. One minute his fiancée is full of humor and instantaneously her emotions overwhelmed her. He was reminded how different the emotional threshold was between a man and a woman.

Jenny heaved with a sigh.

"I should be happy. I should be happy. They're not sending you to Vietnam and here I am getting all upset. It's just the finality of it. You'll be gone for over a year and, I don't know, it's just not what we thought would happen."

FOURTEEN

Despite the long bus ride from Missouri and only a few hours sleep after getting home from Jenny's house, Johnny was ready when the work day began the next morning — though not with the same enthusiasm that he had anticipated. Jenny's anxiety about their impending long separation had put a damper on his spirits. After hooking up the milkers he came back into the house for some breakfast. After the great roast pork dinner the night before, he realized his mother was on mission to spoil him when she slid a plateful of waffles and eggs under his nose.

"I'm not sure I understand how a woman thinks, Mom. Seems like out of a clear blue sky last night Jenny just seemed to fall apart for a few minutes. She just sort of fell apart emotionally at the thought of me being gone for the next thirteen months. Sure, neither one of us likes the idea but it was just like someone had turned a switch on."

Gertie stopped her work at the sink with the totally unexpected statement from her stoic son. She joined him at the table.

"I believe you may be right; you don't understand how a woman thinks. When it comes to relationships women are a lot more inclined to fret. You see yourself going off for a short while taking in a new experience. Oh, the Army may not be something of your choosing, but you see it as an obligation that's no more than a bump in the road. For Jenny it's a whole different way of seeing things. She is most likely concerned that the two of you will somehow be changed in this next year."

Johnny gave a puzzled look and responded with a "What?"

"See what I mean. You and your father. Like two peas in a pod. I've told him, 'Look around, we're seeing the end of some golden years around here.' You and Clark off on your own. Elsie talking like she would like to go to college when the time comes. I'm realizing change is in the wind and he doesn't see it. Sure, he sees the possibility of losing his mother and he sees that we might lose eighty acres of valuable farm land but he's not realizing that the golden years of raising a family are about to become a thing of the past for the two of us."

"I realized years ago that there's just a plain and simple difference in the way a man and woman look at things. Same with you and Jenny. She'll do just fine."

Clark had been working at WWMR for four months. He had surprised even himself. He had acquired an enthusiasm for his work, something that was a new experience for him. Oh, there were two or three times when, what he called the old Clark, surfaced; such as the incident with Andy Quince. But he refocused. He kept his nose to the grindstone, though he was soon reminded that the immediate gratification he was feeling was not enough to help his long-term success.

Frank Smith was an experienced manager. Just as he did with his other employees he left Clark alone as much as possible. Smith did not breathe down a person's neck. If they had a problem they wished to discuss with him his door was always open. Otherwise, he expected his employees to work through to their objectives using their own chain of command. He was especially careful not to be peering over Clark's shoulder. But Smith didn't miss a thing. Every few months he conducted a performance review with each employee on his sales staff. Back in early September he had called Clark into his office. He was as to the point with his nephew as he was with everyone else.

"You're doing well, Clark. I like what I see and my impression is the ad execs are satisfied with your performance. Whenever you've stumbled you've corrected your mistakes." He paused for a moment. "But there are two times you showed up late in meeting an exec for a presentation. Mistakes are mistakes. We all make them. Showing up late is not a mistake, it is negligence. It's irresponsibility."

He did not dwell on the subject, nor did he give Clark a chance to respond. He moved right into a question. "Now, how have you done in getting yourself enrolled in classes this fall?"

Clark could feel himself sinking in his chair. Had there been one available he could have crawled into a hole. He had spent most of his free time having a good time. Other than read a couple of pieces of literature about Carroll College he had not even made the first effort to get himself enrolled for any classes. He'd spent many of his evenings playing cards with friends he had acquired at Kleindeinst Bar and Grill, a restaurant and watering hole across the street from his apartment.

Clark was a work in progress. Yes, he had taken his uncle's challenge to be responsible and unselfish in his work ethic. It was not always easy, for his nature, or at least his habit, was to put himself first. But he was making great strides in the right direction. Now he was face to face with the man who had given him this opportunity, despite what he knew about him. He had just asked him what he had done about getting enrolled in school. How could he tell him he had done nothing?

Clark straightened himself in his chair. He had been hired in the expectation that he would put his boyish behavior away and start acting like a responsible man. Among many other things that meant being truthful.

He swallowed hard. "I haven't done a thing. I've let you down and I've let myself down. I was feeling so good about having this job that I just kept putting things off until, well, before I knew it the summer was gone and I hadn't done a thing."

Smith leaned back in his chair, giving himself a few seconds before responding.

"You said you would make an effort to get enrolled in some classes. The fact that you didn't, well, there's no two ways around it Clark, you were not honest with me."

Smith hesitated again before continuing. He had a knack for using the pause to squeeze the most out of what he wanted to convey.

"But you were forthright enough with me right now, just now, to say what you just said. To lay the responsibility, and the blame, on yourself."

"Yes sir," responded Clark. He felt weak in the stomach and totally defenseless against whatever his uncle might say.

Smith leaned forward with that penetrating eye contact of his. "Clark, do you like what you've seen of this business?"

"Yes, I do." He waited for the ax to fall. He waited to be told he was finished at WWMR.

"I can use you just where you are, Clark. You can stay as an exec assistant and that will work out fine for me." Again the pause. "But did you hear what I just said. I said, 'I can use you.' Maybe that's what you want. To be used by me. Maybe you're willing to be used by myself and any number of other people so that they can attain their goals. In the meantime, you remain as good old Clark, the guy that other people can rely on to use."

"We both know that you came here with a reputation of being a bit self serving. A 'me first' outlook. We've been over that ground and I feel you have worked pretty hard at trying to overcome it. But if you fail to improve yourself, to prepare yourself for something better, then you are just sliding off in the opposite direction. Other people will just be using you. Not because they're out there trying to manipulate you, but because you've failed to live up to your own potential and you're just out there."

Smith's words were a revelation to Clark. Here he was, always believing that he was the one too good for the farm; that he had a special talent for getting what he wanted in his own way. Now his uncle was telling him that the opposite was the real case. That he was the one who was going to be the sap that others could use. These thoughts raced through his mind in the few seconds he had before responding. He clenched his fists as he often did when he wanted to be emphatic about something.

With his uncle saying he could use him just where he was Clark felt safe in offering this thought. But now he offered his words not to maneuver himself into a satisfactory position, or to say what he thought Frank Smith wanted to hear, but because, in these few seconds he realized how true Smith's words were.

"I'd like to do this. I'm going to apply for school in order to begin next fall, a year from now. That will allow me to save more money in the meantime. Does that sound alright with you?"

Smith stood and walked around his desk. "Up to you." With an expression on his face that was unsympathetic, yet showed a willingness to accept Clark's new plans, he extended a handshake. He brought the discussion to a close by changing the subject.

"How is your grandmother?"

Clark almost didn't hear the question.

"Oh! Yes. I haven't been home in some time. Mom says she is not doing well." He hesitated a second and began to speak in regard to his work.

Smith held up his hand to stop him. "No need to talk about this anymore. If starting school next fall works for you that would be fine. Up to you."

FIFTEEN

"Consider it pure joy, my brothers, whenever you face trials of many kinds, because you know that the testing of your faith develops perseverance. Perseverance must finish its work so that you may be mature and complete, not lacking anything."

JAMES 1:2–4 NIV

After his two weeks home Johnny's orders sent him to San Francisco, where his training battalion from Fort Leonard Wood was to assemble for the trip to the Korean peninsula. It had been mildly surprising to them all. When so much of the military's resources, both men and equipment, were headed for Vietnam, it seemed inevitable to them all that they also would go to the war. But the United States considered its continued commitment to the United Nations presence in Korea as essential.

When their son came home on leave and told them that he was being sent to Korea, how relieved Gertie was. To her the Korean Conflict, as they had called it, was only a vague memory. It ended in 1953. It had been over twelve years now. She had paid little attention to it because it was not 'their war.' It was World War II that John came home from. She was busy raising two little boys and a baby girl and keeping a home. She was committed to helping her husband and her in-laws keep Berg Farm a success. The nasty business of Korea was the worry of others.

John Berg Sr. realized that the Korean peninsula was not just any place of American military occupation. The war had no definitive conclusion. The fighting ended in a truce. A cease fire. Twelve years later the peace was still held together only by that truce. From what he knew the situation was still a fragile one, with both sides, the communist North and the democratic South, still armed to the teeth. But still, his son was going to a place of occupation, not the hot war of Vietnam. For this, he too, was grateful.

Throughout the summer months and now into the early fall the land dispute with Gerald Hicks continued to remain a gloomy prospect. From DeVries Real Estate the Bergs had received Hicks' offer for the eighty acres of land back on August 15th. A week later Mack formally refused the offer. Two more offers followed, both again refused by Mack. In mid-October the inevitable notice of a lawsuit filed against Mack Berg by Gerald Hicks came to Berg Farm. It included a court date of November 15th.

Charlie Stroud told the Bergs not to be overly concerned. He would ask for a two months stay to give time to prepare a defense against the suit.

The most urgent concern was Ann. John and Gertie were grateful that Mack did consent to full-time care for his wife. The concern for Johnny's well-being and the land issue paled by comparison to the emotional strain of putting Ann into the convalescent home.

"Just coffee for me this morning, Gertie." Mack had no appetite on this October morning.

John and Gertie joined him at the table. They, too, had no desire to eat.

"Do you think Annie is going to resent this? Taken away from her home. Living with a bunch of strangers. Do you think she is going to feel that I've given up on her and that I'm just dumping her off on a bunch of strangers?" Mack's husky voice had taken on a shallow tone.

A few moments passed when Gertie responded. "When Elsie was an infant her head was so soft that it was forming a little flattened on one side because of the way she slept. You may remember."

"The doctor recommended that she wear a helmet, even when she was awake, to allow her head to regain its proper shape. It seemed like just an awful thing to do. I remember John and I having such a hard time consenting. But then the doctor said, 'It's going to be harder on you than it is on the baby.' Once I understood that I was okay with that helmet."

"The circumstances are different, Mack, but the idea's the same. You need to know that this is harder on you than it is on her."

They dressed Ann warmly for the ride to the Vanstessen Care Home in Madison.

Through the rear view mirror of the family sedan John could see his father with his arm around his wife, supporting her tenderly, in a scene that nearly broke his heart. When they arrived at Vanstessen's front door an orderly immediately arrived with a wheel chair. Though he insisted that, as an employee, he was required to wheel Mrs. Berg into admittance, Mack politely brushed him aside and took charge of wheeling his wife inside.

When the social worker at Vanstessen's recognized the Bergs as a close family, she offered some comforting words.

"I know that this is an extremely difficult day for you. I just want to remind you of something. I know that a close family like yours can feel a lot of pain on a day like this. This is a heartrending experience, bringing a loved one to us. I know your hearts are full for Mrs. Berg. The fact is we receive some residents from families that have little kinship. Now, those families may feel less pain when they entrust us with a loved one, but, well, I think we can agree that a close family such as yours is a blessing."

The three of them spent all day with Ann. Mack stayed the night.

In the days that followed, John and Gertie agreed that they needed to challenge Mack to the day-to-day concerns of the farm. To challenge him, as much as possible, to his usual workload. They both knew that to over empathize with him because of Ann's state would serve no real positive purpose. Besides, he was never one to want anyone doting on him or feeling sorry for him.

In Milwaukee, Clark continued his one man effort at trying to remake himself. Certainly he was making progress. His relationships at WWMR were a testament to this change. He was working with people, considering their needs, helping them reach their goals. Outwardly he seemed to be maturing.

On November 14th, just three weeks after his brother left for San Francisco and the flight to Korea, Clark Berg opened a piece of mail that severely tested his maturation process.

"Greetings from the President of the United States."

Clark was stunned. How could this be? He was eleven months younger than Johnny, yet he was now receiving his draft notice? Surely he had another six months or so before they would want to draft him; if they were drafting at all by then. He had only been out of high school for six months. He was about to apply to four different schools: Carroll College, Concordia University, Wisconsin Lutheran College and even Marquette.

He knew college students were exempt from the draft. Surely there had to be some leeway for a young man who was attempting to enter college?

He paced around his apartment for the next hour. What about his plans? In his mind he took the position all too familiar to him. This was unfair. He didn't deserve this. He was better than being another military draftee.

Finally, he calmed down. It was unusual for him, but he stepped outside of himself long enough to at least realize he was pouting. He wisely realized that a calm approach to this situation was what would help him the most. He would call his draft board officer. Better yet, he would pay a personal visit. The Federal Building was right downtown, only three blocks from WWMR. His draft board officer was there. He would state his case in a calm, rational manner. He planned to start college next September. He already had four applications that he planned to submit. Surely that would make a difference.

And his brother! He had a brother already in the service. Didn't that mean something? He would say he was needed on the farm. He would say he had to get down to the farm on weekends until winter closed in and then he would be helping again in the spring. Surely he could talk his way through this with, who was it, Mrs. Baldwin, his draft board officer.

He had three weeks before he had to report to Camp McCoy. He would get this straightened out.

Two days later Clark found himself in the Milwaukee Federal Building. The place was imposing. Everything about it spoke of the mighty power of the United States of America. He walked up ten steps of elevation to reach one of the four heavy hardwood and glass doors. Once inside those doors he negotiated one of three revolving glass doors, allowing him into a rather austere looking lobby. The lobby extended all the way to the other side of the building where, it appeared, an exact same entrance to the one he had just come through existed. The floor consisted of three foot by three foot squares of highly buffed material. It wasn't marble, noted Clark, but it was a material that seemed as durable and as noble as marble. A battery of four elevators flanked each side of the lobby. Most impressive of all was the high ceiling. The lobby walls went up to the third floor before the ceiling appeared. The whole place was lit by six huge, unadorned chandeliers, hung by thick steel chain link cables. He thought the sound, or the lack of it, had a reverence to it. The voices of people talking, even at the other end of the lobby, echoed, but in a muffled sort of way. Clark felt relieved when he saw the information desk down in the middle of the place.

The sixth floor, he was told. Room 623.

As he approached one of the elevators, he saw a glassed in directory mounted on the wall. He realized this was a place where the hand of Washington rested heavily. The FBI offices. The DEA. Both Wisconsin senators had an office here. Alcohol, Tobacco and Firearms. The Department of the Interior. The Department of Health, Education and Welfare. The Treasury Department. The Internal Revenue Department had an office here. It said Internal Revenue Enforcement.

Clark entered the draft board office of Mrs. Baldwin. It was a small office. There was no receptionist or any other person. Only Mrs. Baldwin. She appeared to be in her mid-40s, platinum bleached hair and dressed in a very proper manner — gray skirt, medium blue jacket, a white blouse with some sort of pink scarf. Her makeup had a decided pink accent to it and her telephone was pink, as well as couple of other items on her desk.

Clark introduced himself, mustering all the charm that had helped him get his way many times before.

Marion Baldwin invited him to sit down. After filing some papers in a folder and placing it aside she gave Clark a courtesy smile and her full attention.

"Now then, Mr. Berg. Is that spelt with an e or a u?"

"B-e-r-g." Clark's voice displayed an upbeat tone. As she looked up his records, he explained his situation.

"I will be attending school next September and I thought I should get down here and try and straighten things out." He immediately thought that the phrase "try and straighten things out" was not the best choice of words.

Without looking up, Baldwin continued to look through her records until she reached Clarence El Berg. Her voice was not unfriendly, but she spoke in a detached manner, offering no emotional understanding to the young man seated on the other side of her desk.

"Yes, here we are, I think?" She looked to Clark with a questioning expression. "I have a Clarence Berg here."

"Oh. I'm sorry. Yes. It's Clarence. Clark is what I go by."

"Yes." She hesitated as her smile seemed to warm up a bit. "May I ask? Your middle name. El is rather different. Does that have some family significance?"

Clark was always sensitive about his name. He considered Clarence an outdated name that, in his shallow way of thinking, was a bit embarrassing. Now he was being asked about his middle name; El. To most people he would just lie. He would tell them the two letter name had no significance. However, he did not want to appear evasive to the woman who now held the future of his next two years in her hands.

"Yes. My great, great grandfather homesteaded here in Wisconsin — just outside of Stoughton. He came from Norway."

Clark gulped hard.

"His name was Elmer and my parents wanted to remember him so, thankfully, they just shortened it to El." He shrugged his shoulders and gave a sheepish look. "That's it."

Mrs. Baldwin stared at him. Though she said not a word her look said, "And why should you, in any way, feel embarrassed?"

She then studied the information in front of her, saying nothing for a very long twenty seconds.

"Your draft notice was sent out six days ago and you say you received it this Monday?" She looked up, offering another cool smile.

Clark leaned forward in his chair. "Yes, I received it on Monday. As I said, I'll be going to school...."

She cut him off with a curt, albeit polite, request. "May I see your paperwork?"

Clark was stunned for just a couple of seconds before returning to charm mode.

"I'm not sure what paperwork you mean, Mrs. Baldwin?"

Marion Baldwin summoned her patience, for she had been down this road before. She clasped her hands together on the top of her desk and politely continued.

"I will need to see your correspondence from the school you plan to attend stating that you have either been accepted or that they have received your application and are reviewing it. If I can see that you have been accepted we can change your classification to II-S. That will rescind your draft notice. If the school, or schools, are reviewing your application at this time I will call them, establish that you are in the process of being considered, and we will put your report date on hold until we see if you are accepted. If you are accepted, your draft notice will be rescinded and, again, you will be reclassified II-S. If you are not accepted, your current status will remain in effect and you will be assigned a new report date."

By now Clark had an unmistakable lump in his throat. He tried to mask his mounting panic with his continued innocent veneer.

"Well, I haven't actually sent out my applications yet. My employer and I discussed my options a short while ago and he encouraged me to work toward a degree. So I really need to get into school. Is there...."

Baldwin cut him off again. "Yes, Mr. Berg, it does sound like unfortunate timing. But your situation doesn't warrant a change in your status, or a postponement of your induction report date."

The color was draining from Clark's face. "But it must mean something that I am planning to go to school?"

She tilted her head slightly, the first indication that she at all sympathized with him. Or was it a gesture that said, "Please, I wasn't born yesterday."

"I must tell you that the intention to attend college carries no weight toward a deferment. If it did the government would lose a great deal of those who receive an induction notice."

"I don't understand," returned Clark, trying to deflect the meaning of her statement. "It is an honorable thing to go to college, isn't it?"

"Yes, of course, Mr. Berg." Her expression turned stony. "However, the government won't allow anyone to use the reason of planning to send out an application to a school or schools as adequate reason for a deferment. Too many people, without the least bit of compunction, would, and do, try to use that as a reason to rescind their induction."

Baldwin flipped the cumbersome records book forward one page and saw John Berg's information.

"I thought your information sounded familiar. John Berg is your brother?"

"Yes. Yes, he is!" Clark sensed an opportunity. "Johnny was out of high school almost two years before he was drafted. Yet I get one just five months after I graduate. That just doesn't seem right."

She seemed puzzled, but just for a moment.

"I see here that you will be twenty years old next March. That does qualify you age wise to be drafted under the current guidelines. It appears you may have fallen behind at some point in school." She raised her eyes to Clark.

He had hit another brick wall. He nodded affirmatively, but did not bother to explain his ninth grade blunders.

Clark turned his vision from Mrs. Baldwin to the floor in front of his feet. His complexion, which had gone pallid just a few moments before, turned red. His friendly visage was melting away. He spoke with annoyance in his voice. "Is there anything I can do about this? Is there anyone I can talk to?"

"You have the option of contacting one of your senators."

She paused for a few seconds, then hesitantly continued. It was now obvious that she was forcing herself to be patient with this young man.

"But I must tell you that you really have no case here. Senators will occasionally, I should say rarely, grant deferments for family hardship reasons, but that's about it."

Clark Berg continued to look at the floor in front of him for another few seconds. Then, without a word to, or even a glance toward, his draft board officer he bolted to his feet and left the office.

SIXTEEN

✦

"Enter into His gates with thanksgiving, and into His courts with praise; be thankful unto Him, and bless His name."

PSALMS 100: 4, 5 KJV

harlie Stroud had familiarized himself with all he could about the Bergs, their land, Midwest Agra Group and Gerald Hicks. Despite his efforts there seemed to be no way around Wisconsin law, which was working just fine for Mr. Hicks.

It had been pancreatic cancer that took Greta Hicks' life. As Betty Smith had reminded Mack and his buddies over their coffee at Rasmussen's earlier that year, the Knudson's other daughter, Maggie, had been killed in a car accident in Georgia. There seemed to be nothing standing in Hicks' way.

One mid-November morning Gertie made her trip to the mailbox. It was going to be a brilliant fall day. The rays of the sun were making their way across the metal mailbox, melting the frost in a steady procession.

Charlie told them to expect a letter formally announcing a new court date for the hearing.

Gertie Berg was the last person to hide from life's problems, but when she pulled out the box's contents and saw the letter from the court she knew immediately it would be the notice of the rescheduled hearing. In a bit of daydreaming over the past weeks, she had tried to convince herself that maybe the Gerald Hicks issue would just go away.

She opened it right there at the mail box, scanning through the legal courtesies and seeing that a court date of January 10th was now scheduled. She knew that unless something fortuitous happened the court would, at that time, order the eighty-acre sale to Mr. Hicks.

Later that morning, Gertie drove out to the fields with John and

Mack's dinner. They were both chisel plowing under a couple sections of corn stubble. On this day she didn't feel it was necessary to mention the letter from the court. Her father-in-law had enough on his mind with Ann's deteriorating health. He would see the notice that evening when he opened the rest of his mail.

She arrived at the predetermined spot where the vehicle trail led to the meeting of two tree lines. The men were not there yet. As she set up the food on the truck's tailgate, her mind drifted back to all the times she and Ann had done this in the last twenty-two years. How young they all had been. Mack and Ann, so full of life and good humor. How she and Mack kidded each other incessantly. It came to her mind about the couple of times she made her announcement of the dinner meal when she shouted "Liverwurst sandwiches."

Mack was a good eater. Never left a scrap on his plate. But he loathed liverwurst. Couldn't stand it. He heard Gertie's announcement as he dismounted his tractor, quietly made his way to the tailgate and found one of his favorites, not liverwurst. A few years later Gertie announced liverwurst again; but this time there they were, liverwurst sandwiches. Not to be deceived again Mack had expected something else. When he saw the liverwurst he allowed himself only a split second of disappointment before taking a sandwich. Seconds before Mack's arrival Gertie had brought Rollie in on the ruse. As Mack went and found a place to sit, Rollie came up to the tailgate, grabbed a hidden sandwich that Mack had not seen and issued a phony, self conscious apology to Gertie.

"Gertie, I love you dearly and you're the best cook I know, but, forgive me, I just have no taste for this type of sandwich."

Rollie walked over toward Mack. "Here you go Thor. How about a trade?"

He dropped the sandwich in Mack's lap as all around—Gertie, John, Johnny, Clark and Rollie rolled with laughter. The puzzled Mack sheepishly opened the wax paper and found one of his favorites—ham and cheese.

They had been good times. Hard work, laughter, love of family, an appreciation that every day was a gift from the Lord. Gertie knew that there would be many more good days ahead. But they would be good times under different circumstances for, except for His promises, nothing stays the same forever. The boys were off on their own. Ann was seriously ill. Someone was claiming the right to buy eighty acres of their land. And they all were getting a little older.

The Thanksgiving holiday was only a few days away. Though Ann and Johnny could not be there, Gertie was determined to make this Thanksgiving as traditional as any. It was their turn to host and that meant that the house would be full of Mehlborgs and Bergs. Clark would be in from Milwaukee and John's two sisters and their families would be there. From Gertie's large family there would be her parents and youngest sister, still unmarried at age 28, and another sister and two brothers, each with their families.

For this large extended family, the special Thursday that was Thanksgiving Day was more revered than it was for many folks. This family lived close to the land. Their faith and the farming heritage of both the Berg and Mehlborg families made them well aware of the blessings to which they owed so much gratitude. For these people, Thanksgiving was no mere kickoff to the Christmas season.

As she did when she previously hosted, Gertie invited Rollie. Twenty-nine people in all. Her two Berg sisters-in-law would bring the pies and her mother and two sisters would bring salads, gelatin rings and dinner rolls. Everything homemade, of course.

Thanksgiving morning dawned with heavy, dark cloud cover and high winds. There was a dusting of snow on the ground. To Gertie this prelude to winter-type weather just meant that the Thanksgiving atmosphere in the house would be that much more homey. She had two sixteen pound turkeys stuffed and in her double oven at 6:00 A.M. In the next few hours she would be preparing a couple green bean with mushroom soup and dried onion casseroles, two baked sweet potato in butter and brown sugar dishes, creamed cauliflower and enough mashed potatoes to, as John would always say, feed an army. She was always grateful for the help from those bringing food, but especially this year. It felt strange to be working in the kitchen on this day without her mother-in-law's help.

The only work that John and Mack did on Thanksgiving Day was to get the milking done. This was finished by seven o'clock. Mack had never lost his appreciation for the automated milk hookups. He traditionally spent the rest of the morning and the early afternoon doing something that was not at all common to him. He was glued to the television.

The traditional Thanksgiving Day Parade from Detroit, sponsored by the Hudson Department Store, came across the air waves at nine o'clock. Mack was delighted by the high school bands, the marching VFW chapters and the many floats with their themes. He especially enjoyed the Detroit Mounted Police Division. The beautiful Arabian horses, all of them either black or a rich chestnut brown, with white at the ankles. The officers and horses were perfectly matched in their unadorned, rugged leather saddles and reigns, with the dark blue with gold trim saddle blankets. What pride, Mack thought, that each officer must take in his work and in the care of his horse. Each man looked proud and dedicated in his high top black boots, his thick and shiny black leather jacket and his perfectly formed campaign hat. He long felt that if he had grown up in the city, a big city like Detroit or Chicago, he would have wanted to be a mounted police officer.

Shortly after the parade, the traditional Thanksgiving Day football game between the Green Bay Packers and the Detroit Lions came on the TV. This was no casual event for Mack. He and Skorpie Johnson had been devoted fans of the Packers since the mid 1930s. In the '30s Curly Lambeau led the team to its best years in the young National Football League. Neither man had ever been to see a Packer game but both, normally placid in personality, had followed the team passionately in the newspaper over the years. Each autumn they had set aside Sunday afternoons, first on radio and then with the coming of television, to follow their team.

The Packers became the doormats of the league for many years throughout the forties and the fifties and the franchise twice came close to leaving Green Bay for a larger city.

But now it was 1965 and the years of a great Packer dynasty were in progress. Vince Lombardi had arrived in 1958 to take over the hapless team and within two years he led them to the NFL Western Division title. Now, the Green Bay Packers became the decade's best and most feared team. Green Bay was "Title Town, USA"

The crowning moment for both Berg and Johnson was the Packers' so called "Ice Bowl" victory over the Eagles in the 1963 world championship game in Green Bay.

Mack Berg and Skorpie Johnson were men who had spent their lives working the land, oblivious to most of the world that went on outside their own responsibilities. One of the exceptions to this was their long suffering allegiance to the Packers. Now they were enjoying the years of sweet success for their team.

This Thanksgiving morning, however, was not to be a traditional one for Mack. After milking he went to Madison to see Ann. The home had arranged an 11 A.M. turkey dinner for patients and their visitors. This would allow visitors time to leave for other Thanksgiving Day commitments, if that was their desire. As he left the house Gertie gave him a big hug, looked him in the eyes and said, "Give her our love." Mack promised he would be back no later than two o'clock.

The Bergs had a large kitchen and a good size dining room connected together. But with twenty-nine people it was going to be a challenge. In her determined mind Gertie insisted that they all sit at one table, that is, one combination of tables. There would be no separate card table or two for the young ones.

The previous Sunday afternoon John borrowed two card tables and chairs from his in-laws. Along with their own card table they could now combine the dining room table, the three card tables and the kitchen table in one straight piece. The width of the card tables did not match the width of the kitchen and dining room tables but, placed in the middle, they did provide the needed room to pass between the arch separating the two rooms. It didn't provide much of a House Beautiful photo opportunity, but everyone would sit together.

As he promised, Mack was back by two o'clock. It was difficult for him to leave Ann, to know that he would be back with everyone while she spent the afternoon in the home's parlor or in her room. But she was having a good day and had communicated well with her husband. She, in fact, gave her husband instruction when they were presented with their turkey dinners in the home's dining room.

"Don't you dare spoil your appetite here," she whispered in her hoarse voice. "You save room for Gertie's cooking. I want you to get back there and enjoy yourself."

Mack kept his emotions in check. "I'm sure it will be a fine day, but it could never be the same without you."

With her waning vocal strength she did her best to cast a positive note.

"I'm going to have a good afternoon just realizing what a grand day it is going to be back at the farm."

When Mack arrived home the place was teeming with family. His spirits were soon lifted. The spoken concerns for Ann, the laughter, the talk. It was all good medicine for him.

Clark had arrived at noon. Both John and Gertie thought they noticed a quietness about him that was uncharacteristic. He seemed to be enjoying himself around so many family members but without his usual brashness. Something seemed to be on his mind.

Under Gertie's direction the women brought it all together. Just before three o'clock John was saying grace and then, like millions of other families across the nation, they celebrated the bounty of this land by eating heartily.

All that work to prepare the Thanksgiving meal and it seemed to be over so quickly. At least it seemed that way to Gertie and, no doubt, to every other woman in America who had worked so diligently putting it all together. But now, before dessert, before those good pies that Gertie's sisters-in-law had made, things would slow down for a Berg— Mehlborg tradition.

Glen Masterson took front and center, as he did every Thanksgiving at this time for the last ten years. He was John and Gertie's brother-in-law. Glen had come up to Milwaukee from Kentucky as a lanky nineteen-year-old kid shortly after World War II to seek his fortune in the north country.

In due time he met and married Gertie's sister, Alice Mehlborg. Though he was now the ambitious head of Milwaukee's Parks and Recreation Department, he had been, for fourteen years now, the loveable hillbilly in a family of Germans and Norwegians. He called himself a rose amongst the thorns.

Glen was happy and proud to promote his country boy demeanor, especially on Thanksgiving, when he made his annual bungling Norwegian award.

He first thought of the idea nine years earlier when Alice had burned, or as Glen would say, destroyed, a corned beef she was planning to have for dinner. She had placed it in a pot of water and initially turned the burner on high. She soon left the house to run an errand, forgetting to turn the burner down. As Glen put it when he made the presentation and every time he had the opportunity to tell the story since, "She went out to spend money we didn't have and came back to a smoke-filled house and a dried up piece of meat that looked, and felt, like a tiny bowling ball."

Now, in these ensuing years, Glen presented the award to a family member who had made, as he called it, "a bungle that would make a country boy like me look smart."

He held up the award, or as it was sometimes called, the Norsey trophy, for all to see. It was a wooden Viking sailing ship with its flat bottom, curved bow and dramatic high prow. It was about eighteen inches long. Standing in the vessel was a little doll. It was a Viking warrior in full regalia — high top leather boots, leather vest and leather helmet with horns. He sported a scraggily beard and wielded his Viking spear held in his right hand that was thrust high above his head. He showed a toothy smile and the look on his face was one of blissful bewilderment.

In his best Hazel, Kentucky drawl Glen began.

"As you may remember last year's winner of the bungling Norwegian award went to my dear mother-in-law, Karen Mehlborg. She may have married a German but she is all Norwegian; and she proved it when she drove into your nice town of Stoughton here one day to pick up some grocery items. Well, somehow she locked herself out of her car. Now, I don't know why anyone would feel like they had to lock their car in broad daylight in Stoughton, but she did."

"Anyway, I reckon ya'll remember what happened next. She got to the pay phone in the grocery market and called the police for assistance. The officer who came was our own Gracie Mehlborg's brother, Chuck Flat. Well, ole Chuck used his special tool to pop the lock open. Karen then dropped her grocery bag…and her car keys…on the car seat and she and Chuck got into an extended conversation about the family until Chuck finally went on his way. Karen then remembered another item she wanted from the market so she locked the door again and went on her merry way back into the market. Well … when she came out she realized what she had done. So it was back to the pay phone to call the police and within a few minutes here comes ole Chuck, in total amazement."

By this time everyone, even though they all knew the story well, were engaged in some form of laughter. Most of them howling. Karen Mehlborg herself was doubled over in her chair, rocking back and forth in self deprecating laughter. Tears rolled down her cheeks.

Glen waited a few seconds before continuing. "Well, Karen was gracious enough to bring the bungling Norwegian trophy with her so that we could give it out on this Thanksgiving Day to this year's recipient."

It suddenly became quiet.

"I and my spies have done our best to keep abreast in this past year of any strange incidents that could qualify and we've come up with three or four. I think the best one involves Ralph Myrdal. Ralphie, you want to come on up here. I reckon it's time to face the music."

Ralph Myrdal was John and Gertie's brother-in-law, husband to John's sister Elsie. With an innocent look suggesting he had done nothing to deserve the trophy Ralph came forward to receive his due.

Masterson launched into his story.

"Most of you don't know about this but last February, I believe it was last February, Ralph and Elsie made a trip to Cleveland, that's in Ohio folks, to attend a wedding. Now, getting from Green Bay to Cleveland should really be no great task. In fact, with proper efficiency and a little discipline I reckon the trip can be made quite easily in less than a day. That is, unless you are Ralph Myrdal."

Ralph was now staring down at the floor, knowing full well that Glen must have done his homework. Those family members who had not heard about this were about to be enlightened. Those who knew about it were already laughing and hooting.

Glen continued. "Well, God bless America and the new interstate highway system that allows us to get around so quickly nowadays. Trouble is when you get to Chicago you have to pay close attention to all those signs to make sure you're headed in the right direction. While Elsie was snoozing Ralphie here was supposed to make his way to I-80 east out of Chicago to get to Cleveland. Well, he found his way to I-80 alright. Trouble is he wound up heading westbound."

"Way to go, Dad!" It was one of Ralph and Elsie's three teenagers. They were all enjoying their father's exposure.

Glen was not finished. "Now wait a minute folks. It gets better. Ralph must have really been in another world because he drove all the way to the first rest area, which is out somewhere near Minooka. At this point he wakes up Elsie so she can take a turn driving. She pulls the car out from the rest stop and almost immediately she sees a west I-80 road sign. Not to mention she is suspicious because the sun seems to be coming up in the wrong direction!"

By now everyone is in stitches. With perfect timing Glen Masterson waited for the noise to subside. "One can only imagine the conversation that occurred at this point."

Applause now accompanied the laughter as he handed the bungling Norwegian award to Ralph Myrdal.

Thanksgiving dinner concluded with hot coffee and the sumptuous pies brought by Catherine Smith and the just mentioned Elsie Myrdal. Blueberry, mincemeat, apple, pecan and, of course, pumpkin. From the Bergs' own heavy cream Gertie had made plenty of real whipped cream with which to smother the pies. On this day those on a diet threw caution to the wind. This was not a day for the fainthearted.

By eight o'clock things began to break up. There were special hugs and handshakes for Mack, everyone offering special concerns for Ann. Gertie had plenty of help cleaning up so once the last of the family had gone she, John, Mack and Elsie found themselves drinking coffee at the kitchen table. Both John and Mack were taking advantage of leftover pie. Mack was feeling especially buoyed by the day as he enjoyed his favorite—blueberry.

"To the hosting family go the spoils. It was a good day, Gertie. Thanks for everything. Ann said she was going to have a good day just thinking about everything here at the house. I think she meant it."

"I know she did," returned Gertie. "What do they call it? She has an indomitable spirit."

She paused. "I'm hoping Johnny had a good day. Are they ahead of us or behind us over there?"

"They're ahead of us," said John. "They finished their Thanksgiving yesterday. You can bet one way or another they had a turkey dinner."

Clark had the long weekend off from work and he would be staying at the farm until Sunday afternoon. His footsteps could be heard as he came down from upstairs to join the others.

"Mom, it was a good day. Is there any pie left or has grandpa and dad eaten it all?"

He cut himself a piece of pecan and sat with the others. For the briefest of moments he just stared at the wedge of pie and cleared his throat, as though he had something important to say. Something that was difficult for his own ears to hear.

"Well…I've got something to tell you."

You could have heard a pin drop. It was not like Clark to say, "I've got something to tell you." He had a history of not telling them much. He would just go off and do as he pleased. If John and Gertie were lucky they would find out later. Now he was sitting at the table with them, willing to take the time to share with them. Yes, he had their full attention.

With both his elbows on the table Clark put his hands to his head, closed his eyes and groaned softly. "Ten days ago I received my draft notice. I have to report to Camp McCoy on December 5."

As he said this, Gertie had her coffee cup raised to her mouth and was peering at her son over the raised cup. There was a few seconds of collective silence. She put the cup down, allowing herself just a moment of frustration. Her tone did not express anger or even annoyance, just resignation. "Goodness knows, it's worry enough having one of you gone. Now both of you?"

She squared her shoulders and questioned her son.

"Well. What do you think?"

Clark should have known that his parents were not about to commiserate with him.

"What do I think? I think it stinks!"

"Here I've got this job and I was planning to go to school next fall. I've been to see my draft board officer. She was a lot of help! There's no getting around it. I think it sucks."

Neither John nor Gertie appreciated the language but they were far more discouraged by their son's reaction.

Gertie dug in.

"And do you think that everything in this life is always going to go your way? Goodness knows it does throw a monkey wrench in your plans but you can be sure that before your life is over there will be many a hurdle to overcome. And some of those hurdles are going to be tougher than two years conscription into the United States Army."

It came upon both John and Gertie immediately. Clark's reaction to his draft notice. Such a different reaction than Johnny's.

John kept it to himself, but he thought how the son who most needed the discipline and denial that the Army had to offer was, of course, now the one who was so distraught about having to go.

"Have you told Frank Smith?" questioned Gertie.

Clark could see he would get no sympathy from his parents. They loved him, he knew. But this he also knew. John and Gertrude Berg were not whiners. He had never seen them feel sorry for themselves, and they weren't about to now encourage their son to feel sorry for himself.

With annoyance in his voice, he answered his mother. "I told him last Friday. I asked him to keep it to himself until after Thanksgiving."

Clark raised his eyes to look at his mother, father, his grandfather and sister. "I'm guessing I'll be going to Fort Knox, like Johnny did, for basic training, but I don't know yet. Anyway, that's it."

SEVENTEEN

T he previous month in San Francisco, Johnny's departure for Korea had been delayed for seven days. So many men were being sent to Vietnam at this time that departures were backed up. This delay was not without design. For six days he and many hundreds of others with orders for Vietnam or Korea stood on a large asphalt parking area of Letterman Veterans Hospital. Every soldier departing San Francisco was required to give blood before departure. The hospital was full of wounded from the war. On the fifth day, Johnny and the others with the same travel orders were called inside to give.

Berg and one hundred and sixty-two other soldiers arrived in South Korea on the last day of October 1965. They landed at Kimpo Airfield in Seoul just as the sun was going down. As they exited the airplane the young men from America were hit with the odor of a large city with a very imperfect sanitation system. It was their first indication that they were now in a poor land.

The air was cold. Johnny reckoned that it was easily as cold as his Wisconsin homeland, even though he later would learn that Seoul was two hundred and sixty miles closer to the equator than Stoughton. The Korean peninsula received the frigid weather that swept down from the huge Siberian land mass across Mongolia and northern China.

Within an hour Johnny and the others boarded Army buses. They traveled in the pitch black darkness of the countryside for two hours, eventually arriving at the gate of a barbed wire fenced-in installation that was illuminated by floodlights. The bus headlights better illuminated a sign at the entrance.

CAMP BURNS
22ND REPLACEMENT DEPOT
U.S. ARMY

All the troops at the replacement depot were assembled twice a day in front of the orderly room on the camp's modest parade ground. On the third morning, Johnny and Tom Bradley, with whom he had struck up a friendship while going through infantry training, and a number of others, were called. They gathered their duffel bags and quickly boarded another bus. On the side of the bus, up near the door, was painted the yellow and black crest of the First Cavalry Division.

The bus traveled on the dusty, narrow dirt road for another forty-five minutes. Johnny saw six U.S. Army camps along the way. Like the replacement depot these compounds were surrounded by two twelve-foot high fences spaced three feet apart. A mass of loosely coiled concertina barbed wire filled the space between the fences. The new arrivals were well aware by now that theft of U.S. Army property was a large problem.

Thatched-roofed, mud-walled dwellings in clusters of three or four appeared along the roadside every mile or so. Johnny estimated the size of these homes to be only slightly bigger than his family's kitchen back at the farm.

After a period of time the bus eased to a stop when it came upon a fairly wide river. Ahead was a cantilever bridge. It was wide enough and substantial enough to accommodate a modern Army tank. On both sides of the entrance onto the bridge were M-60 machine guns. They stood mounted on their tripods, each nestled in a sandbagged bunker. A few feet away from one of the bunkers was a small concrete hut with smoke eking out of a sheet metal chimney. A number of five gallon diesel cans were stacked next to the hut. The two soldiers manning the machine guns and the two soldiers guarding a swinging gate that blocked entrance onto the bridge were American. They each wore the helmet and arm band of the military police. As the bus came to a stop for inspection, Johnny could read the small sign next to one of the bunkers.

FREEDOM BRIDGE
ARMY CORP OF ENGINEERS, 1954
MANNED BY THE 43RD MILITARY POLICE
ALWAYS ON ALERT

After a brief questioning, the bus was allowed to pass onto the bridge. At the north end of the structure the same installations were in place.

The countryside changed abruptly once north of the river. There was no sign of people. There were no rice paddies. The land south of the river was denuded of trees and brush. Here many small trees were evident.

The road off the bridge soon ended at a T. The bus turned right and within five minutes it turned into camp headquarters of the 2nd Brigade, 1st Cavalry Division. Unlike the compounds south of the river, no barbed wire fencing, no fencing at all, surrounded the camp.

The men emptied out from the bus and fell into formation, their duffel bags at their sides. Ten minutes later they were called to attention and then to parade rest as a bird colonel came out of the headquarters hut and mounted a small reviewing stand.

"Gentlemen, welcome to sector A, home of the 2nd Brigade of the 1st Cavalry Division. Welcome to Freedom's Frontier.

"When you crossed that bridge over the Imjim River you entered into a special place. No civilians live here. Approximately three hundred yards to the north of us is the southern boundary of the Demilitarized Zone—the DMZ. The zone is three miles wide and runs across the width of the Korean peninsula. The first mile and a half belong to Republic of Korea and, by virtue of our occupation, the United States Army, serving under authorization of the United Nations. The other mile and a half belongs to communist North Korea. Only so many personnel and so much military equipment is allowed in this zone at any given time. We perform a number of functions to ensure that the North Koreans don't cross that line and that they don't mount a buildup of any sort in the DMZ. You will learn all the details once you arrive at your unit. Just remember this. Hostilities in Korea subsided with a truce twelve years ago. It has been a fragile truce and not one without violence. Not a month goes by without an incident of some sort on the DMZ. Some of those incidents have taken place in the American sector.

"The United States military has 50,000 personnel on the Korean peninsula. It is up to 2,100 of us to keep watch here on the DMZ. Second Brigade has nine camps along our eighteen miles of responsibility, including five miles on our right flank that a battalion from the Seventh Infantry Division occupies. Each of you will be assigned to one of our brigade camps. Gentleman, we have an enemy here that would like to see each one of us dead. I expect each one of you to perform your duties responsibly. That is all."

Johnny, and surely the others as well, were startled at the information they had just received. He immediately thought of Jenny and her concern for his well-being and safe return to her. She had been right, he thought. He realized that his thirteen months in Korea, especially here on the DMZ, was not something to be taken for granted. His old concern for his abilities, a concern embedded in his fragile lack of self-confidence, also began to resurface.

Three hours later Berg had been processed and taken to his camp down the road. Although he kept it to himself, he was happy that Tom Bradley was assigned to the same unit, along with four others. They were now part of Troop A, 3rd Battalion, 2nd Brigade, 1st Cavalry Division.

Later that afternoon the new arrivals were ordered to the Troop orderly room where they received more indoctrination from the Troop's executive officer, a second lieutenant.

"Gentlemen, you are now on the very cusp of the border where the free world meets communism. The physical dividing line of the struggle between good and evil, between freedom and oppression, and between godliness and atheism is now right in front of you. Unless you have grown up under a barrel you have been hearing about the cold war since you were a snot-nosed kid. Now you are at one of the places where the two ideologies geographically meet. Between 1950 and 1953, more than 39,000 American troops died on this peninsula fighting with other United Nations forces and the South Korean Army against invading communist North Korea and, eventually, against communist China. Another 92,000 Americans were wounded and more than 8,000 are still listed as missing. The fighting stopped here, on a jagged line near the 38th parallel of latitude. In the ensuing twelve years South Korean and United Nations forces, most notably the United States, have stood firm in this garden spot to contain the communists."

Everything in Korea confirmed to Johnny Berg how wonderful life was back in Wisconsin. Now he was going to truly learn and appreciate the meaning of freedom, for he was now experiencing the loss of it in two ways. One way was just as his father had said. As a soldier he would experience a loss of personal freedom in order to secure a greater freedom for his country. Secondly, he was seeing the price a people needed to pay to secure their freedom. The people of South Korea, a poor nation where most of the people struggled everyday to meet the necessities of life, had drawn a line in the sand at one of the bleakest places he could imagine. Now, for the next thirteen months, he was to be part of the force needed to maintain that freedom.

The affable Bradley was from Hattiesburg, Mississippi. He and Johnny were assigned to the same squad in the same platoon. They arose that first morning at A Troop and were soon, with the four other new replacements, marched to the supply shed. Here, they shuttled forward in line to receive winter gear — heavy overcoat, two pairs of winter gloves, two pairs of mittens, insulated rubber boots, two pile caps, two pairs of one piece long johns and six pairs of heavy woolen socks. Everything except the boots and the long johns were of the color o.d.; olive drab.

It was only early November but the temperature that morning was sixteen degrees with gray skies. Bradley was in real culture shock over the cold air. Seeking reassurance that someday it would warm up, he worked up the nerve to speak to the supply sergeant, who was behind the counter issuing the winter gear along with one of his subordinates.

"Sarge, when do you believe it's going to warm up here?"

The sergeant, a middle-aged black man of ample girth, looked across at the young man in front of him with a look of exasperation. "Son, where are you from?"

"Hattiesburg, Mississippi, Sarge. The hub city, they call us." Tom saw that designation meant nothing to the sergeant. He quickly added, "The meeting place for a number of railroad lines."

The sergeant tilted his head slightly, now with a look of amused amazement. He spoke with mock irritation.

"Son, I don't care what they claim for your hillbilly town. I'm from Chicago and I'm telling you it gets colder than a well digger's butt in this place. It's not even Thanksgiving yet and you're wanting to know when it's going to warm up? Son, allow me to educate your tender heart and virgin ears. Today is going to seem like a heat wave compared to what's coming up. Hattiesburg, Mississippi? I do believe you're going to be wishing they sent you to Vietnam. Now keep moving, you're holding up progress here."

As he moved along the line Bradley tried to get in the last word. "Yes Sergeant. But we're not hillbillies. They're up north of us. Up Tennessee, Kentucky and Missouri. Flat country where I'm from. We're deep south folk."

The sergeant kept up an irritated appearance. He yelled down the line. "Young man, the only deep you'll see around here is deep trouble."

On just his third day in country, Johnny Berg saw for himself how serious, how immediate, the South Koreans considered the threat from the north. A day patrol from Troop A had run across, and captured, three Korean civilians inside the DMZ. These civilians were searching for and collecting the scrap metal from expended artillery shells from the war. Though these Korean men were undoubtedly South Koreans who had rafted across the Imjim River under cover of darkness, they were now considered under arrest for violating South Korean law and, until proven otherwise, for being possible North Korean infiltrators.

Later that afternoon Johnny was one of four soldiers assigned to guard these men on the trip south to a South Korean Army intelligence unit. Rifles at the ready, Johnny and one other soldier sat on the bench seat in the back of a three-quarter ton pickup, with the three Koreans chained to the bench seat opposite them. Upon arrival the soldiers herded the handcuffed Koreans into a room of what Johnny thought to be a small headquarter's building. In English, one of the three South Korean officers in the room asked Johnny and his three fellow soldiers to stay a few moments.

Without a word yet spoken to any of the captors, one of the officers used his steel toed boot to kick a captive in the shin bone with great force. The helpless victim crumpled to the floor in agony. The process was repeated with the other two men.

Johnny and the other Americans were thanked and excused. As they left the building, Johnny could hear screaming and violence.

First the colonel's warning, then the lieutenant's words, and now this. Berg was aware that he was in a troubled land.

EIGHTEEN

On December 2nd, Clark Berg left for Fort Knox, Kentucky, and basic training. The increased military presence in Vietnam had led to taking both Berg sons in the Selective Service Draft. John and Gertie were grateful that their eldest son had not been sent to Vietnam. Now they would wait while Clark went through training to see where he would be sent.

The young man entered the U. S. Army with a chip on his shoulder. It was simply a continuation of the attitude he had carried for most of his young life.

The experience did not begin well. During the first week of basic training one of the other rookies, having noticed Clark's dog tags, made light of his real first name. They were in the barracks when the troublemaker popped off. "Hey, Clarence. I love it. The only other Clarence I ever heard of was Clarence Birdseye."

Clark did not waste a second as he landed a right hand to the side of the big mouth's head. They rolled around on the barracks floor, neither one of them landing serious blows. They were soon pulled apart by the other recruits as the sergeant, who was charge of quarters that evening, arrived. Clark and the other guy spent four days in what was called a minor detention cell of the Fort Knox stockade. When he got out, Clark restarted basic training. The incident seemed to mellow him out, to a degree. He had no incidents for the rest of basic training.

≠ ≠ ≠

Without the boys, Christmas at Berg Farm was quite different. Mack brought Ann home on Christmas Eve for a two-day stay. She looked forward to it immensely, but it was exhausting for her.

The tenth of January court date about the property sale to Gerald Hicks came and went with dismal results. The district judge shook his head in affinity to the Bergs but he could do nothing but award Hicks the right to buy the acreage in question. It was everyone in Stoughton and environs against Hicks from a populist standpoint, but the words written by Oscar Knudson and signed by Mack Berg, all duly attached into the Knudson deed, gave the court no alternative. Charlie Stroud asked the court for a one year window before the sale took place so that the Bergs could adjust their operation to the loss of eighty acres. The judge gave them nine and one-half months. By October 26, 1966, the Bergs would have to sell the eighty acres to Hicks. Although it now seemed hopeless, it did allow for more time to try and find something that could nullify the sale. Charlie said he would not close the door on the possibility of discovering something, but he was forthright enough with the Bergs to say that the time he devoted to such a pursuit would now be limited.

Up to this time the Bergs had been stubborn enough to refuse to talk about what they would do if they were to lose the eighty acres. Now John and Mack began to talk about how they would manage their herd with the loss of the land.

Mack's sense of pride told him that they could not get along without selling a few head.

"It takes so much acreage to take care of a herd our size. We can't lose eighty acres without making a severe dent in this operation of ours. It's been over thirty-two years since I've had to buy feed and I'm not about to do it now. John, we're going to have to downsize."

John was not so sure. He wanted to consult with the Wisconsin Dairy Farmers Association.

"Hold on, Dad. Let's see what the WDFA has got to say. They might have some new feed techniques that could help us. They're always in close contact with the U of W's Ag Research Department. Besides, let's give it a little time. It's hard to swallow that a man like Hicks can get his way. We've got to believe that somehow the right thing is going to happen."

It was the men who would make the decisions, but it was Gertie who was both the most pragmatic and, at the same time, the most optimistic member of the family. One early February day she took a break from her work around the house when the phone rang. It was her sister Alice. Neither woman had much time for idle chatter. Their conversations were always practical and to the point. But in the last few years they had set aside one time during the depths of the Wisconsin winter when they would just talk about whatever was on their minds.

"Gertie, when are you people going to get your phone system updated out there? I've been getting a busy signal for the last twenty minutes. I'll bet Ruthie Connors has been on that party line of yours." Alice laughed. "We went to private lines about three years ago. It is nice."

"Don't you say a thing against Ruthie, sister. She's one of the sweetest gals around, although she does do her share of talking. Now, how are all the Mastersons doing?"

For ten minutes Alice talked about her kids, their impending trip down to Hazel, Kentucky in the spring and the decision Glen had to make about whether to run for Milwaukee City Council next fall.

"The whole idea of politics just does not set well with me, Gertie. These people are like, I don't know, like butterflies floating around Glen, waiting for him to say yes so they can land on him and be part of the whole process. But you know Glen. He's a born showman, so I know he's interested. We'll just wait and see. How's things at the farm?"

"Awfully quiet, that's for sure. I believe 1966 is going to be a different year around here."

Gertie went on to share about these concerns with her sister, being matter of fact. She told her that based on the progress of Ann's cancer, she thought they could lose her by spring.

"Alice, the Lord's going to do what he sees best. I'm praying for her comfort and for her recovery, but regardless of what happens He's got a place in heaven waiting for her."

"Amen to that," responded Alice.

"It is different around here without the boys," said Gertie. "One day they're both here, going to school, working with John and Mack. It seems like just the next day one's in the Army and the other is working in Milwaukee. Now they're both in the Army. Keep 'em in your prayers. We don't know where Clark will wind up! I'm just glad the Lord's in charge of all this. I sure know that I'm not."

NINETEEN

"Give thanks in all circumstances, for
this is God's will for you in Christ Jesus."

I THESSALONIANS 5:18 NIV

On February 15th, Clark finished basic training. Both John and Gertie were pleased to know that he had controlled his free spirit enough to stay out of trouble. They were mildly puzzled that it appeared to take nine weeks to complete training when they knew that it should take only eight. Clark never mentioned the altercation.

He wrote to tell his parents that his AIT would be medic training at Fort Sam Houston in San Antonio, Texas. He called it a ten-week medical degree. He said he would demand to be called "Doc" when he came home on furlough in May.

Gertie was forever positive about her second born's passage into manhood.

"John, I think the Army is getting that son of ours squared away. I think you'll see some changes for the good when he gets home."

"Yeah. To borrow one of Skorpie Johnson's expressions," said John with a degree of optimism, "I think they'll put some hair on his chest."

When Gertie first read that Clark would go for medic training she was buoyed by the thought that he would be assigned to hospital work. Even if he were sent to Vietnam, he could work in a hospital away from the fighting. But she soon realized what John knew immediately, that he could wind up being assigned to a ground unit. Most medics were assigned to ground units that had potential for combat. She resigned herself not to dwell on the possibilities.

The winter days passed along. For Ann, the situation continued to be agonizingly slow and painful. Mack visited her almost every day. John or Gertie went with him on many of these days. The Gerald Hicks problem, as important as it was, had become an issue of lesser concern.

By this time there had been an increasing number of demonstrations at college campuses in protest to American involvement in Vietnam. They had little influence on John and Gertie. They were not political people. They had an inherent trust in their government; at least as far as the long-term security of the nation was concerned. When it came to the principle of government involvement in the lives of its citizens, they both felt that less was more. The hand of government should stay involved as little as possible in the people's business. Government farm subsidies not withstanding, it was the mindset of the independent American farmer.

Winter's grip along the border in Korea began to soften near the end of March. The second day of April brought a day of welcome warmth for Johnny, Tom Bradley and the others in Troop A. The temperature rose to 60 degrees. There would be more days of damp, snowy weather before spring took hold, but this day was one to be enjoyed.

The entire troop was ordered to assemble in formation at 1500 hours. The runner from the orderly room said that the "old man" was calling for the assembly. Everyone would be there except those on guard post surveillance or day patrol, two of the daylight functions inside the DMZ.

As he and Johnny hustled down to the assembly area, Bradley could hardly contain his joy about the warmth of the sun. "Yes, there is a God. I thought I'd never live to see my bones warm up again, but I think I'm going to make it. Gracious, that sun feels good. I don't care what the old man has to say, nothing can ruin this day."

Johnny just listened to his buddy and smiled. The two had come to be good friends. Bradley had accepted his friend's invitation to visit the farm someday, "but never during winter." He said he never intended to go north of Hattiesburg, except in the summer, for the rest of his life.

Tom Bradley and Johnny Berg's friendship was one that may have never developed save the close contact of young men sharing the camaraderie of the barracks. The two shared very little in common except one very comprehensive thing — a Christian upbringing. The Bradley lineage extended back to Northern Ireland and the family was certain to clarify that part of the emerald isle by referring to it as Protestant Northern Ireland to anyone who might otherwise think them to be Catholic. The Bradleys were Presbyterians.

In 1966, Hattiesburg was a city of marginal prosperity in the economically struggling state of Mississippi. But the Bradleys did reasonably well. Howard Bradley owned one of the town's two wholesale plumbing warehouses. Plumbers from in and around Hattiesburg found at Bradley's whatever they needed in the unending array of pipes, pumps, hoses, clamps, tools, adhesives, filters and fixtures that were the stock and trade of plumbers. The Bradleys were among the town's most prominent citizens.

One would think that Tom Bradley was a young man accustomed to working with his hands, having grown up around the plumbing business. To the contrary, he was much more inclined to pursue music and literature. Here he and Johnny had nothing in common.

Bradley had a full head of curly, reddish brown hair that was not uncommon to those of his Gaelic ancestry. His physique was less than impressive. He was 5-feet-11-inches tall but could only be described as a softie. Even the rigors of basic training and AIT had failed to eliminate the baby fat that described his appearance. It would be very unfair to call him obese for his weight was only moderately out of line. It was just that a lack of muscular development gave him a softie appearance. His jowls sagged slightly and the freckles that were part of his Gaelic complexion did nothing to project a strong masculine image. Here again, the two young men had little in common. Johnny was fit and humbly immersed himself in the physical discipline of the Army while Bradley found it uncomfortable, fearing the exposure of his physical inadequacies.

Despite these differences the two soldiers felt a kinship. And back at

Fort Leonard Wood, during infantry training, something happened that convinced Bradley that he could find no more sure a friend than Johnny Berg.

Someone overheard Bradley singing to himself when he thought he was out of earshot of anyone. It wasn't so much that he was singing, but what he was singing. Tom Bradley liked Broadway show tunes. Hollywood had put many of Broadway's hit musicals on the motion picture screen in the 1950s and '60s and Bradley had enjoyed the music immensely. From Oklahoma, to My Fair Lady, to South Pacific, to the King and I and all the others.

One morning, while on K.P. duty, he was singing "I've Grown Accustomed to Her Face" from My Fair Lady while peeling potatoes back in a corner of the mess hall kitchen.

An Army mess hall is a noisy place. The banging of pots and pans, the hissing of hot water hoses and the shouting and cursing of the others gave Bradley a false sense of privacy.

With his back turned toward the others, he softly, passionately and privately, or so he thought, sang the lyrics of the Lerner and Loewe tune while two others came up behind him:

"I'm very grateful she's a woman
And so easy to forget;
Rather like a habit
One can always break - and yet
I've grown accustomed to the trace
Of something in the air;
Accustomed to her face."

The two guys waited for those words to end before howling with laughter.

By that evening almost everyone in the platoon, and half the training company, was calling Tom Bradley "my fair lady," or just "fair lady." This went on for two days until just before lights out when one of those leading the charge in the kidding tried to draw John Berg into the fun.

"Hey, Berg. I guess you're pretty impressed. Your buddy being such a high class singer and all."

Johnny was sitting on the edge of his lower bunk cot, half undressed. He said nothing for a number of seconds. Then, in his unassuming way, he responded. "Guess I'm not much of an expert on music. Just glad to know I can count on Tom as a friend in the clutch."

There was silence after Berg's response. The next day the "fair lady" jabs quickly dissipated.

The old man was Troop A commanding officer 1st Lieutenant Jacob Flint. He was a wiry, rather bookish looking man in his late twenties but he had given his men no reason to doubt his leadership abilities. A troop or company sized unit should be commanded by a captain, but America was at war and promotions sometimes lagged behind the need to fill responsibilities. It had not been his practice to call for a troop assembly, having done it only once before during his tenure as troop commander.

The first sergeant brought the troop to attention and then parade rest. Flint spoke.

"Gentlemen, I wanted to speak to as many of you at one time as possible to relay some important information. At a meeting at battalion headquarters this morning the other troop commanders and I were informed that 2nd Brigade, 1st Cavalry Division will be leaving Korea sometime next month to join the rest of the 1st Cav. in South Vietnam. In the interim we will continue to perform our duties here to the high standards we have set for ourselves. That is all."

The first sergeant brought the troop to attention and present arms. Flint returned the salute, did an about face and walked away. The first sergeant brought the men to order arms and then commanded them to fall out.

That was it. In less than thirty seconds they were told they would be leaving Korea and going to Vietnam.

Everyone was a bit stunned, but none more so than Tom Bradley. He almost sank to the ground, right there in the remains of the formation.

"We have finally made it through this unbearable winter and they're going to take us away? My bones have been chattering for the last four and one-half months so that they can take us out of here right when spring is finally going to happen?"

Johnny smiled at his friend's dramatic reaction to the news. As they left the assembly area his only comment was, "No more cold weather, Tom."

In the next few days the rumor mill was in full cycle. Exactly when would we leave? Exactly where in Vietnam was the division? Are we going to be operating out of choppers? Most importantly, will our time in Korea be applied to Vietnam?

There was plenty of speculation but these young men knew by now that the Army was not going to give out any more information than necessary. Some were surprised that they were told a month in advance about the move.

Johnny decided to hold off informing his family until the move was imminent. When he told them the news he was hoping to be able to tell them that his time in Korea would be applied to his time in Vietnam. This was information he did not yet have. Berg had been in Korea a little more that four and a half months. The country had made an impression on him, on all of them. He heard someone call it a boil on the buttocks of the world. He understood the sentiment, but he would not express himself that way. He knew he had been blessed to have been born in the greatest nation on earth. He never considered scorning this less fortunate place, or the less fortunate people that lived there.

Now they were going to be sent to the hot war. He simply accepted the news as he had accepted his draft notice. While some around him showed enthusiasm for the opportunity to get into action and a few quietly exclaimed a hatred for "Johnson's war", he carried neither emotion.

"Hey, Berg. What da ya think? You ready to blow away some Viet Cong?"

It was not unusual for the others to prod Johnny for an opinion on things.

"We'll just have to do the best we can. Seems to me that these kinds of things are beyond my control."

TWENTY

Sometimes the sequence of events in the real world can be more amazing than anything the richest of imaginations can create.

Clark finished his medic training on April 22. The next day, a Saturday, his training class graduated. That night he was shuttled into San Antonio where he left at midnight for Chicago by Greyhound Bus Lines. Stopping many times at towns along the way to pick up and let off passengers, the bus traveled through the night and the next day before arriving at the Greyhound depot in Chicago Sunday evening. Clark made himself comfortable on one of the benches in the depot waiting area. He used his duffel bag as a pillow, dozing off and on, until he boarded the 6:00 A.M. bus for Madison, via Milwaukee.

On Monday morning, John Berg drove the twenty-five miles to Madison in a steady spring rain to pick up his son. He quickly took note that it was a different Clark than had left home twenty-one weeks before. He was much more accessible in conversation than John had ever known him to be. Clark asked about Elsie, his mother and his grandparents in a sincere way that was not characteristic of him. He seemed to appreciate every sight along the way as they drove back to the farm. And with a sincere interest he asked about the land sale.

"It's like we told you in the letter," said John. "It seems to be cut and dried. We were given a nine and a half month grace period to adjust our operation. By October 26th we have to sell the eighty acres. Your grandpa and I haven't decided yet what to do about the herd. We don't want to downsize but…I just don't know yet."

John paused and glanced over at his son. "I'm proud of you, Clark." There was an awkward silence for a few seconds and then he continued. "I don't just mean because you made it through your training. You had a lot going for you with your job in Milwaukee. You didn't want to go but you did."

Clark gave out with a soft umph. "I wouldn't give me too much credit, Dad. I didn't have much choice. How do they say it? 'It's either basic training or Leavenworth straining.'"

"That's a new one on me," his father responded.

"I guess you didn't need that one in World War II. Nobody was trying to run to Canada then."

It was the first time in his life that Clark ever acknowledged his father's participation in that war. He looked at his dad and changed the subject. "What do you hear from Johnny?"

"He seems to be doing alright. It's cold there. Colder than here, plus they're out in it a lot. Says it's worst at night when they're out in the field and can't move around to get the circulation going. I don't exactly know what he means by that. He said he'd explain when he got home. Maybe we'll hear from him today. We usually get a letter on Mondays."

John hesitated, then asked the question he'd been wanting to ask. "I know you must have your orders. Where are they sending you?"

"They didn't give us our orders until Thursday night. I figured I'd beat the mail home so I didn't try to write about it." Clark suppressed a smile. "Why don't we wait and I'll tell you and mom together."

When John turned the pickup into the driveway, there was Gertie, in her yellow rain slicker, her short ponytail protruding from the baseball cap that kept her head dry. She was walking back from the mailbox.

She heard the truck coming, turned and produced the biggest smile Clark had ever seen. John brought the truck to a stop and Clark opened the door. In her anxiousness to pile in with her returning son she slipped slightly as she came around the door. The mail flew out of her hands. They laughed as she clambered into the seat and hugged her second born. John went around and picked up the mail out of the mud.

It was coffee and cardamom coffee bread for the next two hours around the kitchen table. Mack kept calling his grandson Doc, wanting to know all about medic training. And they all wanted to know where Clark was being sent.

"Well, I'm not being sent to Vietnam."

His parents and grandfather showed a reserved joy at hearing this news. But inside they were ecstatic. Especially Gertie. She would have accepted the news of Clark's assignment to Vietnam with nothing more than a show of reserved disappointment. But she was a mother, and the news of where her son was not going overjoyed her.

Then Clark told them where he was being assigned. He did not want to tell them until they were all there together, but now he could say.

"It looks like Johnny and I are going to be neighbors. I'm being sent to South Korea." He let a slight grin of satisfaction show.

They were stunned for a few brief seconds. John had his chair leaning back, as usual. When he heard the news he quickly brought the chair to an upright position.

"You're going to Korea? Korea? We're going to have two sons in the same place?"

"That's it, Dad. I hope the place can handle two Bergs in the same place at the same time." With a bit of self deprecation he added, "I hope Johnny hasn't ruined the family name. I'll probably take care of that."

For a few brief moments John felt a closeness and pride that comes sparingly, even in the closest of families. It was a moment when he was reminded what a big world it was and yet the family's two young men were going to represent them in the same place. And, after his own experience in North Africa, he had a thankful heart that God's providence was going to spare his sons the horror and heartache of combat.

"I'm going to write Johnny tonight," said Clark. He spoke with an openness and with an innocent enthusiasm that had always been so unlike him. "I want to let him know we'll be neighbors."

Gertie clasped her hands together. "Oh! What's the matter with me? There's a letter in the mail today from Johnny. I'll read it for all of us."

She grabbed the mud-splattered letter off the kitchen counter and returned to the table with great enthusiasm. As she opened it she asked Clark why Johnny's return address always included the letters APO in front of San Francisco, California.

"I don't know, Mom. Guess I'll find out when I get there."

John had the answer. "All the mail heading to troops over that way has to go through the Army's post office in San Francisco. The APO just means Army Post Office." He had remembered this from twenty-three years before when his address included APO New York City.

Gertie didn't hear his words as she confidently opened the letter and read: "Dear Mom, Dad, Elsie and Grandpa. Big news here. We have been told that our brigade is being sent to Vietnam."

Her voice trailed off at the end of that sentence. She was stunned. For ten seconds she seemed to freeze and no one said a word. Staring down at the table, she pushed the letter over to John. "Why don't you read this."

John took the letter. No one said a word for another thirty seconds when he broke the silence. He read cautiously.

"Big news here. We have been told that our brigade is being sent to Vietnam. We will be joining the rest of the division, which has been there for awhile. They said we will be leaving here sometime after the first of May. We have finally worked our way out of the winter weather. I was looking forward to spring. That's the disappointing part to me. It looks like now we'll go straight to the hot weather. My friend Tom, from Mississippi, says he doesn't care what is going on in Vietnam; nothing could be worse than the cold. Ha! I don't know about that."

John stopped reading and looked up. He felt a need to say something positive. The next paragraph lent itself to that.

"The good news is this. Our time in Korea will count toward our time in Vietnam. I will have about six months in here when we move. So I will just carry on to complete my thirteen months."

John looked up again and spoke with some authority. "That is good news. He'll be home in seven months."

Mack, too, could see that Gertie needed a boost. "That is good news. And Johnny knows how to take care of himself. Seven more months. Before you know it he'll be back home."

He looked to Clark. "Well Doc, it looks like you're going to have Korea all to yourself. It's one heck of a coincidence. You coming home today; telling us that you're being sent there, and then not two seconds later this letter from Johnny. I think it's a moment that won't be forgotten soon around here."

Gertie was sitting back in her chair, arms crossed, looking straight ahead. Her eyes had taken on a glazed over look. There were some brief moments of awkward silence. The silence was not now because of the news they had just received, it was because none of them had ever seen Gertie overcome as she now was. It lasted only a few moments but they all could see her great disappointment.

Now she raised her head. She swiftly transferred her disappointment about Johnny's news to an encouragement for Clark.

"I've got two sons to be proud of; in the service of their country or not. Here at home or wherever in this wide world of ours that the Lord intends them to be."

She then immediately questioned him in an effort to keep her emotions in check. "Do you think you will be going anywhere near where Johnny has been?"

"Nope. He's in the 1st Cavalry Division. My orders say I'm being sent to the 2nd Infantry Division. So, I don't know how close that is to where Johnny is, or, that is, where he was. That is, where he will have been. But wherever I'm located, I was looking forward to the two of us getting together. Looks like we'll have to wait until we're both home for that."

TWENTY-ONE

> "For the wages of sin is death; but the gift of God is
> eternal life through Jesus Christ our Lord."
>
> ROMANS 6:23 KJV

O n May 2nd, the second brigade of the First Cavalry Division sailed
in three Navy transport ships from Inchon Harbor, Korea, for the
war in Vietnam. They traveled as a self-contained unit; men,
equipment and armaments. The voyage took three days.

Johnny had never been on the ocean before. They were under way
no more than twenty minutes and he was sick. He spent most of the
voyage curled up in his hammock or sitting on the deck of the ship with
his head hanging down between his knees. He could manage to eat only
dry toast and drink only water or plain tea. He either threw up or had
the dry heaves a number of times each day. He and the few others with
seasickness didn't care what awaited them in Vietnam. They just wanted
off those ships.

Back home, his grandmother's cancer began to establish its death
grip. By Memorial Day weekend her inability to breathe without great
effort and pain had necessitated her being taken from Vanstessen's and
admitted to the hospital in Madison.

For the second spring in a row John Berg was without the help of his
sons. By the beginning of May, Rollie Leach again started work at the
farm. And when John requested summer help from the University of
Wisconsin, he was delighted to be able to get George Wistoff again.

John and Mack decided to sell eight cows in order to deal with the
coming loss of eighty acres to Gerald Hicks. They arranged to sell four

head each to two of their neighbors. The transactions would take place at the time of the property sale.

Gertie's comment to her sister in February that 1966 would be a different year was proving to be true.

On a day in the middle of June, Skorpie Johnson picked up Mack for the drive to Madison. Over these last few months, Johnson had accompanied his friend to visit Ann about once every two weeks. Despite Mack's heavy heart, the two of them still found moments to chide each other during these trips. It was the way of two old friends who best knew how to console each other through humor.

But now Mack spoke from his heart. "I didn't think it would be this hard." He looked straight ahead while his friend drove. Johnson said nothing.

"She has never complained. But now she can't communicate and I don't have any idea how painful it must be for her."

A good minute went by before Johnson replied. "I don't doubt that Annie is in some pain, but the medicine helps a lot. I don't think she's hurting as much as we think."

He paused for a few seconds and decided to complete his thought. "You know, she's put up with you for about forty-five years and she's had to do that without any medicine at all."

Mack gave back an almost inaudible chuckle. "That she has."

A couple minutes of silence passed when Skorpie ventured another thought. He spoke in the slow, measured cadence that he and Mack had always communicated in.

"When I was twelve, my grandmother died. I remember my mother taking my brother and I into the bedroom in that old cabin of theirs. She told us that grandma was going to die. That we had to go in and see her. That it was the last time we'd get to be with her. I don't even remember what her illness was but I remember that even though her voice trembled weakly she had a clear mind. George and I both started to get tears running down our cheeks and Grandma said, 'Harold, hand me my Bible.'

"So I gave her the Bible, and I've always remembered what she said.

She said, 'Boys, I don't ever want you to be afraid of death. It's getting time for your grandma to pass away, but we are only meant to be here for a while. I'm going to heaven to be with Jesus because I've taken him as my Savior. I want to read you these words. I want you to remember them.'

"Well, she had her Bible marked at a spot so she turned right to it. I found out later that it was from Ecclesiastes. So she read, 'To everything there is a season, and a time to every purpose under heaven. A time to be born and a time to die.'"

Johnson hesitated briefly, but he had not finished his story yet.

"Then, God bless her, it took quite a bit of what little strength she had left, but she found another passage she had marked out. I'll always remember. She read, 'Verily verily I say unto you, he that heareth my word, and believeth on him that sent me, hath everlasting life, and shall not come into condemnation; but be passed from death into life.'"

Not another word was spoken by the two men the rest of the way to the hospital.

Two weeks later Ann Berg passed away. Two days of visitation at the funeral home and the funeral at First Lutheran were as heavily attended as any in Stoughton's recent past. Ann's brother Cal Hopkins and his wife were there as well as three of their four children, Ann's nieces and nephews. They lived in Chicago, Cleveland and Des Moines. The arrival of more distant relatives, four of Ann's cousins on her father's side of the family, was a real tribute to her influence. These two men and two women were the children of George Hopkins' two brothers. Ann had last seen them at the funeral of her mother in 1948.

"Mack, those were special times for us growing up with Annie." It was Lawrence Hopkins who shared his thoughts with Mack. "I don't know what it is about cousins, I guess just, as kids, you know you have that special connection. No matter where life takes us we seem to carry that bond. And the fact that Annie and you could find each other and she could have this life she's had here, well, I guess it was God's reward for the uncertainty she knew growing up."

As they were shaking hands, the man's comment struck a cord with Mack.

"You know, the older I get the more I realize that the good Lord works his plans out when and how he wants to. Ann never lost the joy of the life she had here. To be a wife, mother and grandmother was her greatest joy."

Mack, John, Gertie and Elsie took great comfort in the expressions of all those around them. Elsie especially was comforted by the esteem in which so many held her grandmother. She wanted those in her world to know how wonderful her grandma was and she experienced just that. She missed Johnny and Clark very much at this time. In a way she felt alone, because her two brothers were away in the service and it was they who knew the loss of grandma at her level.

John and Gertie did not know the military's policy regarding the death of grandparents. John had called Camp McCoy to ask whether the boys were eligible to come home for the funeral. The answer was no. For overseas personnel, emergency furlough for death in the family covered only immediate family. The Armed Forces defined immediate family as parents, siblings and children. For personnel stationed in the continental United States, emergency furlough for death of a grandparent would be granted, but not for personnel overseas.

John thought it just as well. Both boys had been well aware of the severity of their grandmother's cancer before they left. The quick trip home and the immediate return to Vietnam and Korea would probably be more of a strain than just receiving the news by mail.

John and Gertie would look forward to their permanent return.

TWENTY-TWO

After Ann's passing, Mack took up a renewed energy against the sale of the acreage. Even though he and John had resigned themselves to having to sell the eighty acres, he now became increasingly agitated. He tried to get through to Gerald Hicks a number of times but Hicks never responded to his calls. He then called DeVries Real Estate and demanded to talk to the owner, Robert DeVries. Mack read him the riot act, unfairly chastising him for "being in cahoots with a no good swindler like Gerald Hicks."

He called Charlie Stroud with no other purpose than to tell him how unhappy he was about the whole thing. Charlie was at Ann's funeral and told Gertie he would be calling them about a week prior to the time Hicks could make his offer. Now, with Mack calling, the lawyer went ahead and explained the strategy on how to handle the offer. He would rather have spoken to John about it, but here was Mack, on the phone and in no pleasant mood.

"When you receive Hicks' offer from the DeVries agency let me know immediately. If you don't like the figure, I will take the offer before the judge and he will determine how equitable it is. No doubt Hicks will low ball you. Under these circumstances, with it being a mandatory sale, the judge may have to determine what a fair price is."

Mack said he wouldn't like the offer no matter what Hicks said. But he also said he understood what Charlie meant. Speaking to Stroud seemed to be good medicine for him. He returned to a quiet resentment about the whole thing.

Mack went in to Eastside Cemetery faithfully once a week to visit his wife's grave. These trips were not maudlin for he knew full well that Ann was not in the grave, but in heaven. Each time he recalled many treasured memories and left the place with an uplifted spirit.

He had a small headstone placed at the grave. It was profound in its simplicity.

ANN BERG

1898 -1966

SHE WAS LOVED BY ALL

It was around the second week of October when Mack was visiting Ann's gravesite that he discovered a curious thing. He decided he would make this his last visit of the season and, in fact, visit only once or twice a year from now on. He had needed these visits, but now he decided it was time to let go a bit. On this afternoon he took a nostalgic walk among the grave markers, recalling old friends and family. He quietly spoke to some of them, smiling as he recalled so many things.

He came upon the Knudson gravesite.

"Well, Knuddy, we're in a fine fix now. I know you had only good intentions when you included that note in our property sale. I'm sure you didn't know that your son-in-law was going to come up with all this stuff thirty years later. It has been good acreage, Knuddy. I sure don't want to give it up but, I guess, it won't be the end of the world."

"Margaret, I know that you're planted down south somewhere, but I want you to know we are sorry to learn that your Greta passed away. I guess it's not so bad as far as you're concerned though. I mean, she's with you now. Both your girls; Greta and Maggie. Eternity is a good thing, isn't it?"

As he walked out of the cemetery Mack felt as though the world had been lifted off his shoulders. Somehow his decision to stop visiting Ann's grave so often and his walk around recalling old friends left him with a mellow feeling.

As he got back to his pickup, a strange feeling came over him. It was the Knudson gravesite. Something wasn't right, but he couldn't place what it was.

He walked back over to the graves. There was one modest ground level sandstone marker of rectangular form that served to recognize both graves. Mack read the inscriptions:

Oscar Alec Knudson	Margaret Elizabeth Meyers Knudson
Born March 12, 1875	Born Dec. 6, 1876
Died Sept. 18, 1952	Died

Margaret's date of death had never been inscribed.

Mack was almost back to the farm before the possibility dawned on him that the date of death might be missing because Margaret was still alive! Nonsense. He remembered reading about her passing in the obituaries years ago.

That evening, Mack and Gertie enjoyed a soft autumn rain as they sat on the front porch. John was in the tool barn changing the oil and filter on one of the tractors. Gertie didn't allow it to show but Mack knew her boys were on her mind. Especially Johnny. He was in harm's way. He thought it would do her good to be able to talk about it.

"Here we are sitting in comfort on this old porch of ours and my two grandsons are trudging around on the other side of the world. It might be raining where they're at, but I don't think they're able to enjoy it like we are."

Gertie grabbed the opportunity to respond. "I think we can be sure of that. At least it's not too cold yet for Clark in Korea. But I'm sure it is more than just warm for Johnny. Downright hot and humid, I'm sure. I'll bet that when they get back, sitting here on the porch like this, or any of a hundred other things, will be something they'll never take for granted."

She looked at Mack with a soft smile that conveyed optimism. "I think Clark might start appreciating things more."

Mack rocked in the swing and took his time responding. "I do think you could be right about that."

At no time during that evening did he think to mention about the Knudson gravestone.

≠ ≠ ≠

At Berg Farm, breakfast on Sunday, before heading out to church, was always extra special. The family always ate supper together, but Sunday was the only time they ate breakfast as a family. Gertie and Ann had always prepared two, sometimes three, different items. It might be oatmeal and poached eggs with toast and cardamom coffee bread, or waffles with sausage and eggs, or any number of combinations of things. Fresh fruit was always a part of it; grapefruit and oranges in season, plums and peaches in August and September, their own blueberries in July and August and their own fresh raspberries from July into early October.

Now Ann was gone and the two boys were in the Army, but Gertie carried on just the same. Sunday morning was still a breakfast feast.

Mack was just finishing his poached eggs and a Danish roll when he remembered to mention the gravestone. John was curious so after church service he, Gertie, Mack and Elsie stopped at the cemetery.

John was puzzled. "That is a little strange. I'm going to call Charlie Stroud in the morning. We'll let him know."

Mack gave a puzzled look. "You think he should know? How is that going to help anything?"

"I don't know, Dad. Charlie has always said he wants any information we can give him."

John spoke with a hint of frustration in his voice as he tried to be patient with the hopelessness suggested by his father's question. "You did say you remember that she died?"

"Sure, I remember. I've been reading those obituaries for a long time. Like I've always told you. I want to be sure my name's not in there."

The next morning, John found himself much too busy to take time out to call Charlie Stroud on something that probably did not mean a thing. They were now less than three weeks away from the sale of the property.

Both John and Mack worked all morning in the tool barn repairing a three-point hitch bracket. They came in for dinner at eleven o'clock.

Rollie Leach was already at the table.

"Chicken sandwiches, tomato soup, lemonade. If you behave yourself, oatmeal cookies for dessert," announced Gertie.

"What? No liverwurst sandwiches?" Mack playfully asked.

Rollie chimed in. "You're just too sharp for us, oh mighty Thor. Gertie figures she has to allow a little more time before she can pull another liverwurst trick on a sharp cookie like you."

Mack grunted. "Rollie, you know, I'm your boss and you should be showing me a little more respect."

"This is true Mr. B. But what fun would that be, eh? The season's almost over for me, you know. Heck, I'm not here for all the money you're paying me. Got to have a little fun with you. That and Gertie's cooking are the only things that keep me coming back."

John had gone straight to the phone. Charlie Stroud was in his office.

In a manner that was somewhat apologetic, John offered the information about the incomplete gravestone. Charlie, on the other hand, was encouraged by the information.

"You did the right thing in letting me know this. I'll follow up on it." He asked John how his sons were doing overseas. They spoke briefly in that regard before hanging up.

Charlie Stroud was disappointed that he was unable to help the Bergs. They had been faithful in paying him for the hourly work that he and his staff put toward the case. They were low maintenance clients, not constantly looking over his shoulder. He regarded them as salt of the earth people that had put their trust in him.

Now Charlie had a new thread to follow. Mack said that Margaret Knudson had been dead a number of years. Now there was a gravestone for her with no death date inscribed. The most likely thing was that Margaret was buried down south, as had been thought. Even so, it was common practice for a previously engraved headstone to be completed with the date of passing.

Charlie was able to reschedule the two appointments he had the next day. He drove over from West Allis to the Pleasant Springs Town Hall. He needed to reexamine the recorded deed of the Knudson sale. He remembered a second addendum to the deed that he had paid scant attention to when he originally examined it. It might now, just possibly, hold some significance.

When a request is made to view a deed of public record, it is common practice to require the signature of the person requesting to view. The signatures are on a page that remains a permanent part of the deed. When Charlie first signed in he remembered that Gerald Hicks was the only other signature on the page. This had been no surprise to Stroud. Hicks had come from Chicago to view the deed. It is likely that it was at this time that he confirmed the addendum showing the "family right to buy property" note.

When he arrived at the Pleasant Springs Town office, Charlie was greeted by the receptionist, Tom Evans wife, Agnes. She immediately offered him a cup of coffee.

"Yes, this is somewhat a family affair here in Pleasant Springs. A pretty low key operation." She gave out with a hardy guffaw. "I remind everyone that I'm the only full time employee here and that my husband is just a part-timer. There's just three of us, Tom, myself and our clerk, Bev Fehlsig. May I call you Charlie? We're pretty informal around here."

Agnes Evans was a robust and engaging person. By the time she retrieved the deed in question and offered the conference room for him to read in, Charlie felt right at home. The cover page of the document did indeed indicate that there was a second addendum. It was the last page of the document. It was dated January 14, 1937. This was one month and nine days after the deed had been filed. The addendum was short and to the point, although, unlike the first addendum, this was typed in legal parlance.

"If a member of the Oscar and Margaret Knudson family (hence known as the Party of the Third Part) should want to buy the acreage sold to Mack and Ann Berg (Party of the Second Part), as agreed to by the Party of the Second Part as per the hand written and signed and notarized addendum titled "Family Right to Buy Property" of which said document is also incorporated into the formal deed as an addendum, such a sale will be prohibited if either Oscar or Margaret Knudson (Party of the

First Part) indicates the desire to prohibit such a sale. The desire to prohibit such a sale by the Party of the First Part must be presented in writing with signature and notarization by the Party of the First Part or their representative. Party of the First Part must be of sound mind.

Signed on this day of January 14, 1937

Oscar Knudson

Margaret Knudson

Notarized on this day,
January 14, 1937
Thomas L. Evans
Supervisor, Pleasant Springs Town
County of Dane
State of Wisconsin
Thomas L. Evans

Charlie felt a charge of intrigue go through him. This would mean nothing if Margaret Knudson was dead, as Mack had said and everyone else had presumed. But with the gravestone showing no date of death it was something to be pursued.

The lawyer then allowed himself a quick smile. He speculated that Oscar may have been less than impressed with his young son-in-law at the time. He may have felt that he needed to have a say over whether one of his family members could buy back the eighty acres from the Bergs or the other eighty acres from the Piersons. Stroud was fairly convinced that this had been Knudson's thinking.

Charlie was anxious to visit the Knudson gravesite, but first he wanted to see Tom Evans.

"I'm expecting him any minute," said Agnes. "But you know these part-timers. Just can't depend on them."

Just at that moment Tom Evans came through the door. Although the two had met only briefly when Stroud first came in to examine the deed, Evans recognized him right away.

After a hand shake and exchange of greeting Evans immediately humored his wife.

"Did this wife of mine offer you a cup of coffee, Mr. Stroud? She's

Norwegian, you know. A little stiff on the hospitality."

Agnes retorted. "Ha and ya to you, Mr. Evans. It's a good thing you finally got here. The people of this community deserve a little service. And I think you can call him Charlie."

Back in his office, the supervisor was reflective.

"Good people out here. All of Stoughton. All of Dane County, actually. Can't hardly believe I've been doing this more than thirty years. The Bergs are great people. What's happening stinks. The date where this Hicks guy can buy the acreage is coming up, isn't it?"

"It sure is," Charlie responded. But I'm here following up a curious lead. There is an addendum to the deed that says either Oscar or Margaret Knudson could forbid the purchase by one of their family members if they saw fit. It was an addendum that you notarized."

Evans raised his eyebrows. "Yes, I saw that when Hicks made his claim on the other addendum. If only old Oscar or Margaret were here now they could put a stop to our Mr. Hicks."

"Sure. But the reason I even bring it up is that the Bergs just informed me on Monday that in the cemetery here in town, at the Knudson gravesite, Margaret Knudson's name is engraved but there is no date of death. There was either neglect in engraving her death date or," Stroud hesitated, "she's still alive. Now, Mack has always insisted that Margaret is dead. He saw her obituary. But I need to follow this up."

With his arms folded in front of him Evans leaned forward on his desk. A look of delicious curiosity crossed his face. He now leaned back in his chair.

"I don't remember her being buried up here, but then, they had no family left and the funeral, no doubt, took place down south. Have you been over to the cemetery?"

"I'm going there next."

"I'd like to go with you, if you don't mind; and then we should go to city hall to check the burial records."

"Exactly," Stroud responded.

Eastside cemetery was within the Stoughton city limits, so, after confirming for themselves the missing death date on the gravestone, the two men immediately went to city hall.

Though Stoughton was considered a small town by almost any standard, the impressive city hall was abuzz with activity in comparison to the little Pleasant Springs Town office. Evans was greeted warmly and quickly received permission for he and Stroud to investigate the town's burial records, located in a records room in the building's basement. Here burial records went back to 1852, five years after Luke Stoughton founded the community.

"Mack says that she died twelve to fifteen years ago," Stroud said.

"Yes. Here." Evans handed him the folder containing burial information from 1954 through '58. Evans took the folder from '50 through '53. Within five minutes they confirmed that there was no record indicating Margaret's death and burial anywhere.

The men expanded their search to adjacent years and still found nothing.

"I do see Oscar's burial record here in 1952," said Evans. "It indicates a double-wide plot with a double-wide ground level headstone with a pre-inscription for Margaret Elizabeth Meyers Knudson. It indicates that Margaret purchased the headstone, including the future cost of her death date inscription. There is no paperwork here stating that Margaret was buried somewhere else, and that's a requirement since she does have a headstone here."

Evans hesitated, gave out with a slight grin and looked at the lawyer. "Charlie Stroud, it looks like you have yourself a real mystery here. Unless, of course, she's listed in one of the more current folders.

"And that's not likely, is it?" Charlie's words were more a statement than a question. "I'd go to check all the folders for the following years. Just to be sure."

"Oh, and Tom. When the Knudson's retired down south, do you know where they went?"

"Yes, I do. They went down to Gulf Shores, Alabama. That Fjordland retirement place down there where all the Swedes and Norwegians go." He smiled. "I hear it's a real swinging place."

TWENTY-THREE

Late that afteroon Charlie Stroud called the Bergs from a pay phone in the Stoughton City Hall. When he spoke to Gertie, he informed her that he had some new information to give them. She insisted that he come for dinner.

"Gertie, I don't know what you call this exactly, but it's one of the most flavorful meals I've ever had. With your cooking, I don't know how these two guys of yours keep their weight in line."

Gertie was up and about. "They work pretty hard, Charlie. Burn it off, I guess. It's called a New England boiled dinner. Ann found it in a cookbook, years ago. You just throw everything into a covered pot; a small butt ham, whole potatoes, carrots, onion. No salt necessary. You fill the pot about a third of the way with water and you let it cook on the stove top on low heat. I like it because the cleanup is easy." She slid a large square of her homemade gingerbread cake with a mountain of Berg whipped cream under the lawyer's chin.

"Oh, my! You may have to roll me away from this table."

John was emphatic. "You're going to finish that gingerbread before we talk business. Now, eat up."

After dessert Gertie served more hot coffee. Stroud was a satisfied man. "I may go into a stupor before I can bring you up to date."

They all laughed a little. Over the last eleven months, despite the lack of progress against Gerald Hicks, the Bergs and Charlie Stroud had grown close. This evening was just another example to the lawyer of how at peace with themselves this family was. He had important news to share with them yet first they shared their supper with him, never asking a single probing question. He himself was a Christian, but he knew of few people who demonstrated the Holy Spirit in their lives as much as these folks. They seemed to have an assurance about things that impressed him greatly.

"I did some digging today." He went on to tell them about the deed addendum and the lack of a burial record for Margaret Knudson. He told them that Tom Evans knew right where the couple had retired to. "I'll make a phone call in the morning and see if they know anything about Margaret Knudson."

Both John and Gertie reacted with measured enthusiasm. "Do you mean to say that if you can find Mrs. Knudson, that if she is still alive, she could deny Hicks the right to buy the acreage?" asked John.

"That undated gravestone and no paper work in the town records tells us there's a chance she's still alive, and that second addendum to the deed tells us that, if she's of sound mind, she can put a stop to Mr. Hicks. Yes, John, that remains a possibility."

Mack was skeptical; emphatically skeptical. "All this is fine, but like I said before, Margaret is dead. I read her obituary notice in the paper."

There were a few seconds of silence before Charlie responded. He could have given out with a cliché comment, something like, "We have no reason to doubt your claim, but…" However, he knew these people deserved his forthright response. He looked Mack straight in the eye.

"We have an undated gravestone in Eastside Cemetery and no record of burial there or at any other location. I would not be doing my job if I did not pursue this. Now, having said that, we have to realize that she's most likely planted down south somewhere. Tom Evans tells me that this sort of thing happens occasionally. One spouse is brought back for burial then, later on, for one reason or another, when the other one dies the body is not brought back. It's a sorry state that the wishes of the deceased are not granted, but it does happen."

"Heck, it's not likely, but she could have been the one to say, no, I'd rather be buried down south than back in Wisconsin."

"And then there's this. If she is alive she may be in no condition to understand and sign a document forbidding Hicks from purchasing your acreage. We have to realize she'd be into her nineties by now. Alabama law is most likely similar to ours. As such, a notary witness is required to be present at the signing to be sure the individual is of sound enough mind to be able to understand what she is signing."

"No doubt she wouldn't remember about the addendum to the deed," said John. "Or even that there is a deed. She may not even remember that she lived in Wisconsin."

Stroud reinforced the cautionary thought. "Besides, we're assuming a lot here. Old Margaret, if she is alive, may think that Gerald Hicks is as fine as warm bread pudding after a cold supper. She may want her son-in-law to have every opportunity. Hard to believe, but it's possible."

The next morning Stroud called the Fjordland Retirement Community in Gulf Shores, Alabama. He asked if Margaret Knudson was a resident there. If necessary, he was prepared to identify himself. It was not.

The bright voice of the receptionist was straight forward and emphatic.

"She certainly is. Margaret Knudson, bless her heart, has been a resident here longer than anyone else. Would you like to speak with her?"

The revelation was so immediate that Charlie came close to stumbling over his own thoughts.

"Uh. Oh, no, no. I have something I need to discuss with her. I'll stop by."

"Thank you, sir. Just a reminder that our visiting hours are from 10 A.M. until 7 P.M., with special arrangements for any earlier or later time. Thank you."

Charlie hung up the phone and tingled with excitement. Just like that he had confirmation that Margaret Knudson was alive and, apparently, well, in Alabama.

He called the Bergs immediately. Gertie was upstairs putting clean sheets on one of the beds. She made a mad dash down the stairs to the kitchen, picking up the phone on the fifth ring.

Stroud spoke plainly. He made no attempt to contain his excitement.

"Gertie, she is alive, and apparently well. She is living in the same retirement community where she and Oscar went thirty years ago!"

"Oh, Charlie! That's wonderful news. That's just wonderful. I can hardly wait to tell the men. I'm taking dinner out to them at eleven o'clock. They'll be very pleased."

Charlie was emphatic. "Gertie, you need to tell Mack that it's vital that he go down there with me. I should have mentioned this last night. When we explain this thing to Margaret she has to be reassured about all this. If Mack is there with me, we have a chance of getting her to understand what this is all about."

"I'll make sure he understands that." Gertie felt another surge of excitement.

"Charlie, taking a trip like this, such an important trip, will be wonderful medicine for him."

A short while later, Gertie was setting up dinner off the tailgate of the Ford station wagon. The location was under a line of red oaks that separated two forty-acre sections at the southwest corner of the farm. Over the years, the trees had become fairly large so that the shade they rendered inhibited nearby growth in the field. Mack and John had talked for the last five years about the need to cut them down. But it was a big job. More than that, Mack had a soft spot in his heart for these oaks, though he would never admit to it. He had watched them grow since the day he helped his father transplant them there as saplings in the spring of 1913. This was a spot that the Bergs had rendezvoused at many times during field operations in order to break noontime bread.

Gertie held her tongue until John, Mack and Rollie grabbed their sandwiches and the coffee that had replaced the ice tea and lemonade of the summer months. The Bergs did not always say grace at these on site meals, but today was going to be special.

"The three of you can just hold on a second before you eat. I want to say grace today."

"Our Lord, you have blest us beyond measure. You have blest us far more than we can begin to appreciate. We have always enjoyed a wonderful life, and even when the occasional tough time comes along we have been fortified by Your presence in our lives to help us through the circumstances. And now, on a day of great excitement like this, we pray that we will have the humility to accept hopeful news with a calm nature and a thankful heart. We bring this prayer to You with confidence because we come to you in the name of our Lord and our Savior, Jesus Christ. Amen."

There was a cautious silence. John peered at his wife, then spoke guardedly.

"Thank you, Gertie." A few more seconds of silence ensued before he asked, "You mentioned about some great excitement. Is there something that we ought to know about?"

"There just might be."

She held back a smile and could not help being a little smug. She then put her hands on her hips and beamed with excitement. "Charlie called this morning. Margaret Knudson is alive! In Alabama!"

John, Mack and Rollie stopped chewing at the same time. John, completely on instinct, closed his eyes for a split second and quietly said, "Thank you, Lord."

For a brief moment the news was a blow to Mack's pride. "Alive? How can that be? No. No. All this time and I've been wrong?"

He then quickly put aside his pride as he realized the significance of this bit of good news.

"What in the Sam Hill! Just like that? He already found out? Why, like Skorpie would say, 'That's better than a check from home. Ha!'"

"She is down there at that retirement home—Fjordland." Gertie spoke emphatically to her father-in-law. "And you, Mr. Berg, need to be prepared to make a trip down there."

She stopped short, letting the statement sink in.

Mack set his rugged jaw and a questioning look came over his face.

"I've heard of that Fjordland place. Inga has a friend from Chicago who's down there. But what do you mean, I need to get ready to make a trip down there? This is great news, but what do you mean, I need to make a trip?"

"Charlie says that if we want to have Margaret sign something that puts an end to Gerald Hicks, you have to go down there with him. And he's right. She won't know him from Adam. Charlie says that if she's clear enough of mind at all to understand what's going on, she'll need to see you and understand that this is something important to you."

Mack's face went from curiosity to concern. "Well,…well." His eyes drifted to the ground. "The work we've got right now. I can't leave the farm right now. Look at the work we've got."

John was not surprised by his father's reaction. In a lifetime of working this land and caring for this dairy herd, Mack had never been away during the spring, summer or fall for more than a few hours at any given time. He immediately dispelled his father's uncertainty.

"Dad, we just heard some of the best news we've had in some time. We're going to get along just fine while you go down there and put an end to Gerald Hicks. Going down there is going to be the most important work you can possibly do for the farm now. The fields are in good shape. We've got no equipment problems. You need to go with Charlie."

Rollie didn't mind putting in his two cents worth at a moment of such good news.

"That's for sure, Mr. B. It'll be tougher than wind sprints on the first day of training camp, but John will get along. And I'll get down here if he needs me."

The hockey analogy may have not registered with any of them, but that didn't stop Rollie.

"It's like when you Vikings used to take those boats of yours and sail over to England. You know; all that pillage and rape stuff, eh. Only now you're just going south to get a signature. Piece of cake."

Mack couldn't help but crack a smile at Rollie's humor. He said nothing immediately but, in due time, he responded.

"Yeah, I guess your right. I'm just a little stuck in my ways." He lifted his gaze to the others and his eyes lit up. He was realizing what a great opportunity was in front of them.

"Ha! I do believe we can put Mr. Hicks in his place. Ha! This is going to be great stuff!"

≠ ≠ ≠

Two days later, Mack and Charlie were on their way to see Margaret Knudson. It was essential for them to obtain her signature without undue delay. The sale to Hicks was only eight days away.

The two men journeyed south in the Bergs' sedan, a 1962 Dodge Duster. They were able to travel much of the way on the fairly new I-65 interstate highway, stopping overnight in Nashville, Tennessee. It was the first time Mack had done any long distance travel on the interstate system. It rained the last two hours before reaching the city and now it poured buckets as they secured a motel. Mack began to relax. He began to realize how little his own world extended beyond Berg Farm.

"What's so funny?" Charlie was wondering what had Mack smiling as they brought in their bags.

"Oh, I guess I haven't been out and around much. It's just the way the clerk talked at the front desk. 'Yawl and I reckon.' Just different words than we're used to up north. Where's this place we're going to, again? Golf Shores?"

"That's it. But it's really Gulf Shores."

Mack turned and gave the lawyer an odd look. "Isn't that what I said; Golf Shores?"

"Well, yeah, but it's not golf, as in the game of golf, it's gulf, as in the Gulf of Mexico."

Mack was insistent. "Yes. I know. Golf Shores. Not that crazy game they play. Chasing a little white ball all over the countryside. Never could see the point to that game. Waste of good farmland, if you ask me. How much farther tomorrow, until we get there?"

The lawyer did his best to control a smile. He felt at home and relaxed with Mack, but he in no way wanted to offend him.

"We're half way down there. Before we get to Mobile, we cut off and head straight down along the water to Gulf Shores. It's right at the bottom of the state. Right on the water."

TWENTY-FOUR

The day after the revelation that Margaret Knudson was still alive, Gertie made her occasional check of the big farm calendar that was mounted at the head of the basement stairs. She liked to see the progress of time in regards to the return of her sons.

With his time in Korea applied to Vietnam, she was reassured that Johnny had only six weeks to go. Clark had arrived in Korea on May 14 and still had a long way to go. In either case the revelation that Margaret Knudson was alive and could possibly short circuit Gerald Hicks' plans had buoyed her with optimism about the safe return of her sons.

Clark had written home and informed them that in a move of logistical inefficiency all four hundred men in his training brigade from Fort Sam Houston, although trained to be medics, had been reassigned to the infantry. What he did not tell them was that, in a bit of irony, his 2nd Division brigade had been brought up to the DMZ to replace his brother's 1st Cavalry brigade. He just felt that his parents had enough to be concerned about with Johnny in Vietnam.

Clark's company's camp was just to the west of the camp that his brother had been at. Home was now a group of corrugated metal huts on a gradual hillside. In front of them lay the DMZ and North Korea. At their backs, on the other side of the hill and down the steep embankment, was the Imjim River. The place was called Camp Johnson, named posthumously for a Korean War Medal of Honor winner.

Johnny had given his impressions in the letters he wrote home from Korea, but Clark had been in Milwaukee, in his own world. He had seen only one letter from his brother. He had not paid much attention to it, reading it only as a courtesy to his mother. Now he was seeing for himself what he had ignored from his brother's written words.

On just his second day in camp, Clark was part of a four-man detail that traveled south to another camp to pick up some heavy-duty equipment. From the back of the two and a half ton truck that he and the others rode in, Clark saw the intensive physical labor of those working the rice paddies. When he saw one man, walking along briskly, tipping two buckets of sludge like material that hung from a wooden yoke across his shoulders, he questioned the soldier next to him.

"What's going on with that guy?"

"I thought you said you were from Wisconsin, man. That's the Korean version of fertilization. And you can bet it's not likely to be some animal manure. Beyond a few plow oxen you're not likely to find any farm animals over here. They save their own logs over here, man! Not exactly a John Deere operation."

Clark was also awakened to his own narrow inadequacies while on his first assignment to guard post detail.

The battalion had responsibility for four guard posts along the demarcation line with North Korea, deep within the demilitarized zone. A guard post, located on a prominent hilltop that had been denuded of vegetation, was about twice the size of a baseball diamond. It was surrounded by a chain link fence and concertina barbed wire. Two men inside a wood frame hut, manned with binoculars, scopes, maps and descriptions of Russian-made vehicles and equipment, watched and reported back to battalion headquarters any suspicious movement they observed on the North Korean side of the border. A narrow five-foot deep trench snaked around the hilltop, connecting the observation hut to a widened out, sandbagged sleeping and eating area for the six other men, who rotated guard duty and routine maintenance from the trench. Guard post duty consisted of a twenty-four hour cycle.

"Where yawl from, Berg?"

Clark had already determined that Ike Spencer, a kid from somewhere in Arkansas, was a backward hillbilly that he in no way planned to align himself with. He answered Spencer, but though he would spend the next twenty-four hours with him on this hilltop he made a conscious effort to distance himself from any sort of friendship.

It rained during the day. That night the humid spring air was ripe for mosquito activity.

"I've never in my life seen mosquitos like this. This repellent is strong enough to take my skin off, but these things are the size of birds." Clark's frustration had him lacing his comments with oaths. He and Spencer, having just been relieved from guard duty, were sitting in the sleeping area.

"I reckon this is about as bad as I've ever seen when it comes to mosquitos," replied Spencer. "But... I reckon we can make it through until daylight."

In the dim light provided by the kerosene lantern Clark could see that Spencer's face was swollen with bites, just as his was. Yet the hillbilly kept his misery to himself while Clark continued to whine and come close to panicking.

In the next couple of days, back at Camp Johnson, Clark came to realize that Spencer had shown a great deal of maturity on the guard post. It was a maturity that Clark found greatly lacking in himself.

By October, the bite of the autumn morning warned of the bitterness of the Korean winter that lay ahead. By this time, Clark hoped he had gained enough grit to exchange mosquitos for the numbing temperatures of the coming Manchurian clipper.

In Vietnam, Johnny's First Cavalry unit operated outside of Bien Hoa, a city only twenty-five miles north of Saigon. Because the division was so mobile — helicopters and armored personnel carriers — they had a large range and were often used to help other units that needed assistance. Johnny had seen fighting a few times. Twice the troop had the harrowing experience of close-in combat. He knew he would never forget it and he decided it was something that he would never want to talk about.

His gift of calm served him well on a number of occasions, but none more so than on an afternoon in August.

His platoon had engaged the enemy along the edge of a woods when the man just ahead of Johnny was struck in the neck by a bullet. Fortunately it was a glancing strike, yet the impact on the stricken blood vessel was so immediate that Johnny saw blood squirt twenty feet. He immediately crawled forward and applied one of the sterile bandage pads that every soldier carried. Within less than a minute, that pad was soaked with blood as the wounded man heaved in pain and panic. Amid shouts by others for the platoon's medic, Johnny had the wherewithal to find and apply the wounded soldier's bandage pad. Again, that bandage quickly became a sopping, useless mess. By now another soldier had crawled to Berg's assistance and, at Johnny's instruction, continued to keep pressure on the wound with his bandage. Johnny Berg stripped off his equipment and fatigue shirt. He took off his undershirt and rapped it as tightly as he safely could around the wounded soldier's neck. This slowed the blood flow enough to buy some time. As the medic approached three minutes later, the shirtless Berg was so smeared with blood that the medic's initial impression was that it was Berg who was wounded.

The stricken soldier eventually survived.

The two brothers exchanged letters about once every three weeks. Johnny would say that the incessant heat and humidity were not good, but there was a certain beauty about such a tropical place. He wrote about the good things back home. How he missed the farm. How he missed the Wisconsin countryside and the four seasons. How time was so rapidly changing things. Grandma now passed away. The two of them gone. How they might lose the eighty acres. And Elsie growing up. She would be out of high school and probably into college before they got home. That is, if Mom and Dad could come up with the money to help her go to college.

He wrote about Jenny. He told Clark about how great she was and about how they planned to get married when he finished his time in the Army. How the two of them looked forward to carrying on the work of the farm.

He encouraged Clark. He told him how there was a law that said employers had to take back service men when they returned to civilian life. Not that he would need the law to get back his job. He heard from Mom that he had been doing a fine job at the radio station. And he told him that somehow, some way, their experience in the Army was going to help them. He thought the experience would help Clark in his career at WWMR. He would probably be able to stare down Uncle Frank when he got back. No more intimidation! Ha!

As Clark read these things one afternoon, one of the others could see the amused look on his face.

"What gives, man. Good news from back home?"

"No. No, it's my brother. Can't hardly get a word out of him back home. So quiet it's frustrating just to be around him. Now here he is in Vietnam, writing to me like some kind of motor mouth. At least by his standards a motor mouth. Except for our farm ole Johnny has never shown a vision about anything and yet he gets a pen and paper in his hand and all of a sudden he's a major deep thinker."

Clark thought to himself for a moment before sharing more.

"I guess I've been a little tough on him over the years for being square around the edges, but, for sure, he does have some certainty about what he wants when he gets home. Gonna marry his girl, work the farm. He's always been that way. Always figured that no matter what booby traps are out there things are going to work out just fine."

Clark wrote back. He was shocked at the poverty. That people lived like this, in these conditions, and he had been so unaware of it. He said he was realizing what a brat he had been for so long. He wrote that for the first time he was realizing what America had for them all in regard to freedom. Here he was on the Korean DMZ, nose to nose with communism and yet, until now, he hadn't even bothered to understand what the word communism stood for. Communal. That was the root word. A communal way of life. Nobody really owned anything. The government would supply everyone's needs if they would all just behave themselves and perform their jobs for the good of the community. One big utopia. He thought about how, under communism, the farm back home would not belong to the family, but to the government. The great pride that men like Grandpa and Dad, and now you, Johnny, had in the farm wouldn't mean anything. The motivation for personal effort and personal pride would be gone. He wrote of how these poor people in South Korea had so little, yet how fiercely they defended themselves against the communist way of life. Freedom meant everything to them, yet he had never given it a thought back home. Yes, Clark even admitted that his army time, despite how much he wanted it over, despite how tough it had been to accept the discipline and the unquestioned allegiance to orders, was going to help him in his life.

He was also careful to ask Johnny not to indicate to their parents that he was stationed on the DMZ.

A turning point for Clark occurred on his first trip to the "village." After four weeks at Camp Johnson, he was given his first overnight pass.

In this sparse land, an overnight pass meant only one thing to anyone who wanted to get away from camp. It meant an overnight at the "village." For soldiers on the DMZ the village was Munsan; pronounced *Moonsan*. It was the first settlement south of the Imjim. Amongst the little buildings that hugged the road in the village were bars and houses of prostitution. For a trifling of money, an American soldier could satisfy his urges in one of the dimly lit back rooms.

Clark wanted to get away from the isolation of Camp Johnson. He was curious, and from all he had heard from the others he could have a good time. He and two others rode the Army bus into Munsan. They entered one of the bars and they were each immediately approached by a girl. The one that latched onto Clark could have been as young as eighteen, though her occupation had aged her face markedly.

In her broken English she immediately asked him if he wanted to go to the back room for, as it was called, a "short time." Clark hesitated and she suggested he buy them a beer. It was the worst beer he had ever tasted. A far cry from Milwaukee's finest.

Within a few minutes he knew that this was not for him. He thought of home. He thought of his mother and father and the faithful relationship that they had to each other. He thought of the two sexual experiences he had in high school. They had satisfied his curiosity and his immediate urges, but afterward they had been meaningless. He had thought he would feel a sense of bravado, but in both instances he felt sheepish. Now, how much more pathetic would this be.

For two dollars he could have his way with a girl he didn't know and didn't want to know. A girl whose few English words allowed her to ply her trade.

It was embarrassing because his buddies were right there with him, but he excused himself. He walked out and caught the next Army bus back to camp.

Back home they continued to notice a change in Clark. They could see that his eyes were being opened. He apologized to them for, as he described it, "a lifetime of snotty behavior." He said that he wanted to live differently when he got home.

Gertie, the woman who always had such control over her emotions, suffered tears of joy when she read these things.

TWENTY-FIVE

"The man of integrity walks securely, but
he who takes crooked paths will be found out."

PROVERBS 10:9 NIV

Mack and Charlie arrived in Gulf Shores, Alabama, in the late after-noon. They found a motel four blocks up from the shore. It was about half the price of, as Mack called them, the "jazzy" places along the water. They would wait until the next morning to see Margaret.

Across the street from the motel was a Waffle House restaurant. For dinner Mack enjoyed two of their large waffles, eggs and plenty of cof-fee. For Charlie it was a continuous battle with his waistline. He had a bowl of what the menu called grandma's grits, plus a fruit cup and cof-fee. As they finished, Mack made an observation.

"I've got to give you credit, Charlie. You said you were on a diet, but grandma's grits and a fruit cup? For supper? I guess that's fine discipline. Or maybe it's like a friend of mine, Skorpie Johnson says: 'Your taste buds are drifting through the sewers of life.'

"Anyway, I've got to admit that I was kind of looking forward to eat-ing out a bit on this trip, just for something different, but it gets old pretty fast. I miss that home cooking."

The lawyer may not have heard the part about home cooking because he had begun to chuckle. He lowered his head, his chin on his chest. His shoulders began shaking from a soft, uncontrollable laughter that he did his best to muffle. After a full minute of this, he raised his head. He had tears in his eyes as when the funny bone is caught by sur-prise.

He started to repeat the expression he had just heard from Mack, but before he could get half way through he returned to more muted laughter. In an attempt to mask his loss of control he put his right elbow on the table and rested his forehead in his hand. Another minute passed before Charlie could take some deep breaths and regain his composure. He had gotten sufficiently watered up to where he needed to blow his nose before speaking.

Mack took it all with hardly more than a quick smile as his mind drifted to the next day's meeting with Margaret Knudson. He spoke somewhat rhetorically.

"Charlie, do you think a ninety-one year old is going to remember something that happened in 1936? Sometimes I can't remember what happened yesterday."

Charlie Stroud was still enjoying the humor. "Your taste buds are drifting through the sewers of life? That's not bad, Mack."

"Are you up for a walk down to the water, Charlie? We've been cooped up in that car for two days and my legs need a good stretching. I've never seen the ocean. It can't be as nice as Lake Michigan, but what do you say we go take a look?"

Charlie had regained some self control, but was still curious.

"Sure, Mack, but I have to ask you. Who is Skorpie Johnson? I mean, where did the name Skorpie come from? It must be a nickname."

"Oh, yeah. He's Harold Johnson. Been a friend of mine since we were kids. His mother made some of the best Swedish cardamom coffee bread you could ever want. Skorpie loved his coffee bread. He'd eat the whole loaf at one time if his mother didn't stop him."

The two men began their walk, but Charlie's question had not yet been answered.

"Okay, but I don't get why you call him Skorpie?"

"Oh. Okay. You see, when a loaf of coffee bread starts to get old and dried out you put it in the toaster and let it get good and toasted — sort of burnt. Then you slap a mountain of butter on it and eat it with plenty of coffee. Sometimes you just dunk it right in the coffee. Softens it right up. It's called a skorpa. Don't know where the name came from. Anyway, we started calling him Skorpie. The name stuck."

As Mack finished his explanation, a questioning look came to his face. "Now, with the Johnsons, I really don't know. The way Skorpie ate the stuff I don't think they ever had any of it to get old. Ha!"

The street led straight down to the water. It was lined with a blend of retail shops, restaurants, small offices and motels. There were also several groupings of three or four elegant old two- and three-story stucco homes; mansions in their day. They had been built by the wealthy from Mobile as ocean retreats from the heat of the city.

Just two blocks from the beach, the men came upon the gated entrance to a group of well kept buildings. A somewhat weathered, but still impressive looking, hand-carved sign stood next to the gate. The countries that form Scandinavia were chiseled out and painted. The words, also chiseled out, said:

WELCOME TO OUR LITTLE CORNER OF HEAVEN ON EARTH
FJORDLAND RETIREMENT COMMUNITY

"Looks like we found the place, Mack." Stroud hadn't bothered to look up the street address yet, but now they had walked up upon it. He read aloud from a small plaque next to the sign.

"This retirement facility was built by Edgar Olmstead. Mr. Olmstead was a bank financier from St. Paul, Minnesota, who, with his wife, each year enjoyed a retreat from the cold winters of the north to the sunny skies of Gulf Shores. In 1925, Mr. Olmstead brokered a financial arrangement that created this facility. Construction began in 1926. Fjordland Retirement Community officially opened in October, 1928.

"Mr. Olmstead was born in Skive, Denmark, and felt an affinity with all of Scandinavia. He named this facility for the rugged coastline of Norway."

"Yup." Mack stood there with his hands in his pockets, rocking gently back and forth. Gertie had gotten him to distance himself a bit from his work attire to make this trip, but there was no mistaking that Mack was a man from the land. He stood there in his khaki slacks and short sleeved plaid shirt. He had left home wearing a belt to please Gertie, but by now had exchanged it for his more familiar suspenders.

"Looks like this is the place. I hope Margaret can help us out tomorrow." His words drifted off as though he were talking to himself. "I hope we didn't come all this way for naught."

The next morning Mack and Charlie approached the woman at the receptionist's desk of the Fjordland Retirement Community. She received them with the same bright, friendly voice that Charlie had heard when he first telephoned the place.

"Yes, Margaret is here and I'm sure she would love to see you. She is such a dear. She hasn't got any family left to visit her, yet she is one of the shining lights at Fjordland. Always in a good mood; always doing what she can to cheer up other residents. I will have her escorted into the community room where you can meet her. Oh, and yes. You should speak to her a bit loudly and distinctly. She has hearing aids, but still has a bit of trouble."

As they waited for Margaret in the community room, both men were occupied with the same thought. Was Margaret Knudson really as well off mentally as they were being led to believe? Would she remember Mack? It had been thirty years. Would she be sharp enough to grasp the Bergs' plight and be willing to help them?

Margaret arrived presently. She was accompanied by an aide, but was managing on her own with the help of her walker. Before acknowledging her visitors, she centered herself with her back to an easy chair and eased herself down.

The aide gave a short introduction.

"Margaret, these are the men who have come to see you."

She had yet to look up, but now shifted her gaze to the aide. "Thank you, dear."

Mack and Charlie were still on their feet as Margaret shifted her gaze onto them. She offered not even a flicker of recognition, but she spoke with humorous self deprecation.

"I'm a little slow, boys. I need to sit down. These bones of mine need all the help they can get."

She looked quite amazing for a woman in her nineties. She had shrunk a little from when Mack knew her, but still maintained a frame that a woman twenty years her junior could be happy with. She wore large, fairly thick glasses through which her marvelous blue eyes showed. Her pure white hair was done in curls, and once she was situated in her chair a bright smile of greeting lit up her face.

She spoke slowly, in measured rhythm, but other than a slight tremble her voice was clear and strong. "Well, this is a pleasant surprise. I have many wonderful friends here, but it is so seldom that I can receive visitors."

The men sat down. It was Charlie who responded. "Mrs. Knudson, you don't know me, but this man here is an old friend of yours."

Margaret shifted her gaze from Charlie to Mack. She stared hopefully, but without immediate recall. But as soon as she heard his gravelly voice she showed a glimmer of recognition.

"Hello Margaret. We've come some way to see you. Do you remember me?"

Stroud had suggested to Mack that he give her an opportunity to recognize him before he introduced himself.

She raised her hand to her mouth as though trying hard to pull out the name of the man seated before her.

"Oh dear. I just…" She reached out her left hand toward him. Mack extended his arm and she grasped the back of his weathered hand with a firm grip. "Ann. Ann. How is dear, sweet Ann?"

Mack almost melted. She could not quite come up with his name, but she remembered Ann. He gently squeezed her hand.

"Ann passed away a short while ago. She's gone to be with the Lord, just like Oscar."

"Oh my, yes. How wonderful for them." She held on to Mack's hand with a determined strength as her mind searched to come up with his name.

"Oh, my. Wisconsin. How young and strong we all were. I just. I just can't…"

"It's Mack. It's me, Margaret. It's Mack Berg."

"Oh, my. Oh my goodness. Mack and Ann Berg."

Tears immediately streamed down from her eyes. She quickly glanced at Charlie Stroud as though to say, "Do you realize who this is? This is our old neighbor. This is our old friend, Mack Berg."

For the next hour and a half Margaret Knudson did an amazing job of remembering the past. She spoke of how Mack's father and mother, Gus and Ruth, had been such a help to her and Oscar after they bought their place from Oscar's uncle. She could not quite come up with the word "depression" but she spoke of how everyone struggled through the hard times between the wars; yet how fortunate they were as farm people who never lacked for food to eat. She even recalled details of Mack's wedding to "dear, sweet Ann." How the Steingirds were so pleased to see their granddaughter marry Mack. She remembered a number of the farms around them, including the Johnson and Pierson places. She remembered how special Saturday nights were. Taking their two girls into town, where they would all enjoy just walking along Main Street, being amongst the people. How much it meant to them, after the isolation of the farm all week. And then Sunday morning. They, too, were Lutheran. The four of them, being able to be there together in church.

She was well reflective.

"It is amazing how back then I just never gave a thought that those good days would ever come to an end. I just thought that those times would go on forever."

"Tell me, does Axel still have his bakery?" She turned to Charlie, speaking slowly, but quite distinctly. "When Oscar and I came down here we so missed Kronberg's. There is nothing down here like Axel Kronberg's bakery. Just a marvelous place."

"A lot of years have passed, Margaret," said Mack. "Axel died some time ago, but John, his son, has carried on the business wonderfully. Hasn't changed any of the old favorites."

Since coming to know the Bergs, Charlie had become familiar with the bakery and could honestly report his delight with the establishment.

"I agree. I've gotten to where I can't come to see the Bergs without stopping there for something. It's a wonderful place."

All of a sudden Margaret drifted off a bit, just for a second or two. Her body clock seemed to remind her that lunch time was approaching.

"Won't you both join me for lunch? It would be such a treat to show you off to my friends at the table." The thought left her fairly beaming.

At lunch Margaret went on at length about her life in Wisconsin. Though others at the large table were in different stages of mental decline, the elderly seem to have a special ability to communicate with each other. She spoke haltingly, and in a volume not always audible to everyone, but still, Mack, Charlie and everyone else were well entertained by her memories. A full hour passed when, again, her sense of routine kicked in. She repeated the thankful comment she had made when she first welcomed Mack and Charlie.

"I have so many wonderful friends here but it is so seldom I get visitors. I always take a nap after lunch. Will you come back and see me sometime?"

"That is a kind offer, Margaret," said Mack. "If you feel able right now, we want to take a minute to explain something to you. Could we go back and sit for a few minutes?"

Her face took on a serious look that indicated a concern about disrupting her routine. "Well then, we should go back to my room."

Margaret did not ask what brought Mack and his friend down to Alabama to visit her. As can happen with older people, even those doing as well as she, time and location can lose their context. She just saw them as visitors casually stopping by to see her. Returning to her room, she struggled with her walker, obviously getting tired. Once in her room, she plopped into her wheelchair. Fatigue had her staring blankly, straight ahead.

Now Mack brought up the name of Gerald Hicks.

"I want to ask you about something, Margaret. Your son-in-law, Gerald Hicks, wants to buy some of my land. Oscar and you sold your land to myself and to Bobby Pierson when you retired here to this place. Do you remember that?"

Margaret's expression took on a frown. Her fatigue seemed to fade. She paused for a number of seconds between sentences, but she made her point.

"Gerry." She shook her head negatively. "He is not a nice man. How poorly he treated our Greta. He never wanted any children. Can you imagine? He just made up his mind. Greta wanted to have children. He spent so much time away. Work, work, work. But not like on a farm, where you work so hard, but you are right there with your family. He left Greta alone so much."

She grasped Mack's hand. "Did you know my Greta died?" She stared up into his eyes. "She died a while ago. He didn't even tell me until after. He called on the telephone and told them here; after she was buried. I would have wanted to be there. Gerry never told me."

Margaret was now visibly shaken. Her fatigue came back upon her. Mack and Charlie both realized that the moment to explain the need for her signature would have to wait. They helped her out of her wheelchair and into bed. She fell off to sleep immediately.

For a few seconds Mack stood at the bedside, looking down at this woman and feeling how rapidly all the years had passed. "Life moves along quickly. Life moves along real quickly."

Charlie knew that Mack was speaking as much to himself as he was to him. He just nodded his head in agreement.

The lawyer now felt it was important to speak to Fjordland's administrator. He needed to explain the purpose of their visit and to learn if a notary or a lawyer were easily available if Mrs. Knudson was willing to sign a statement regarding the addendum.

Mrs. Betty McCallum, Fjordland's administrator, made herself very accessible.

"Yes, it's a notary that you want, Mr. Stroud. We have occasion for a notary from time to time and I should have no trouble having someone here this afternoon. You will also need a second witness. Someone here from the home who can testify later, if the need arises, that the resident was in no way coerced into signing anything. I would be happy to witness the procedure."

Betty McCallum paused, as though not sure to continue.

"It should not be my place to add a personal comment, but I must say that I am not surprised to hear that Margaret's son-in-law, Mr. Hicks, is trying to take advantage of this situation. He was less than compassionate with Margaret when her daughter died. All I mean is that he never informed her until after the funeral. Even then, he refused the opportunity to speak directly with his mother-in-law. He told me on the phone that he would send a copy of the death certificate. Margaret would not have been up to the trip to Chicago but...can you imagine? It seemed very callous not to let her know immediately about her daughter's passing."

At this point a lesser man than Mack might have jumped all over the opportunity to smear Gerald Hicks. He simply said, "Yes, we're hoping to put a stop to him."

As the two men left the building, Mack asked Charlie to hold on a second. "Could we sit on this bench for a minute?" There was something on his mind.

"Ever since you found out that Margaret Knudson was still alive I have been trying to figure out how I thought I saw her obituary all those years ago. Now I understand. It was her daughter's obituary. It was Maggie. I guess I read it and somehow thought it was Margaret. Do you know how close I was to messing up everything? Me being so sure and telling everybody that she was dead. If it hadn't been for that gravestone..."

He stared blankly ahead, shaking his head. "When I was a kid my father used to call it a brain cramp."

"That could happen to anyone, Mack. What's it been, fifteen years since the daughter died. And the same first name. You can bet that the obit listed her as Margaret, not Maggie. The important thing is we are here and hopefully she is willing to sign our document. And I'll say this. She's none to pleased with Hicks. And...she remembers the Bergs fondly."

Later that afternoon they returned to Fjordland. With Betty McCallum and a notary officer in attendance, Mack explained the entire situation to Margaret. She was now well rested. She listened attentively as Charlie Stroud read.

"I, Margaret Knudson, expressly forbid Gerald Hicks from purchasing the eighty acres of land sold by Oscar and Margaret Knudson to Mack and Ann Berg on December 5, 1936, unless Mack Berg, or a member of his family to whom said land is bequeathed, is willing to sell said land to Gerald Hicks."

"I acknowledge that my signature to this document is in direct knowledge of the addendum inclusive to the deed of sale of property to Mack and Ann Berg on December 5, 1936. This addendum was filed on January 14, 1937."

"I, Margaret Knudson, being of sound mind, do put my signature to this document on October 13th, 1966."

After reading, neither man said anything to make the document more meaningful to Margaret. They hoped she could grasp its meaning without what might come across as a condescending explanation. It was a wise decision, for Margaret Knudson had always been a woman of independent spirit. Now, even in her advanced years, she retained that spark. If she needed an explanation she would ask for it. She not only understood the document read to her, but she was amazingly perceptive.

"I am glad Oscar included this in the sale of the farm. He must have known what the passing years allowed us to understand. Gerry Hicks is not a good person. Oscar must have realized he needed to have the last say." She looked at Charlie Stroud and her eyes danced. "Only now it is me that gets the last say."

She reached out to receive the paper. She was given a pen, but hesitated long enough to look over to Mack. With a subtle smile she said, "Try not to get old, Mack." She pointed to her heart. "At least we can stay young here."

Mack and Charlie stayed with Margaret for the next hour. She spoke one moment about her life in Wisconsin and the next about her life at Fjordland. In both realms, she said her life had been blest; "mightily blest," as she said the pastor used to say.

As they sat there with Margaret Knudson, Charlie Stroud knew again that his experience with this case was more than just academic. These were special people. He had come down to Alabama with a friend as well as a client, hoping to acquire a signature from an elderly woman from Mack and Ann Berg's past. He was about to leave with a great deal of admiration for this woman, who was a shining example of optimism and thankfulness in the closing years of her life.

As the men departed, Mack had a question. "Margaret, did you and Oscar ever make that visit to Norway? I remember now. It was one of the things you wanted to do when you retired."

"Oh, my goodness! Yes. That was something we wanted dearly to do."

She thought for a brief second. "We waited too long. Oscar started feeling bad and it just seemed to go on for years. Before we knew it we were unable to go."

She struggled to put another thought together. She looked at Mack with a look of mischief in her eye and spoke with good humor.

"We have happy hour here. I think the closest I ever got to Norway was a bottle of that Finlandia Vodka."

The three of them shared a good laugh.

TWENTY-SIX

"I sought the Lord, and he answered me, and
delivered me from all my fears."

PSALMS 34:4 KJV

Mack and Charlie were excited that evening. They had Margaret
Knudson's signature in hand. They would leave for home first
thing in the morning, but tonight Mack insisted that they cele-
brate. He wanted to buy dinner for his lawyer. He said it was going to be
someplace fancier than the Waffle House. Right down on Ocean Shore
Drive they found a Howard Johnson's nestled amongst the elegant high
rise hotels.

"No grandma's grits for you tonight," he told Stroud. They both
enjoyed a straight from the Gulf of Mexico shrimp dinner.

The next morning they left for Wisconsin. When they arrived in
Chicago about 2:00 P.M. on the second day, Mack found a pay phone. He
called the farm to share the good news.

"Gertie, we're in Chicago and we should be home shortly."

"Tell me, Mack Berg, did you find Margaret in good spirits? Don't you
dare keep me in suspense."

Mack gave his rumble of laughter and teased a bit. "Sure have been
missing your cooking. What's for supper tonight?"

"You know better than to ask. In fact, if you want any supper at all
you had better tell me about Margaret Knudson."

Mack gave his daughter-in-law the good news. Gertie was so
delighted that she let out a squeal; an expression uncommon to her.

"Oh, Mack! That is such good news! I can't wait to tell John. You get
home quickly and you come hungry. And you tell Charlie Stroud to come

hungry. He's not getting away from here until he has supper with us."

Gertie took out twelve links of her homemade brats from the Kelvinator's freezer compartment. It was one of John and Mack's favorite suppers. With a small amount of water she slow cooked the sausage in a covered pot with carrot slices, green beans, diced onion, salt and pepper. Enough of the juices from the sausage leeched into the water to create a light, translucent gravy full of flavorful vegetables. She served this with boiled potatoes and big slabs of her still warm homemade bread and the Bergs' fresh churned butter.

This was Rollie's last day at the farm before returning to work at the university. He, of course, eagerly joined the celebration dinner.

John used a most appropriate Bible verse in saying grace. "And we know that all things work for good to them that love God, to them that are called to his purpose."

It was a special time around the table. The good land that they cared about would remain intact. Gertie and John both thought about their boys and how much they would have liked them to be here, sharing these moments with them. They both also thought how good it was to have Charlie Stroud and Rollie Leach sharing their table. It was good to know that family could extend beyond those who were united by blood.

Dessert was simple and delicious. Homemade vanilla ice cream with homemade chocolate sauce. The ice cream was made with the Bergs' fresh cream and had real bits of vanilla in it. Charlie Stroud's dieting campaign once again lay in shambles.

"I need to get this Gerald Hicks business resolved. I can't lose any weight as long as I'm around you Berg people." Everyone laughed. "Gertie, that was most delicious."

"I'm glad you enjoyed it. Now tell us, what do you need to do to settle things with the court?"

"I'm going to present our document and my copy of Oscar's addendum to the court clerk as soon as I can get an appointment; either tomorrow or the next day. I expect to get a phone call soon after that. The judge will convene a hearing with Mack, John, myself and Mr. Hicks and his lawyers. At that time he will present Mr. Hicks with some bad news."

None of the Bergs gave a haughty response to Stroud's words. It was just not their way. Rollie, on the other hand, was willing to be smug for all of them. "Oh, I'd love to be there to see the look on that chap's face when he gets the news. And what's this? You say he couldn't even tell Mrs. Knudson when her daughter died?"

Rollie had more to say. It took him a second to work up his nerve, but he caught everyone by surprise. He spoke shyly, looking at no one, but toying with his spoon and empty ice cream bowl.

"We boys had a Sunday School teacher back in Hespeler. He was one of the hockey referees in town, too. Mr. Fraser."

Rollie cleared his throat, for these words were not easy for him to share. "We were kids, maybe thirteen, fourteen years old. Over the years I had been mad at him a few times on the ice. For sure, every kid who ever played hockey was mad at the refs from time to time. But he taught us something in Sunday School class that I always remembered. He had a Bible verse he wanted us to remember. In fact, he was wise enough to write it out on a three by five card for each of us. He told us to find a special place to keep the card so we would always have it and never forget the verse. It was Psalms 34:4. 'I sought the Lord and he answered me, and delivered me from all my fears.' I've still got that card...somewhere."

It became perfectly quiet.

The Bergs knew Rollie had a good heart. They knew him to be trustworthy and unselfish. He had never demonstrated a self serving bone in his body. But in the years they had known him they never heard him speak of any relationship with the Lord. He had never mentioned any church background. Although he had always shown a great spirit of optimism and seemed to enjoy just being alive, he never once said anything to them that confirmed to them that he might be a Christian.

Rollie continued to toy with his spoon. He declined to look at anyone around the table. He was showing a vulnerability and a shyness that was foreign to him. Rollie Leach was anything but a shy man.

"Anyway." He paused to compose himself. "Anyway, when I think of the Bergs it makes me think of that verse."

He let out a deep breath. "You folks are a God fearing group. And you have a way about you. I mean, you don't seem to get excited or pan-icky when things go wrong, eh. It's like you have this strength that car-ries you through things. Anyway, that Bible verse just reminds me of you."

A few more seconds of silence followed. Sure, they were all a bit stunned to hear these things from Rollie, but also there was a realization that in some way, over these last nine years, maybe their behavior had served as a witness to him. Charlie Stroud heard these words and knew they conveyed the very thoughts that he felt about the Bergs. It was he who broke the silence.

"I say, amen to that."

Elsie got up from her chair and walked around to Rollie. She was seventeen years old now and turning into quite an attractive young lady. The no nonsense feistiness she showed as a youngster was still a part of her being. She put an arm around Rollie's neck and kissed him on the cheek.

"I didn't know hockey players could go that deep."

Rollie's face turned red. "I'll have to go deep more often, eh!"

Five days later, Mack and John were with Charlie Stroud in court in front of Judge Theodore Stillwell.

The judge had advised Gerald Hicks' lawyers by phone of the doc-ument now in hand that prevented him from acquiring the eighty acres from the Bergs, but Hicks insisted on the hearing.

The icy cool and confident appearance that Hicks displayed seven-teen months earlier at the Pleasant Springs Town administration build-ing had vanished. He now had a look of frustration and even desperation. He broke from his practice of allowing his lawyers to do all the talking with a pathetic plea.

"Your honor, I have the foresight and initiative to offer progressive changes for this community. To forbid this sale based on a thirty year old note of an infirmed, elderly farmer is just not a practical solution to this community's future."

Judge Stillwell made the obvious response.

"Mr. Hicks, the very written documentation that you used to file your claim you now are claiming, in part, should have no bearing on this procedure. I think we can all agree, Mr. Hicks, that you cannot have it both ways."

No amount of posturing or indignation on the part of Hicks' lawyers could sway Judge Stillwell from the obvious decision. The whole farming community around Stoughton, with the exception of Midwest Agra, was gratified by the outcome of this land dispute. In his final statement on the matter, the judge couldn't help but add a dig toward Hicks before slamming down his gavel.

"Based on the signed statement from Mrs. Margaret Knudson, you are forbidden from purchasing the property in question, as per the addendum to the deed in question."

The judge folded his hands together and looked directly at Hicks. "Mr. Hicks, you live by the letter of the law and you die by the letter of the law. This case is closed."

The days immediately following the court decision were a special time. John canceled the sale of the eight cows to his two neighbors. He had spent the last few months thinking of all the adjustments the farm would have to make to the loss of the eighty acres. Now he was free from that concern.

For Mack the discovery of Margaret Knudson's undated grave marker, the trip to Gulf Shores and the eventual court decision had, indeed, been a good tonic for him. He was better able to deal with the sadness he felt from losing Ann. His inner voice now spoke to her in an uplifting way as he went about his daily work. If his mental state regarding Ann could be called daydreaming, it was daydreaming in a healthy way.

This release from grief allowed Mack's mind to better grasp other thoughts. He realized, more so than at any other time, the dangerous situation his grandson Johnny was in. He was in the service barn one morning, sharpening the blade on the bush hog, when this revelation hit home to him. He stopped what he was doing and ambled toward the house.

Gertie was outside hanging bed sheets on the clothesline. Two years previous she and Ann had bought an automatic dryer, but she still liked to hang some items, like towels and sheets, outside. It was a chilly, but blue-sky, October morning. She knew that as the sun got higher there would be plenty of warmth to dry the sheets with a freshness unmatched by the dryer.

As Mack surprised her from behind, she whirled around and put her hands on her hips. She had a clothes pin clenched in her teeth and a look on her face that said, "Now, Mack Berg, what in the world do you want?"

Some may have seen the humor in the moment, but Mack only saw the daughter-in-law he held so dear.

Gertie quickly took the clothes pin out of her mouth. "Not like you to be showing up at this time of the morning. Dinner won't be for another hour."

Mack said nothing in response to her comment, but stepped straight up to her.

"Gertie."

She maintained a puzzled look, for she had rarely heard him speak her name in such a solemn tone. He had said only one word, but it got her complete attention.

He stood there for a second or two with an apologetic look on his face. Gertie put her hand to her chest, just below her throat, in a gesture of surprise. She tried hard not to laugh in her father-in-law's face, instead managing a question.

"Well, what in the world is wrong with you?"

Mack did something that was completely out of place for him. He gave Gertie a hug.

He backed off and Gertie looked at him with wide, wondering eyes. She put her hands back on her hips. She still wanted to laugh, but did not dare.

"Why Mack Berg, what has gotten into you?"

Mack retreated a step or two. He spoke in his rumbling manner. "Can you forgive a guy who's been lost in his own thoughts?"

Gertie was at a complete loss to know what he was up to. They stood there, motionless, for a good five seconds before she responded with a frustrated sounding, "What?"

"You and John have two sons on the other side of the world. My grandsons. One of them is in the middle of a war and here I've been with all my own concerns and you've gone right along doing your best to help an old bird like me. Ann is gone and I'll probably never get used to that, but what's important now is those two young men of yours. Of ours. I've been selfish in my own thoughts. I know you probably don't think of it that way, but it's true. I have been. The most important thing in the world to me right now is the safe return of those two boys. I mean those two men."

Though Gertie had been stunned, it was only for a few seconds. Her response was firm. "Now, what's this about? Mack Berg, you've never been selfish in your own concern."

She stopped for a second to gather her thoughts.

"A big part of what goes into those boys comes from you. They are strong and I know we can be proud of their performance. We may never know what they are experiencing, but I know they are well grounded, and much of that comes from their grandfather and grandmother. Oh, I know Clark has been a handful at times, but I can see in his letters. I can see that he's growing up."

Mack took a deep breath. He knew his no nonsense daughter-in-law would always be straight with him.

Gertie folded her arms. "Now, back you go, Mack Berg. I suppose you have more work to do in the barn. And I need to get in the kitchen and put some dinner together for you and John." She spoke commandingly but was really doing her best to hold back her emotions.

With that, Mack turned to go back to his blade grinding, but he stopped short.

"What's for dinner?" It was his way of putting an end to the conversation and accepting Gertie's response.

"Leftovers. Last night's ham, escalloped potatoes and some tomato soup."

She hung her last item on the line and went into the house. In the kitchen, she worked in slow motion for several minutes as she thought about the conversation that had just transpired.

TWENTY-SEVEN

"Let your light so shine before men, that they may see
your good works, and glorify your Father which is in heaven."

MATTHEW 5:16 KJV

Young John Berg continued to find himself very much in the crosshairs of war.

Coastal Binh Dinh province was the division's designated area of responsibility, but their mobility continued to subject them to providing help in many other places. As such, officers' map reading and communication skills were severely tested. If a comfort zone could ever be achieved in Vietnam, such as knowing landmarks, understanding the vagaries of streams and rivers, learning the temperament of one village compared to the next and other essentials of warfare, such a comfort zone was most difficult to achieve for the 1st Cavalry Division.

For Troop A, 3rd Battalion, 2nd Brigade, it was no exception. Johnny Berg and his fellow soldiers found themselves in unfamiliar and dangerous situations a number of times. He continued to perform admirably.

On July 1st he had received a letter from his father telling him of the passing of his grandmother. John Sr. left most of the writing to Gertie, but when his mother died he felt a strong need to inform both of his sons himself. Johnny had prepared himself to receive this news, but he still had some difficulty with it. His initial reaction was one common to most people. He felt if that if he were home he could have made a difference. But the feeling did not last long. He had seen young men in his troop, even his own platoon, die. This proximity to death snapped him back into reality very quickly. Besides, as Tom Bradley reminded him, he had not chosen to be away from home.

Bradley and Berg's friendship only got stronger over the weeks and months. Bradley went from amazement to admiration for his friend's demeanor. Johnny never seemed to let anything faze him while they were in Korea and now, in Vietnam, it was just the same. Bradley knew that when the platoon was in a tight spot Berg was scared, just like the rest of them, but he had an ability to control his fear. He had an ability to think clearly. In their time together Bradley had yet to see his friend show any sign of panic. And he never showed an ounce of self-indulgent attitude. John Berg was the most self-effacing person he had ever known.

Each in his own way, Berg and Bradley were affable with and well liked by their fellow soldiers, even though they refrained from some of their buddies' recreational pursuits. Their common solid backgrounds helped them buttress each other. Having a friend of common scruples made it a bit easier to resist the vices that were so easily available to the American soldier.

While on K.P. duty one morning in June, Johnny was severely challenged by one of young men who saw his quiet nature as an easy target. As was customary for those on K.P., the six soldiers that had gotten the mess tent squared away after the breakfast sat down together to eat their own meal.

"So Berg, what's a guy like you do for fun back on the farm? Do they have any senoritas back there, or maybe you get your kicks squeezing those cows' teats. Hell man, all this time, in Korea or here, I haven't seen you check out the action yet."

Johnny did not like being mocked, but his soft spoken manner was allowing for him to be verbally trampled on.

Alberto Cruze sensed easy prey. He prodded Johnny again.

"Hey, man. The good thing about these women here, you don't even have to sweet talk them, man. That should be cool for you, since you don't ever open your mouth. Hey muchacho; two bucks and it's all yours, man."

Because the others liked and respected Johnny Berg, they kept their snickers to themselves. Still, Johnny felt humiliation for not knowing how to handle Cruze's verbal bullying.

"Guess I'm not much of a ladies' man, Cruze. I'll leave that up to you."

"Sure, man. Hey, I like you, Berg. I'll tell you what. You come down to Florida when we get out of this hell hole and I'll show you around; introduce you to a few ladies."

In deference to Johnny one of the others deflected the talk to another subject. But it was not an easy moment for Johnny Berg.

It was in mid-August, on a night of extreme anxiety, when Johnny Berg put into words the Christian witness that was so well demonstrated in his behavior.

At this time Troop A had, for three days, been on a First Cavalry fire base seven miles from the Bien Hoa installation. These fire bases were manned by a troop size unit, about a hundred men. Every ten to twelve days this troop unit was rotated back to Bien Hoa. From these fire base locations, patrols were sent out to probe the surrounding area.

Berg was part of a forty-man unit that was humping five miles back to the fire base in the twilight hours of one such patrol. As the two-track dirt road they were on descended to low ground they were cut off by a force of Viet Cong or North Vietnamese regulars; they knew not which. They were forced to take a defensive posture. Because of the lateness of the hour, the Americans knew they were in trouble. The enemy had learned that by forcing the Americans into a standoff at night, it was difficult, almost impossible, for helicopters to aid a unit in trouble. Such was the case here, for by the time the patrol realized it was surrounded, darkness had closed in. They called for assistance and were advised to hold their position. Helicopter gunships would arrive at daybreak and a platoon from the fire base would also be choppered in.

The men hastily dug in for the night, forming a defensive circle about 150 yards across, with the narrow, two-track road intersecting the circle.

It was a long, dark, humid, mosquito infested night of terror. Three attempts by the enemy to broach the thin line were made and beaten back.

Johnny shared a position with none other than Alberto Cruze. The foxhole they scrambled to dig was nothing more than a soupy depression in the marshy ground.

They were as different from each other as the worlds from which they came. Cruze was a kid from the Puerto Rican community in Jacksonville, Florida. As he had demonstrated in the mess hall, he was never hesitant to try and promote his own masculinity with a cynical worldly attitude. Now he was plenty scared.

As the night wore on Cruze became increasingly desperate. In his heavy accent he whispered to Johnny. "Hey, man. What the hell is with you, anyway, Mr. Cool? Yeah. Mr. Cool. Man, aren't you afraid of dying out here in the mud on the wrong side of the world? They keep saying you are like the ice man. Always cool, man. Well, Mr. Cool, you and me are maybe gonna get blown away before we see daybreak. What the hell is with you, anyway?"

Cruze mumbled some oaths to himself, becoming more panicky by the minute.

Johnny said nothing for about five minutes but he was becoming acutely aware of something. He realized that if there ever was a time when he needed to verbally express what it meant to know the Savior, that time was now. He had been taught since he was a youngster that it was his responsibility as a Christian to share his faith with others. To witness. To witness by how he lived his life and by actually sharing the Gospel—the Good News. Never had he verbally spoken of his faith. Ha! People could hardly get two words out of him on any subject. Now, here he was, realizing that if anyone ever needed to hear from him what it meant to be a Christian, it was the young man that now shared this miserable foxhole with him. He had asked, "What the hell is with you, anyway?"

Berg realized he had been brought to this time and place for a reason. He was now almost as scared about what he should say to Cruze as in facing those who were trying to kill them.

"I'm no expert on things, Cruze. All I can tell you is that the difference in me is Jesus." Johnny was watching his field of fire as he spoke.

Alberto Cruze sat low to the ground in the muddy foxhole, his helmet off, his hands pressed to the sides of his head in confusion and fear. When Berg spoke Cruze looked up and the two young men stared at each other for about ten seconds.

Cruze spoke with not only a frightened, but also a confused tone in his voice.

"What the hell you mean, man?"

Johnny pulled his thoughts together as best he could.

"All I know are two things. Whenever and wherever I leave this world, I'm going to heaven. And while I'm here in this world the Lord's given me a peace I know I wouldn't otherwise have. He's right there with me. Every step of the way. Every day. Just like the Bible says."

Rifle fire erupted briefly on the far side of the perimeter. Both men kept vigil on their field of fire until Cruze eventually flopped back down into the depression.

After a few minutes his nerves were settled enough to speak.

"The Bible? Man, the Bible. That's for the priests to read, man."

"No Cruze, that's not right. It's there for everybody. You and me. Everybody."

Cruze could only respond with a long, "Maaan."

At daybreak, helicopter gunships arrived. The enemy was severely punished and they soon withdrew. The men loaded their three dead and seven wounded into the choppers. They then humped the remaining distance to the fire base.

Berg and Cruze never spoke about these things again.

During this year of 1966, America's involvement in Vietnam continued to increase. Though he spoke mainly of home in his letters, even Johnny Berg showed a hint of frustration.

Dear Jen:

…We are doing our best to accomplish the day to day things they want us to do, but I have no real idea of how it all fits into the grand scheme of things. There is no front line here. We seem to gain an inch over here while we lose it in another direction. It's hard to know if the people here like us or hate us. The best we can hope for is to accomplish what we are supposed to do on the day at hand, even if we don't see the progress of it on the next day…

Yet, in the coming days, political movement in the "grand scheme of things" would have an effect on the Berg family that no one could have imagined.

TWENTY-EIGHT

In Korea, Clark suffered his own battles. After his initial mosquito infested experience on the guard post, he vowed to better handle the frustrations of whatever he might be confronted with. His second operational assignment was stakeout patrol. From the sound of it, this duty did not sound too bad to Clark.

"Hey Berg. You better dress warm, my man. It gets cold out there at night."

Clark was not impressed by the advice he received as he geared up alongside a more experienced buddy for what was sometimes called the ambush patrol.

"You've got to be kidding, man. It must have been 85 degrees out there today. It's nearly the middle of June."

Clark learned another lesson that night; if you're given reasonable advice—take it.

Each night, sometime after sunset, at least one patrol of from eight to twelve heavily armed men from each company was trucked out along the barrier road that ran parallel to and just outside the edge of the DMZ. The men were dropped off and they walked into the zone. The patrol leader found a location that he thought to be adequate and the men set up in a circle; low profile, facing outward. There they sat on the ground for from four to eight hours, depending on the orders they had been given. The idea was to surprise North Korean agents as they tried to enter South Korea or as they were returning north.

Five hours into this stationary patrol, Clark knew that he should have listened to the advice given him. As he sat there on the damp ground, as motionless as possible, he began to feel the effects on his body of a heart at rest. If he could just get up and walk around. He began to rub his arms with his hands. He moved his arms briskly at his sides. He even laid on his back and raised his rifle up and down as though he was doing bench presses. None of these things helped very much because his body temperature had already gone down significantly.

Throughout that night the messages of propaganda broadcast by the North Koreans from loudspeakers embedded in the mountains seemed especially loud to Clark. It seemed as though he could almost reach out and touch the speakers. Though he could not understand the words, he soon was well aware of the message. "The Americans were imperialist pigs that should be banished from Korea and all of Korea needed to be united in one mighty communal workers party."

When, in due time, the patrol finally got to their feet and walked to the road to rendezvous with the truck, Clark felt precious warmth flood throughout his body. Despite the frustration of that night he never made an issue of it. He had learned his lesson with Ike Spencer.

In his letters home, Gertie was very encouraged to see the change in her son. A letter received in late September was especially encouraging.

> *Hi Mom, Dad, Elsie and Grandpa:*
>
> *Hope everyone is doing fine. I know I've said this before, but this is a strange, strange place. When the North Koreans broadcast their hate messages from their mountain loudspeakers I'm told that on a still night the message can be heard for miles down the peninsula. They sometimes speak in English to us. They tell us that we are a bunch of colonial occupiers that are preventing the two Koreas from uniting. They say that we are a bunch of war mongers in Vietnam and that if we don't leave Korea we may be responsible for reigniting the war here.*
>
> *Sometimes, in the morning, we find propaganda leaflets scattered over the ground. Some are written in Korean, others in English. Hard to believe, but they send up hot air balloons that are timed to drop these propaganda leaflets. If it wasn't so pathetic it would be funny.*

Actually, being right here on the border, doing the surveillance activities that we do, is probably the only thing that is keeping me from climbing the walls. Special Services brings a movie and projector about once a month so that gives us something to look forward to. I've taken up reading a little. Oh, yeah! About every three months the doughnut dollies show up. These are Red Cross girls who bring doughnuts and some decent coffee for us. If I'm lucky enough to be in camp when they come I sit there with the other guys, drinking coffee, eating doughnuts and talking to and looking at American women. Ha! The Army makes sure we never get too friendly with these girls. They are always gone before night fall.

You might not be too excited to hear this, but the thing that helps me most to pass the time is playing poker. Don't worry. I learned my lesson during my first month here when I lost my whole month's pay. I've since found a nickel, dime, quarter game that I can live with.

I can't get over how different these people have to live compared to us back home. In the south they are so poor and yet they consider themselves so lucky because they are free. In North Korea they have even less and their lives are dominated by the communist regime. Everyone works for the good of the commune they live in. Nothing belongs to the individual and his family. The government controls it all.

I used to snicker at how Dad would always take time to just stare out at the farm, sometimes just stand up on the tractor and look around at what he had. I think I understand now.

When I start to get down a little about this place I think of Johnny and how I know he's got it a whole lot worse. It helps me realize this is not so bad.

Looking forward to the day I come home,
Clark

As October gave way to November, Clark could begin to imagine the unpleasantness of the coming winter. As the daylight hours grew shorter and the temperature began to slide, he was determined to mentally fortify himself for the coming winter.

On Monday, October 31, Clark spent nine hours on a daylight patrol in the DMZ. He knew this to be good duty compared to stakeout patrol or guard post. On day patrol a unit of ten men humped the empty terrain inside the DMZ, alert for any sign of North Korean infiltration. It was, as the men called it, cake duty, or getting over.

As they had been instructed, and as common sense dictated, Clark's patrol stayed off the high ridges where they could more easily be seen and they stayed out of low spots where monsoon rains could have washed still lethal land mines from the war. Clark had always cared little for history, unimpressed by even his own family's legacy of five generations on the farm; but each time he humped through this eerie land he felt as though he was walking through a dismal record of history. He could see reminders of both war and civilization, for prior to 1950 this land was occupied by people eking out a living. He and his buddies occasionally came upon rusted out equipment or weapons from the war. They stayed clear of these relics. North Korean agents were known to have booby trapped such things.

In this ghostly land, Clark saw the signs of extinct villages where the forces of nature had not yet completely removed the signs of human life. The remains of collapsed thatch-roofed domiciles that had been so undisturbed that the grass thatch still lay in place on the ground. Iron pots, primitive oxen-pulled plows, stone fences barely visible through the tangle of grass and bramble that had long ago grown up through them. As the men moved along they often trampled through tiers of extinct rice patties.

Yes, Clark knew the day patrol to be good work. The fact that it was a moving patrol, a patrol where a man could keep his heart pumping warm blood to his extremities, was all that was needed to make it good duty.

What Clark did not know was that events taking place during the previous week, events far beyond his control, were to have significant consequences on him and some of his fellow soldiers.

TWENTY-NINE

I n that summer and fall of 1966, public pressure continued to mount against the Vietnam war. In late October President Johnson traveled to Manila, the Philippines, for a conference with South Vietnamese leaders. During one of these days Johnson made an unannounced trip to Vietnam. He inspected the troops at the American installation at Cam Rahn Bay. With Vietnam Commander General William Westmoreland standing at his shoulder, he exhorted the troops to "nail the coonskin to the wall." After completion of the conference in Manila, the president traveled to South Korea where he met with President Park.

The president's excursion into Vietnam and his trip to Korea incensed the North Korean communists. The regime in Pyongyang held little influence in the worldwide court of public opinion so their vocal objections to the "American imperialist pigs" drew scant attention. They knew only one way to make an effective statement against the Americans. That statement was through violence; and they knew just how far they could push.

It was now Tuesday morning, November 1st. Clark had some maintenance duty to perform at camp that morning and then he would have the afternoon off. It was that evening that he was not looking forward to. He was assigned to go on stakeout patrol. The cool fall temperatures felt refreshing during the day, but he knew the night patrol would be bone chilling.

That night the eight man patrol met in Company B's armory and briefing hut at 2200 hours. Clark locked a magazine in his M-14 rifle, stuffed additional magazines in his belt pouches, clipped grenades on his harness straps and wedged a couple of flares inside his canteen belt. He wore long johns, fatigues, field jacket with liner, flak jacket, winter overcoat and finger access mittens. The old reliable Army pile cap kept head and ears warm. He and the other men put aside their combat boots in favor of their "Mickeys." These were rubberized, insulated boots developed during the Korean War that looked like Mickey Mouse's feet. When a soldier was moving, the insulation created a great deal of heat within the boot. As they sat on the ground soldiers learned to wiggle their toes to maintain at least some warmth.

As per usual, the briefing was conducted by the lieutenant who was on charge of quarters duty that night. On this night it was Lieutenant Randy Jones. Jones had been at B Company for two months. Amongst themselves the men had gotten to calling him Lieutenant Fuzz. He was a graduate of the Army's rugged ranger school and a competent soldier, but his idealistic attitude and his peach fuzz baby face earned him his handle.

On the map of their sector of the DMZ, Jones indicated where the drop off point would be. From there the patrol would enter the zone and make its way to an adequate spot and set up. The lieutenant reviewed the radio identification password and radio calibration was established with battalion headquarters. Berg was relieved to see that John Benton was on the patrol that night and had been designated by the patrol leader to be RTO, or radio-telephone operator. He was quiet and unassuming. He took his work seriously. He reminded Clark of his brother.

Jones then went through the litany of dos and don'ts that was standard procedure during these briefings.

"No smoking, no talking, no standing once in position, no squelch on the radio, avoid often used locations, circle formation only, rifles on safety and no early arrival at the pick up rendezvous. Don't take anything for granted out there."

He also reminded the men that it was a moonless and cloudy night. Silhouette visibility would be very poor.

Clark had heard it all before. This was his twelfth stakeout patrol. But he had learned to take the instructions and warnings seriously. On just his third patrol, there was an incident that taught him to take nothing for granted.

It was sometime past midnight when the men on Clark's part of the circle heard movement about fifty yards out from their positions. The moon was crescent that night, offering just enough light to make things eerily visible. For three minutes the men sat crouched or lay prone, frozen in their positions. When movement finally occurred again, the two soldiers next to Clark opened fire. They rattled off six rounds each before stopping. They all then immediately heard the sounds of an animal writhing in pain. Wild boars roamed this deserted land and they had just shot one. It was that three minutes of apprehension that stayed with Clark. It was enough of an experience that he never approached these patrols flippantly. Some of the others around him may be willing to compromise the patrol, but he disciplined himself not to be one of them.

It actually made him shake his head and give himself a little smile. Clark Berg, the family rebel. The one with no discipline. The good time Charlie who never thought about the consequences. Now here he was, taking his responsibilities seriously.

Jones told the men what they were most interested in hearing; the duration of the patrol. The length of the stakeout patrol varied to avoid creating a repetitive pattern. The operation could last from four to eight hours.

"Rendezvous at 0500."

The men groaned. This stakeout patrol would last for six hours.

At 2230 hours, while President Johnson slept at the Walker Hill Resort near Seoul, Clark Berg and the other seven members of the patrol were trucked out to their drop point.

Sgt. James Hensley of Swartz Creek, Michigan, was the patrol leader. Hensley was in his tenth month in Korea. He had proven himself to be a good soldier; well disciplined and unwilling to join the others when the inevitable gripe sessions took place. At twenty-three years of age he was an old man compared to many of the men in the company. Clark felt good about having a competent patrol leader.

Over time the men began to know the more convenient locations to set up for the stakeout. These were places where visibility was good, where access to and from Barrier Road was easy and where the ground was dry and protected from the wind. Two of the men on this patrol had been on a stakeout patrol just two nights before and it had been an especially cold night for the end of October. There had been a steady rain all afternoon and into the evening. A short time into the patrol, the wind had come up and the rain turned to snow.

Now it was just two nights later and those men were in no mood to freeze again.

The patrol was dropped off on the road not far from a location in the zone that they knew to be relatively comfortable. Over time the troops had come to call it the Riviera. Though the location was one that many patrols had used over the years, that is where they went. It was a mistake. They had followed a predictable pattern.

North Korean agents that were sent into the south were not average soldiers. These men were highly trained, highly motivated, politically indoctrinated career soldiers. It was these soldiers that had made an assassination attempt on South Korean President Park late that summer down in Seoul. The attempt failed. In the aftermath, a number of the assassination squad engaged in an hour long gun battle with Park's security force and South Korean soldiers before being killed. North Korean agents possessed a hatred for South Korea's democracy and the United Nations soldiers, especially the Americans, that occupied the country. They were trained to kill.

At some time after 0200 hours, an unknown number of North Korean agents attacked the eight man patrol. Surprising the American's circular formation from the rise that offered the Yanks protection from the wind, the North Koreans had the advantage of not only surprise, but an elevation that gave them a great tactical edge.

The North Koreans lobbed a number of grenades into the patrol before charging down the slope with automatic weapons firing.

Shrapnel from a grenade ripped into Clark's right leg, though in the utter surprise and fear of the moment the pain did not even register. He turned and fired his M-14 rifle toward the oncoming weapons fire of the North Koreans, terrified not only by the attackers, but by the possibility he might hit one of his own men. Amid shouts of panic and confusion by the Americans, Clark had the presence of mind to snap another twenty round magazine into his rifle after emptying the first magazine. American soldiers had always been taught the tactic of fire superiority. Clark knew this and in these few terrifying seconds began to fire again at the weapons noise and the crackle of brush under foot of the oncoming enemy. He got only two shots off before being hit in the right collar bone. He was thrown back by the impact. He convulsed in pain, giving only one scream before throwing up and then passing out in shock.

PFC Benton got off a brief message back to battalion headquarters, saying the patrol was under attack. The radio operator at battalion later testified that weapons fire could be heard during the message. The attack was brutal and cold blooded. When troops, including the battalion commander, arrived they found some of the men shot many times; as though the North Koreans stood over the bodies and continued to fire. Some corpses had also been bayoneted many times. Some had fingers cut off where the North Koreans had taken the men's rings.

Miraculously, there was one survivor.

The United States was engaged in a war in Vietnam. At the same time it was helping to hold together a thirteen-year-old truce in Korea. Now North Korea, in an effort to show its hatred for America, in an effort to show its seething resentment for the American president's visit to Vietnam and South Korea, had attacked and murdered a U.S. Army patrol.

Within a few hours, radio bulletins announced the incident. Soon newspapers, via International Press, Associated Press and Reuters, carried the story around the world.

"A few hours before President Johnson left Seoul for home today, at the end of his Asian journey, six American soldiers and one South Korean of a United Nations Command patrol were killed by North Koreans… This is undoubtedly the gravest incident in the series of clashes near the uneasy zone…it was believed to be the most brutal incident since 1953."

"…the Communists charged into the United States sector lobbing grenades, using submachine guns, finally coming to grips in a brief but savage hand to hand combat…"

"…the Communists fired forty to fifty bullets into the bodies of the dead Americans and mutilated and bayoneted the corpses."

The North Koreans had ambushed an American ambush patrol. It was tragic and embarrassing for the U.S. Army. For the Johnson administration it was infuriating and frustrating. The United States could not afford a military response in Korea. For the families of the dead it was shocking. Their husbands and sons and brothers had been sent to Korea. They were safe, away from the fighting in Vietnam; or so they thought. Now six American families were going to receive the awful news.

When the incident took place at 2:30 A.M. Wednesday morning in Korea, it was 11:30 A.M. on Tuesday at Berg Farm. John and Mack had been working diligently the last few days harvesting corn. The weather cooperated wonderfully. The corn was as dry as a bone and would store beautifully. Early that morning they worked in tandem to complete the last remaining partial section of corn. Their timing was good, for a driving rainstorm began just as they put their crop and their tractors under cover.

With the hard rain pounding heavily on the barn roof, the two men spent the remainder of the morning doing some ongoing work replacing the brakes on their old, but still reliable, Allis- Chalmers. The tractor was in semi-retirement now, used only occasionally in place of one of the Masseys.

It was now dinnertime. The wind was blowing the rain very hard as the two men came up the steps of the back porch. They left coats and muddy boots outside, under the cover of the porch overhang.

"I'm so hungry I could eat the horns off a billy goat," said Mack as he and John went directly to the kitchen table.

Gertie did not look up from the fried egg sandwiches she was preparing. "That sounds like something Skorpie Johnson would say. That man's full of more nonsense expressions than anyone I could ever hope to know."

It was John who answered. "You're right on both counts. Dad stole that one from Skorpie." He looked to his dad. "What's he call it when it's raining like this?"

Mack had a bit of an annoyed look on his face as he could again see that he would get no credit for any of Skorpie Johnson's old folk sayings. "He says it's raining pitchforks and billy goats."

"Soup and egg sandwiches," announced Gertie. "Applesauce cake if you behave yourselves." She slid the sandwiches and the steaming bowls of her homemade cream of celery soup under their chins.

John squeezed her arm as she started to walk back to the sink. "Wouldn't the boys like to be eating like this right now!"

Gertie quickly returned to her counter work, but looked over her shoulder at her husband.

"Well it won't be long for Johnny. His thirteen months will be up at the end of November. That's just four weeks." She spoke with a tone of resignation in her voice that proclaimed a certainty for his safe return. She stopped her busy hands and turned to the men.

"I know how Johnny will be when he gets home. Same old Johnny. But I know Clark will be different. I mean changed. He's grown up a lot. I know from his letters that it will all be for the good. You just watch and see."

She smiled as she turned back to her work.

At that very hour Clark was fighting for his life.

THIRTY

The Bergs' Philco radio sat atop the refrigerator. Gertie liked to catch up on the news each evening as she put the finishing touches on supper. The Bergs' television never got turned on until after supper. Such was the common practice for many families, for, though it was not necessarily verbalized, the T.V. was still considered a luxury. Its enjoyment was limited to one or two hours in the evening, and then only if there was something on worth watching.

She generally had the radio tuned to WWMR. The station's strong signal came in more than adequately from Milwaukee. After all, she had a son and a brother-in-law who worked there. At five o'clock the network newscast originating from New York came across the airwaves.

Gertie was so used to hearing the daily report on U.S. casualties and enemy body counts from Vietnam that she almost missed the broadcast's lead story.

"In Korea last night, North Korean soldiers attacked an American patrol inside the Demilitarized Zone. Seven American soldiers and one South Korean soldier attached to the American unit, which was on routine night patrol, were brutally attacked in the predawn hours. Only one of those soldiers survived the attack. In the previous thirteen years, since the fighting was halted in Korea by the uneasy armistice, nine Americans had died at the hands of the North Koreans. Only once had as many as two American soldiers died in any one incident."

"In Tokyo, Eighth Army Commander Dwight L. Beach gave this statement a short while ago. 'Last night, at approximately 0230 hours, an American patrol from the Second Infantry Division, operating in accordance with the Joint United Nations — North Korean Armistice

Agreement, was brutally, and without provocation, attacked by agents of the government of North Korea."

As soon as Gertie heard the words Second Infantry Division, her hands stopped their work. The radio had her full attention.

General Beech's statement continued. "Military commanders on the ground in South Korea have informed me that all indications show that the attack was premeditated. This was not a random encounter of U.N. Forces and North Koreans. This was a purposeful attack by specially trained North Korean agents who came across the border and attacked and murdered an American patrol performing routine surveillance in the Demilitarized Zone, well south of the demarcation line between North and South Korea. Six American soldiers and one South Korean soldier were killed in the encounter. One American soldier, though severely wounded, survived the attack. At this time that is all I have to report."

The network newscast continued.

"Reporting from the president's location at the Walker Hill Resort near Seoul, South Korea, press secretary Bill Moyers said that the president will speak to the nation over the radio and on the television upon his return to Washington tomorrow regarding what he has described as a very grave development on the Korean peninsula. The press secretary said that American, South Korean and other United Nations troops stand ready to counter efforts of aggression by North Korea."

"As always, the Pentagon will not release the names of those killed, pending notification of next of kin."

Gertie closed her eyes right there at her kitchen sink. She whispered a short prayer for the families of those lost in this attack and she prayed for Clark and the other American soldiers in Korea.

John and Mack would be in for supper in thirty minutes. She spent that time continuing to get supper ready and thinking about how her faith had taught her to understand and submit to God's perfect will. That was not always an easy thing to do. She felt a chill across her back. What if one of her sons were to die?

Gertie decided to keep the radio on while she, John, Mack and Elsie ate supper. A short recorded message from the president regarding the incident was soon played. It had been made from the runway at Kimpo Air Base before he departed Korea.

"He sure sounds tired," remarked Mack.

John let thirty seconds go by before saying anything. "They all age quickly, that's for sure. Especially one leading a highly criticized war."

The president made no mention of the specific unit that suffered the attack, saying only that it was a Second Infantry Division unit.

"Those young men, their families. What a shock this is going to be for them. I'm grateful Clark is not right on that border." Gertie looked for reassurance, while at the same time making a firm statement. "His unit is well away from the border."

Mack immediately offered the comforting thought. "Yep. Says he's a ways from the border, south of that Imjim River."

In Vietnam, Johnny heard the news at seven o'clock that morning. Along with his partner he was on perimeter guard duty during the night in a sandbagged bunker along the fence line at the First Cavalry's big Bien Hoa base.

Their replacements arrived at dawn.

"Good chow, Berg. French toast, bacon. Eggs too, if you want'um."

It was eighteen-year old Andy Becker who informed Berg about breakfast. He was a skinny wisp of a kid who had volunteered for the Army right out of high school.

Johnny gave an affirmative head shake to acknowledge the scouting report. His guard duty partner, however, had plenty to say.

"Becker, where are you from?"

Johnny gave himself a little smile as he knew Sal Bucci was going to give Becker an earful.

"Parsons, Kansas." Becker answered with an expectant look at the worldly Bucci, ready to humbly accept whatever he said.

Bucci peered directly into Becker's face.

"Do they ever feed you people out there in Parsons? No matter what the mess hall shovels on your plate you seem to think it's good. Becker, where I come from we wouldn't feed army chow to a dog. And you talk like it's the best stuff you've ever shoveled into your mouth. Do you know where I'm from, Becker?"

By now Andy Becker was staring at the ground, doing a slow burn at the humiliation being inflicted on him. His country Kansas upbringing hadn't prepared him to joust verbally with the likes of Sal Bucci. He stood there in silence.

"Queens, my friend. Queens, New York City. And my mother cooks like you wouldn't believe. I could stand here and give a list of her specialties that would make you drool like a baby."

"I'll tell you what, Becker. When we get back to the world, you come to Queens and I'll see to it that you get plenty to eat. And it won't be that hayseed chow you get out in hicksville. Plenty of Mama's good cooking and I'll take you out to eat, too. On me. Restaurants where you won't even understand what's on the menu."

Bucci stared at his prey while announcing his departure.

"Come on, Berg. Let's get out of here. We've got to get some of that good French toast before it's all gone!"

The two soldiers began to walk back to their company area. They hadn't taken but a few steps when Bucci let out with a quick laugh and a smile. "Becker. Ah! He's a good kid."

Sal Bucci was tall and muscular. He had the swarthy complexion and dark flashing eyes of his Mediterranean ancestors. Always with the dark shadow of a beard, even just an hour after a fresh shave. He was good looking by any standard and, no doubt, well experienced with girls. His black hair was cropped closely now, but back in New York it was a thick, wavy magnet for the opposite sex. He was twenty, only two years older than Becker, but much more worldly. How Bucci could run roughshod over a kid like Becker and then consider it just a bit of humor? It made Johnny realize, all the more, how different they all were.

"Hey, Berg."

Johnny wheeled around. Andy Becker's partner had caught up with them. "Thought you'd want to know. Some guys got waxed up in Korea.

DMZ. It was on the radio. I know you said your brother's there. Thought you'd want to know."

For a few seconds, Johnny stood perfectly still. He felt immediate anxiety and any interest in breakfast was gone in an instant. He made a deliberate and speedy trip to the tent that served as barracks for the platoon that he, Tom Bradley, Bucci and Becker were a part of. He needed to get to the radio that he and Bradley had bought.

The tent that the men called home had wooden floor slats that kept the mud at least partially at bay. Long extension cords running from A Troop's generator provided electricity for the dim lights and for the little radios that many of the men had. Berg and Bradley had their radio on a little lamp table that separated their two cots. It served as a link to home. The one English speaking station they could receive was Armed Forces Radio in Saigon. The music, the news from home and the letters from home program where girl friends, wives and parents back home sent song dedications to their young men were all meaningful. Back home such simple entertainment would hold little interest. But here, more than 8,000 miles from Stoughton, Wisconsin, knowing the threat of death lurked just outside the Bien Hoa compound, any time on base in the company of the radio was considered a luxury.

But now Berg was listening for the news he had just been told about. Many of the guys in his unit had arrived since the brigade left Korea. News of seven soldiers killed in Korea meant little to them. In Vietnam they were surrounded by the prospect, and sometimes the reality, of death on a daily basis. From a geo-political standpoint, those who had been stationed with Johnny in Korea surely understood the gravity of such an incident, but, other than the fact that they had served there, they had no emotional attachment. But Clark was there; right there.

Johnny Berg now found himself in a condition very foreign to him. He was in a state of worry and tension. He stuck by the radio, waiting for the hourly newscast.

"In Korea, just eight hours ago, an American patrol of the Second Infantry Division, serving under the United Nations peace keeping authority, was attacked in the Demilitarized Zone. Six American soldiers and one South Korean soldier were killed in the encounter. There was one survivor. The attack took place at approximately 0230 hours Korean time, which is two hours ahead of us in Vietnam. This was the most flagrant incident involving American troops to occur on the Korean peninsula since the truce between North and South Korea was implemented thirteen years ago. We have no further details at this time, but we have been told that a press conference detailing the incident in the DMZ will be forthcoming from either Second Division headquarters or from KMAG headquarters in Seoul sometime this morning."

Johnny thought of Clark one minute and his family back in Wisconsin the next. He could not now relax until he knew which unit had taken the hit. He knew that it was Clark's regiment, the 23rd Infantry, but needed to know that it was not Company B, 3rd Battalion. Thirty-five minutes later Tom Bradley came into the tent. He had been on a work detail most of the night. One glance and he could see the look of apprehension on his friend's face.

"What in the Sam Hill is bothering you?"

He got no response.

"I've known you for more than a year and I've never seen you with a worried look. Am I now to believe that you are actually human like the rest of us; that something is bothering you?"

When Johnny could give him only a blank expression, Bradley tried a little humor.

"Hey man, what's going on? Did one of the Holsteins die back home?"

That got a little puff of laughter out of Johnny. He went on to explain what he had heard on the news.

Bradley did an immediate mathematical analysis.

"Okay, I'm reckoning the regiment that took our place has about seven hundred line troops. So there's about a one in seven hundred chance that your brother was on that patrol. Now, I ask you, are not those pretty good odds that your brother was not involved?"

Bradley, always expressive with gestures, held out his hands, palms up, in a way of saying, "am I not right?"

But then both men immediately realized the miscalculation. "There were eight guys on the patrol, Tom. That makes the odds less than a hundred to one." Johnny threw back his shoulders. "Clark's in B Company, 3rd Battalion. If it's not them…then I'll know he's okay."

THIRTY-ONE

Harvest was in. The Bergs had come to call this day of relaxation after the last of the corn was in krumkake day. For years, Ann, and now Gertie, baked a traditional Norwegian krumkake dessert for the supper meal. It was the family's own small tradition. Krumkake day was their way of recognizing that they had met their responsibilities for another season on the farm. It was a way of thanking their God for another year of blessing on their land. And, it was a day that they slept in and allowed themselves to relax for the entire day.

So on that morning, the third of November, a Thursday, Mack assumed his Sunday routine. While John and Gertie slept and Elsie caught the bus for school, he walked out to the mailbox to retrieve the Madison State Journal. The November sun was just making its appearance on the horizon when he returned to the house and found his easy chair in the parlor. More often than not Mack would get no more than a paragraph or two read before his head tilted to one side or the other and he was softly snoring. But on this morning the headlines held his attention. The incident on the border between the two Koreas filled most of the front page. The headline story concerned the political fallout. A sidebar article addressed the nuts and bolts of the actual incident as it had been pieced together by U.S. Army authorities.

Mack Berg was not a man easily disturbed, but when he read that the Second Division soldiers killed were part of B Company, 3rd Battalion, 23rd Infantry, he was stunned. He had read all the letters that both the boys sent home and he had written to them a few times. He had an uneasy feeling that the unit mentioned looked familiar. He sat motionless for a good ten minutes.

Gertie kept both of the boys' letters in an informal pile in an out of the way corner of the kitchen counter. Neither Mack nor John asked her why she didn't file them away somewhere for safe keeping, but they both rightly suspected that just seeing them sitting there in a pile was a source of comfort for her. Besides, the kitchen had always been Gertie and Ann's domain and they knew better than to question anything that went on there.

Mack knew he had to check the return address on one of Clark's letters to see if it matched the unit mentioned in the paper. He finally stood and walked into the kitchen. He hadn't felt this much weakness in his being since the day Ann died.

Pfc Clark Berg
Co. B, 3rd Batt., 23rd Inf.
2nd Inf. Div.
APO S.F. 31 Calif.

The unit designation was exactly the same.

He stood there with his hands on the counter, leaning into it. Mack was never eloquent of tongue but he closed his eyes and prayed aloud, right there.

"Oh Lord. Keep our Clark safe, Lord. We are so blest to have those two young men. Bring them both home safely to us. I know that when we leave this world we're going straight to your heavenly kingdom, but please Lord, let these young men live to know the joy of the love of a woman and children before you take them. Amen."

Weak-kneed, Mack sunk into a kitchen chair and stared again at the newspaper to be sure he had seen the unit designation correctly. He looked back and forth, from the paper to the return address on the letter. Clark had said he was stationed well away from the border. Yet here it was in black and white. He then thought about the notification of next of kin. Could it have been accomplished yesterday? He hoped it had been accomplished yesterday. But what did he know of such things? He then gathered his thoughts and began to think pragmatically. He reckoned that the odds that Clark was on that patrol were fairly slim. But even as that thought calmed him down he decided not to mention his discovery. There was no point in giving his son or daughter-in-law an unnecessary start. He put the newspaper out of sight.

For fear of not being at home should the family receive a terrible phone call about their son in Korea, Mack almost canceled his invitation to have noontime dinner with Skorpie and Esther Johnson. As time permitted, Mack's friend had been working on a project in his basement and the two of them planned to spend the afternoon doing just that. To Mack's delight Esther had promised to make one of his favorites: meat pie. It was a specialty of Esther's that Mack and Ann had enjoyed a number of times over the years.

He did his best to ease his mind about the welfare of his grandson. He, as it is said, put it in the Lord's hands. He did not mention it to the Johnsons.

John and Gertie spent the morning in town. They strolled up and down Main Street with no particular objective in mind. This was a rare activity for Gertie and something almost unheard of for John. His visits into town consisted of church on Sunday and the occasional trip to the hardware, the implement dealer or the feed store, as the need arose. They treated themselves to lunch at the Koffee Kup restaurant. John had his eye on a chocolate milkshake to go along with his corned beef sandwich, but Gertie swayed him.

"Go ahead and have your milk shake if you want, John Berg, but I've made something for you back at the house."

He looked at his wife knowing full well that she wasn't going to give him anymore information, but he questioned her anyway.

"We're having krumkake tonight, aren't we?"

She gave him an expression of mock frustration.

"Yes, John, we are having krumkake tonight. That's no surprise. This is krumkake day. I said I have made something for you now."

John chuckled to himself but said nothing more about it. He forgot about the milkshake and settled for coffee.

They returned to the house under heavy gray clouds and high winds. Once in the kitchen, Gertie revealed one of her husband's favorites. She had made him a Boston cream pie; the two layered yellow cake with vanilla pudding filling and dark, semisweet icing. This was indeed a decadent day for John Berg.

At about three o'clock there was a knock at the front door. John was upstairs in the bedroom in a comfortable chair which he used for the few moments of reading that he allowed himself. Like his father, it actually became a contest between reading and dozing off to sleep. Gertie was in the kitchen taking mental notes on what she needed to buy the next day at the grocery store. Even the self-sustaining Bergs bought their share of store items. She hurried to the door and when she opened it there stood two men in military uniform. Gertie's heart caught in her throat, but in the split second that followed she refused to believe they could be there with bad news.

She stared at them for a good five seconds before offering a cautious, "Hello."

The two men were assigned to the Army's R.O.T.C. training program at the University of Wisconsin. One was an officer, a captain, the other an enlisted man, a staff sergeant.

The captain responded to Gertie. "Yes, mam. Is your husband home?"

When she heard that sentence, Gertie knew for certain why these men were at her doorway.

They all stood there awkwardly for the next ten seconds. She then gave a slow affirmative headshake and, without a word, leaving the men on the porch with the door open, she retreated to call for John.

Gertie walked to the stairway that she had climbed a thousand times before. She ascended only three steps before sitting, leaning into the step above her. She made no attempt to call her husband for more than a minute. As she did her best to pull herself together a desperate hope came to her. She knew the Army would give notification not only when a soldier died, but also when a soldier was missing. Missing in action they called it. She did not know if the Army used the same notification procedure for missing in action as they did for killed in action, but in these terrible seconds she clung to the possibility that they did. It was absurd desperation; hoping that Johnny was not confirmed dead, but only missing, somewhere in the Vietnamese countryside.

Finally, she raised her head and called John's name.

In twenty-one years of marriage, John had never heard his wife's voice sound so strange. So weak. She was the most forthright person he knew and now her frail sounding voice drew his immediate attention. As he came down the stairs, Gertie came to her feet. She always looked people straight in the eye when she spoke, but now she failed to raise her eyes. "There are two men at the door."

She then raised her head and grasped John's arms at the elbows as hard as she could.

"They're from the Army."

He grabbed his wife to him. He knew immediately why the men were there.

John Berg was married to a very strong woman. He had always been happy to allow Gertie all the independence her spirit required. He had always been comfortable enough in his own skin to not feel the need to be a controlling husband. He was wise enough to know that if he tried to run their lives with a dominating hand theirs would have been a woeful relationship. But now, with the heartache they were about to step into, he knew he needed to take charge.

"We are going to invite these men into the parlor and you and I are going to sit and hear what they have to say." He took Gertie by the arm and walked purposely to the front door.

"Come in. We are going to take a seat." John closed the door behind the two soldiers and the noise of the high winds outside was now shut off. The house was silent except for the footsteps of four people as they walked on the hardwood floor into the parlor.

The captain questioned them. "Are you Mr. and Mrs. John Berg?"

As he and Gertie sat on the edge of the davenport, John nodded.

Though the captain made every effort to be respectful and empathetic, he refrained from any emotion. He spoke the memorized script as prepared by the Army's Casualty Notification and Assistance Center.

"Mr. and Mrs. Berg, the Secretary of the Army has asked me to express his deep regret that your son, Clarence El Berg, was killed in action in South Korea on November 2, 1966. Your son was killed while on patrol in the Demilitarized Zone. The secretary extends his deepest sympathy to you and your family in your tragic loss."

He paused briefly. "Mr. and Mrs. Berg, we are very sorry for your loss. The Army will be in contact with you regarding the arrival of your son's body. The Army will be contacting you to provide any assistance you would desire regarding arrangements for your son."

The captain placed an official letter essentially stating what he had said on a nearby lamp table. He excused himself and the sergeant and they retreated without further word.

That was it. As simply and quickly as that, the Bergs were told of their son's death. It had happened countless times before in the country's history and now it was happening to them.

But now mother and father of the deceased were stunned not only with grief, but they were also stunned with confusion.

The captain had said Clarence. He had said Clarence, not John. They looked at each other in a split second of utter bewilderment.

John rose to his feet and without a word to Gertie he followed the two soldiers, stopping them at the bottom of the porch steps.

"Wait. Wait I…We have two sons. One is in Vietnam. One is in Korea. You said Clarence. He's in Korea. Are you sure it's Clark? Are you sure it's Clarence? We thought he was safe."

The two soldiers glanced quickly toward each other. From his breast pocket the captain took out his copy of the letter he had read to the Bergs. He slowly read the name to himself.

"Yes sir. Clarence El Berg." He hesitated. "Mr. Berg, your son was part of the Second Division patrol that was attacked in the Demilitarized Zone in Korea two nights ago."

A few seconds passed, and John simply nodded his head. The two men quietly withdrew to their vehicle. John put his hands on the porch railing for support. Clark had told them he was well south of the North Korean border. Clark had done the same thing that he had done twenty-three years before in North Africa. He was in the thick of the fighting in Tunisia's Kasserine Pass, but he had written his parents, saying he was far behind that spearhead.

For the rest of that afternoon it was difficult for the Bergs to grasp a sense of their own emotions. They felt confusion as much as they felt pain. They had each prepared themselves, steeled themselves, for the possibility of losing Johnny in Vietnam. But Clark was in a country where the fighting had stopped thirteen years before. It was a fragile truce, yes, but he was reasonably removed from the border. Or so they had thought.

John called the Johnsons to tell his father. When Esther Johnson called down the basement to tell Mack that John was on the line, his shoulders slumped. John would not be calling except with important news. Skorpie Johnson recognized the body language immediately.

"What's wrong?"

Mack said nothing, but went upstairs to take a phone call that he dreaded.

When she arrived home from school Elsie burst into tears hearing the news. In her youth, she had not allowed the thought of losing either of her brothers to enter her mind.

That evening John gathered his thoughts well enough to deal with the need to let their son in Vietnam know what had happened. Without some prodding by him, the Army might not research the fact Clark had a brother in Vietnam. The irony of it. They had enough information to inform the family back home, but maybe they did not know that Clark's brother, who wore the same uniform, who was drafted by the same army, was in Vietnam.

He wanted to speak to Johnny on the telephone. He didn't even know if that was possible. He took the letter left by the two soldiers and called the Randolph Casualty Notification and Assistance Center at Fort Knox. He received no answer, for the office was closed for the evening. A second number put him in contact with Fort Knox headquarters. He was told the center would open at 8:00 A.M. and that someone would phone him first thing in the morning.

John slowly sunk into a kitchen chair next to Gertie, Elsie and his father. Certainly, for Johnny's sake, he wanted his son to hear the news from him. But this was also an unconscious form of therapy for John. It was as old as the grieving process itself. The attempt to accomplish something, in this case the notifying of his son, took the spotlight off his own grief.

By eight o'clock that evening, the Bergs had yet to notify any of their extended family. They sat at the kitchen table, sometimes going fifteen minutes at a time without a word being said. Gertie pulled herself together in her usual deliberate style, only to lose composure when she began to speak of her son. When she attempted to talk about how she could see in his letters how Clark was changing, how he was growing up and appreciating things he had always ignored, her voice was a roller-coaster between blessed assurance and the trembling emotion of grief.

She took out one of Clark's letters; the only one that she had placed safely in a kitchen counter drawer. The others had all read it before, but she wanted to read part of it to them. She composed herself, showing a brief smile of a proud mother.

. . . "I want to ask your forgiveness for the way I have acted for so long. When I look around me here at the poverty in this place and have become aware of the importance of the prosperity and freedom that I have always taken for granted I know what a jerk I have been. Yet you have always stood by me. All of you. Grandma and Grandpa, being so patient with me. Poor Elsie, putting up with the selfish behavior of her brother. And Johnny, just being Johnny. He's never tried to show me up. He's never talked down to me. Yet there I was, jealous of him because of my own crummy behavior, resenting him because he was not the self serving person that I have always been. . . ."

Gertie was not finished reading, but she put her hands over her face, just briefly, before continuing. Tears streamed from her eyes. Her voice trembled at a high pitch.

"And you, Mom and Dad. You have always worked so hard to give Johnny, Elsie and me such a great home. You gave us great security and love. But there I was; manipulating and calculating and thinking only of myself. Some of the guys I am here with come from homes

*where the father mistreated them or where the parents divorced, and
yet I see a lot better behavior in them than I see in me. I want to come
home and be a different person. I want to be the kind of son you can
be proud of. I think about all those basic rights and wrongs we learned
in Sunday school and church. It takes some of us longer than others
to learn those lessons."*

Tears streamed from Elsie's eyes.

Gertie beckoned her daughter to her. Elsie sat in her mother's lap, as
she had done when just a young child. The two of them buried their
faces in each other's shoulders. They sobbed very quietly.

In due course Gertie raised her head, and through her grief she stated
that she needed to contact her family.

"No. Gertie. No. I'll make the phone call." John's voice was adamant.
"I've let you carry more of the emotional burden of this family than I
should because you just, you just don't need me there to lean on. There
will be plenty of time for you to talk to them."

Gertie squared her shoulders. "I can let the Mehlborgs know." She
gave her husband a weak smile. "I know you're trying to help me out, but
the best thing I can do is to let my family know."

The next morning, John paced around, first outside in the darkness, then
inside the house, waiting for the eight o'clock hour and the call from
Fort Knox. He could not recall a time when he felt so anxious. When he
had not heard from the Casualty Center by eight thirty, he called. He
spent the next five minutes either waiting or being shuffled between three
different people.

Finally a woman came on the line who introduced herself as Florence
McIntyre. Her sincere voice carried a soft mountain drawl. John recognized her as being, as they say, very down home. He felt that he had
reached someone who could help him.

"Yes, I see you did call last evening. I'm sorry you had to wait until this morning to speak with us. Now, Mr. Berg. How can I help?"

"We have a son in Vietnam and I urgently need to speak with him. Is there anyway you folks can arrange for that to happen?"

"We occasionally arrange for folks to speak to loved ones but it must involve an emergency, that is to say, the passing away of a family member or a situation where death is imminent. I hope you'll forgive me, Mr. Berg, I don't mean to sound callous, but I am required to ask you what the need is?"

After a few seconds of silence, Mrs. McIntyre spoke again. "Mr. Berg. Mr. Berg?"

John gathered himself. "Yes, I'm here. You see, we have two sons in the Army at the same time. One is in Vietnam. That's the one I need to speak to. Our other son is…Our other son was Clark. He was just killed in Korea and I need to let our son in Vietnam know. He has to know his brother is gone."

As an employee at the Randolph Casualty and Assistance Center, Florence McIntyre knew immediately that Clark Berg must have been on the DMZ patrol that was attacked. From the folders of casualty information on her desk she quickly retrieved the information that listed the American soldiers killed in Korea less than forty-eight hours before. There was the Berg name. She resisted the common human response to express her sympathy at this moment.

Instead, she explained to John the procedure that would take place in order to get hold of his son.

"Mr. Berg, in a situation like this it is the Red Cross that takes care of notification to a soldier. They may have already notified him. If you will be so kind as to give me your son's unit in Vietnam, I will forward the information to the Red Cross. They will use their infrastructure on the ground there to arrange a phone call. When we are told the status of that arrangement we will surely get back to you."

After getting the information, the woman retained a professional composure.

"Mr. Berg, from the time we pass this information on to the Red Cross, it can be anywhere from two hours to possibly a full day before a phone call can be set up. With your son being in Vietnam, he may be in the field, which would require the longer time."

She paused only a brief second before asking John if he had any questions.

"No. No, I think I understand." The sincerity John felt in the woman's voice prompted him to add a comment that he would otherwise not have shared. "I'm just hopeful that I can speak to him before he hears his brother's name over the radio. We do appreciate your help here. God bless you."

John's comment of "God bless you" prompted Florence McIntyre to speak from her heart.

"Mr. Berg, this is such a tragic and unexpected event for your family. I am sure you have been so shocked to have lost a son who you thought was safe. If there..."

In the woman's hesitation John sensed that she wanted to say more. He knew, however, that in her position she must be careful in what she said. John spoke, doing his best to retain his composure.

"Mrs. McIntyre, I want you to know that our son was a Christian and we know that he is now in heaven."

There was a moment of silence before she responded. "Mr. Berg, I do believe that at a time like this for your family, that is the only thing that can sustain you."

Up to this moment John had yet to shed a tear, despite the heartache and shock he was feeling. He was trying to be as strong as he could be for his wife and his daughter. But because a woman in Kentucky, a woman he had never met, but by whose humility and concern in her voice he had identified as a Christian, he had broken down. He turned so Gertie, Elsie and his father could not see his face.

THIRTY-TWO

The special day of November 30 was drawing closer for young John Berg. It was the day he had been pointing toward since he first arrived in Korea and then Vietnam. His rotation day. The day his tour was finished. It was the day, as some of them liked to say, that he would "return to the world." In his troop, he and Tom Bradley and the four others who had been assigned to Troop A that first day back in Korea were still in one piece and they were "getting short."

Twenty-seven hours had now gone by since Johnny had received word about the incident in Korea. He, Tom Bradley and a number if others were spending the day on a work detail, filling sandbags at the Bien Hoa base.

"What do you think, Tom. Do you think that I would have heard by now if my brother was hurt?" Johnny used the word hurt. He couldn't force himself to use the word killed.

As Johnny Berg held open sandbag after sandbag, Tom Bradley shoveled in the sand. He purposely downplayed the possibility of Clark's involvement.

"Man, what's happened to the guy who always handles trouble like it was a Sunday walk in the park. All of a sudden you're tied up in knots when the odds are that right now your brother is up there counting the days he's got left. Just like us."

Sal Bucci was sandbagging nearby and overheard the talk. "That's right Bergie. If he's not sitting there counting the days, he's sitting there wondering what kind of slop the mess hall is going to throw at them tonight."

"Yeah, I'm sure he's okay," responded Johnny without a whole lot of conviction. "It's just that I thought, I thought that when we got home things might be different for the two of us. What I mean is that we might have a bond that we haven't had before."

In his New York way, Bucci offered a way for Johnny to stop worrying. "I'm telling you, man. It's not going to help your brother one bit by you dragging around here worrying about him. Stop thinking and start pulling your weight on these sandbags."

It was after midnight when the Red Cross made contact with Troop A. The charge of quarters runner from the orderly tent quickly entered fourth platoon's tent looking for John Berg.

"Berg. Where's Berg?"

The runner was none too delicate as he ran his flashlight up and down the two rows of cots that flanked the walls of the tent. Men groaned and cursed at the awakening.

He spotted Johnny, beaming the flashlight into his eyes.

"Yeah. What is it?"

"How should I know, man? They told me to come get you. I think maybe you got a call on the land line. On the double."

As the runner left, he responded to the grumbling, cursing men by flashing his light into the faces of as many of them as he could. "Get back to sleep, gentlemen. This platoon has perimeter patrol in the morning. I'll be back to wake you low-lifers at 0500. You will rise and shine!"

Johnny sat on the edge of his cot in the dark. With a very weak stomach he slowly pulled on his fatigues and boots. Tom Bradley lay in his cot staring at his friend in the darkness. He knew what was going through his mind. He felt it best to say nothing.

THIRTY-THREE

"But as it is written, Eye hath not seen, nor ear heard, neither have entered into the heart of man, the things which God hath prepared for them that love him."

1 CORINTHIANS 2:9 KJV

Two days later, Berg was back home in Wisconsin. He exited the plane and walked the covered ramp onto the gate area at the Dane County Regional Airport. He looked up to see his mother, father, Elsie, Mack and Jenny Watson. The emotional stability that all parties had gained in the time since they learned of Clark's death came unraveled quietly as the six of them gathered in one large hug. Not a word was spoken. Johnny had tears in his eyes and his body shuttered. He felt that if he separated from their collective embrace too soon he would just sink to the floor. After these few moments, they exited the gate area, Johnny with an arm around both Jenny and his mother. Still, no words were exchanged.

Once back at the farm, Jenny excused herself, insisting that Johnny have time alone with his family. They would see each other later that evening.

It wasn't until Johnny, his parents, Elsie and Mack were all seated around the kitchen table that any real conversation occurred. It was Johnny. He looked down at the kitchen table and spoke in a measured cadence in order to get his words out.

"It must have been...such a shock. When they told you it was Clark."

Gertie responded weakly, but still in her pragmatic way.

"We were shocked, yes. Heartache's the same."

She had more to say, but it took a moment before she could let her human grief give way to her Christian reassurance.

"Your brother's life has been cut short, but he's with his Savior now. For that we can be forever grateful. It is the only consolation I could ever hope to know."

A short while later, Johnny phoned Jenny. When he heard her voice he lost his composure. By now it was seven o'clock in the evening and Jenny could hear the exhaustion in his voice. She said he should get some sleep and come over in the morning. He would have none of that. He was soon over at the Watson house. They sat there, alone on the couch in the parlor, mourning quietly together. Whatever emotions he had been able to control in front of his parents now came totally unraveled in front of his fiancée.

His tears flowed as he tried to get out his words.

"This time I've been gone, the greatest thought I've had… just how great it would be when I got home to you and to everybody. Never did I ever think it would be like this."

It broke Jenny's heart to see the young man she loved in such pain. They mourned there together until Johnny fell into a deep sleep.

Since America's involvement in Vietnam first began, no one from the Stoughton area had yet to lose his life. Now Clark Berg, stationed in Korea, had been killed in what most everyone thought was a safe place. The community was stunned.

The day after Johnny got home, Clark's body arrived at the airport. A crowd of about ninety people—family and friends—were there. A military escort took his body to the Holzhuter Funeral Home in Stoughton. The Army officer that escorted the body from California advised the officials at Holzhuter's to recommend to the family that the casket remain closed.

What happened in the next three days was a testament to a family's, and a community's, faith. John and Gertie insisted that the funeral be one of hope. Despite their heartache they made sure that everyone who came to share in their sorrow knew that they believed that the Lord had fulfilled His promise and taken their son into heaven.

The Bergs asked Glen Masterson to take up his guitar and sing his rendition of "There Will Be Peace in the Valley." Red Foley himself could not have done a more sincere arrangement than Clark's uncle. Carl and Flo Feskreig sang acappella "It is Well with My Soul." Both of these offerings could not have been more perfect.

Pastor Mantlund's words were clear and strong.

"The Bible tells us that once a person has truly received the Lord Jesus as his Savior, He will not let that person go. We all stumble, we all sin. He has left the Holy Spirit with us, yet none of us, even the most determined Christian, can live a life totally pleasing to Him. Some of us drift farther away from Him in our behavior than others. Yet He loves us and He will not let go of us.

"The Bergs are not a family to readily share their family concerns with others, even with their pastor. But I know that John and Gertie gave great concern to how their son struggled with his faith. How he seemed unable to bask in the contentment that the Lord wants for his followers. How, in trying to find a replacement for that contentment, he became increasingly irresponsible and, at times, self indulgent. But the Lord is true to us, even when we fail to be true to Him. And be assured, all of us, to one degree or another, are guilty of being untrue to Him. And so our Lord would not let Clark go.

"I was here at First Lutheran only about a year or so when Clark, in confirmation class, confessed his faith in Jesus Christ as his Savior. He received the gift of salvation; salvation from eternal death, by confessing that he was a sinner and confessing his belief that Christ came as the Son of God to die on a cross—taking on his sin.

"Our Lord, on His own timetable and in the way He chooses, brings each of us back to Him if we truly have confessed our belief in Christ. And so He sent Clark away from us. He sent him away from his wonderful family, away from this bountiful land that He has so wonderfully blest, to an austere and struggling place. John and Gertie have told me that during Clark's time in Korea he found what he called the key to satisfaction. It was in his last letter, where Clark said he was realizing it was not the circumstance that provided contentment, but rather a relationship with his Lord. That even in an austere place like Korea he could begin to find satisfaction by just allowing the Savior into his life in a day by day, step by step relationship.

"And so we are here and we grieve. We grieve because God has given us the capacity to love and along with that love we can't help but grieve, especially when we lose someone so young, at such an unexpected time and in such a violent way. But as those who belong to Him, He has given us expectation of the great reward.

"We can leave here today with two verses from our Bible. One is a verse of great comfort and one is a verse of great excitement. The verse of great comfort is this, spoken by Jesus in the book of John. '...I am the resurrection, and the life: he that believeth in Me, though he were dead, yet shall he live.'

"Clark Berg is alive today in heaven.

"And the verse of great excitement is this. I Corinthians 2:9. 'But as it is written, Eye hath not seen, nor ear heard, neither have entered into the heart of man, the things which God hath prepared for them that love Him.'"

Clark was buried close to his grandmother in Eastside Cemetery. They were the first of the Bergs buried there. The old Skaalen Cemetery, a gentle slope near the northwest corner of County Road N and Skaalen Road, was the burial sight for the generations past of the Bergs. Elmer and Muriel Berg were laid to rest there. So were Gus and Ruth Berg. Other family members as well. That old cemetery, closed to further burials in 1939, was on property donated by Oscar and Sonia Skaalen, a couple that Elmer had become friends with on his journey from Norway.

Life went on for the Bergs. Though they had lost Clark in a far away land they never showed bitterness toward America's occupation in Korea or its war in Vietnam. As the protests against the war increased through the rest of the 1960s and into the '70s, they refused to adopt the attitude of those who held America's leaders in contempt.

Johnny had twenty-seven days left in his tour of duty in Vietnam when he came home for Clark's funeral. The Army's policy was that if an overseas stationed soldier came home for an immediate family member funeral, he would return to that duty station, Vietnam or otherwise, if he had two or more weeks remaining at that station. But because his brother had been killed in action, they made an exception for Johnny. He was sent to Fort Benning, Georgia, where he completed his military obligation.

Johnny Berg and Jenny Watson were married upon his return to civilian life. They built a small home on Spring Road, at the northeast corner of the farm. Johnny never wavered from his commitment to carry on the tradition of Berg Farm.

Mack lived another fifteen years. They were productive years. He continued to work the farm with his son and grandson until he was eighty-two. He spent his final days at home. In those days he grew fond of using the old expression that he was about "to be called Home." When his lifelong friend Skorpie Johnson, hail and hardy in his eighty- second year, visited him in those final days, Mack would always chide him, saying that he, Mack, would be called Home first.

"I always did lead the way for you, Johnson."

Harold Johnson gave his gruff and hardy chuckle. "If He lets in an old Norseman like you, I know I've got it made."

Elsie, married and the mother of two, visited her grandfather's bedside one Sunday afternoon. She was sitting there with Gertie and John when Mack asked her to read the passage from the Bible that Fred Mantlund had read at Clark's funeral years before.

"But as it is written, Eye hath not seen, nor ear heard, neither have entered into the heart of man, the things which God hath prepared for them that love Him."

A very contented look came upon his face. He gathered enough energy to speak.

"I know you're going to put me in the ground next to Ann. That's a good thing. But I want you to know that I'll not be staying there. Like the word says, we hardly know how great it's going to be in heaven. I'm believing that she and I will be a part of it together."

Two days later, Mack Berg passed from this world into the next.

≠ ≠ ≠

John and Gertie remained the same shining example of the unchanging, down to earth couple that they had always been. As youngsters they had grown up in the Great Depression and then been part of the great effort of World War II. Since then they had raised a family and met their responsibilities as diligent contributors to the American way of life. They stood on their own two feet, meeting life's challenges, overcoming its disappointments and accepting its rewards with thankful humility. When they were given praise for their accomplishments, they were able to deflect that praise to their God.

The loss of their son was something they never were to forget, but it was something they kept to themselves, accepting it as one of the many disappointments that a family experiences. When acquaintances brought up the loss of Clark, they never turned their eyes away. They looked optimistically at the person and said how grateful they were to know that he was in Heaven. Never did they speak of the great confusion of that day when they braced themselves for the death of one son, but were told of the death of the other.

John and Johnny continued to partner in the farm. John and Gertie invited Johnny and Jenny, with their three children, to buy the homestead; provided, of course, that they could continue to live there. It was a cycle familiar to this family. Now six generations on the land.

Twenty years after their Army days, Tom Bradley made good his promise to visit Johnny. As he pledged while in Korea, he came in the summer. The closest he wanted to get to a Wisconsin winter was to look at the family's photos of the farm in its snowy landscape.

One afternoon he sat privately with Jenny on the Berg porch, saying that her husband was the best friend and the best soldier he ever could have hoped to know. He told her how he could never understand it. How his friend could be the most unassuming, self effacing, reliable and contented person he ever knew, when all about them seemed so out of control.

Then he told her that he now knew the answer.

"In these last twenty years my faith has come a long way. Johnny was so quiet he never expressed it, but he had a great inner peace that he could only get from his God."

Jenny nodded. "Yes, I see it in him all the time."

She then reflected for a moment.

"But you know, Tom, he must have spoken up at least once when you guys were over there. He got a letter a few years ago from Florida. A man named Cruze. He wrote to thank Johnny for what he told him that night in the marsh. That's how he said it; 'That night in the marsh.' He said it led to changing his whole life. He said it led to the most important decision he ever made."

THE END

Though this is a story of fiction, the events leading up to and including the morning of November 2, 1966 are factual. The news wire quotes reporting on this incident are factual.

In memory of those American soliders who died the morning of November 2, 1966:

Sergeant James Hensley
Private First Class John Benton
Private First Class Robert Burrell
Private Morris Fisher
Private Les Hasty
Private Ernest Reynolds
Survivor: Private First Class David Bibee

In the ensuing years, the free and democratic country of South Korea has become an economic powerhouse. Communist North Korea remains a land where its people live in fear and abject poverty.

MY BIBLE

hen I became twelve years of age, our Sunday School presented me with my own Bible. Now, these many years since that day, I still have that Bible, and though there has been many a day that I have failed to open its pages and many a time that I have failed to heed its advice, it always has been, and always will be, the most important book that I'll ever own.

The Bible is the Word of God, and in its pages He tells me how to live in this world and what I must do to live forever in Heaven when my life on this earth is done.

When I am feeling insecure, discouraged or afraid He tells me in the Book of Psalms, the thirty-fourth chapter, the fourth verse to "seek Him and He will hear me and deliver me from my fears." In Psalms 27:14, He tells me to "wait patiently on Him and be of good courage and He will strengthen my heart."

The Lord tells me in His Word that "He is my refuge and my strength, a very present help in trouble." He tells me to "rest in Him and wait patiently for Him."

His Word even says to me that if I "delight myself in Him He will give to me the desires of my heart."

My friend, you may feel very far away from God. You may have spent much of your life pursuing the things of this world. Possibly along the way you have been less than honest, less than unselfish. You may have even hurt the people who have cared about you the most. Sometimes you may feel very, very empty and you wonder what does it all mean and where in the world are you going?

Well, sir, you may want to heed a couple of Bible verses in the Book of Proverbs—that's chapter three, verses five and six. There it says, "Trust in the Lord with all thine heart; and lean not unto thine own understanding, in all thy ways acknowledge him, and he shall direct thy paths."

That's good news. That's good news for all of us, for, you see, we are all sinners—from the most sincere preacher in the land down to you and me.

And here's the best news of all. The Bible tells us that "while we were yet sinners Christ died for us." God has provided a way for us to be freed from our sin; to have our sin completely washed away so that when we leave this world we can stand before Him and be welcomed into his kingdom of heaven and live there in perfect peace and joy. You see, the Bible tells us that God sent His Son Jesus into this world to die on a cross, taking on the sin of all mankind. The Bible tells us that if we will believe this, if will accept Jesus Christ's sacrifice, then we shall live eternally in Heaven.

My friend, it is right there in the greatest Bible verse of them all, John 3:16.

"For God so loved the world that he gave his only begotten Son, that whosoever believeth in him should not perish, but have everlasting life."

SOURCES:

The Holy Bible, New International Version ® Copyright © 1973, 1978, 1984 by International Bible Society

The Ryrie Study Bible © 1976, 1978 by The Moody Bible Institute of Chicago

"© Alan Jay Lerner and Frederick Loewe 1956, Copyright renewed. Excerpt issued with permission."

Lyndon Baines Johnson Library and Museum 2313 Red River St. Austin, Texas 78705

Fighting Brush Fires on Korea's DMZ Richard Kolb

The Forgotten DMZ Major Vardon E. Jenerette

/